THEY CALLED HIM SUDDEN

0713-BENN

THEY CALLED HIM SUDDEN

Ben N. Field

0713-BENN

To order additional copies of this book, contact:
Xlibris Corporation
1-888-7-XLIBRIS
www.Xlibris.com
Orders@Xlibris.com

CONTENTS

0713-BENN

CHAPTER 1

"Time and events, boy, time and events." That's what my Pa would always say when something untoward would happen. Pa had lots of coal-black curly hair and wore a big full black beard that framed piercing sharp blue eyes that would look right inside you, so that right off all you noticed was those bright, intense eyes. Now my Pa was dead. That such a thing as this could happen had never ever once crossed my mind. But it had happened, and suddenly I was all alone. In my mind I could see Pa standing there shaking that big shaggy head and telling me, "Time and events, boy, time and events." It wasn't quite sunup yet, and there was a grayish cast to a cheerless rainy morning. From our cabin's door, I could see the wagon coming. The team was straining hard, pulling uphill like that. The wagon jolted back and forth, its ironbound wheels sinking deep in the muddy ruts, leaving long, snake-like tracks stretching as far as the eye could see back down toward the Weaver farm. I could see the pine board box in the wagon bed. It held the body of my Pa. The man holding the reins of the team was Old Man Weaver, the farmer Pa had been working for when he was killed.

I pushed back the tears. I needed to buck up and be the man Pa always said I was. I had the burying to do. If'n this had happened back home, there would be family and friends lined up fifty or sixty wagons deep coming to the burying. But we weren't back home and I didn't even know how to get word to any of the folks back there about what had happened. There weren't no one but me, 'cause we were just passing through.

I didn't go with Pa yesterday to work on Mr. Weaver's water well. We hadn't had meat to eat for awhile and I was hungry for some meat, so I went looking for a deer. Now I feel powerful bad for not being there with him. Maybe I might have seen that the board was about to drop down on him and got to it in time to grab it, or maybe even been down in the well, diggin', instead of Pa.

There ain't much room to move about when you're in the bottom of a hole diggin' for water. The ones on top are supposed to be pulling the dirt out and looking out to be sure nothin' is gonna fall on you. We had put a board across some posts we'd set in the ground and had a pulley with a rope hung on the board. When the bucket was full of dirt, the ones on top would haul on the rope and pull the bucket of dirt out. But the edge of the bucket got stuck on the side of the well as it was being pulled up, and it pulled the board off the posts. The board and all of the rest of it, the pulley, the rope and the bucket full of dirt, it all fell on Pa.

When Ma passed on, we were expecting it for a spell beforehand. Pa's accident was so sudden, I couldn't take it in. I looked at Pa laying there in that box, and I couldn't believe it. Pa was always so much bigger than life. How could this have happened? How could it be? Last night after I'd come home with my deer, happy because I knew Pa would be glad to see some meat on the table, I found Old Man Weaver waiting for me to get home so he could tell me about Pa being dead. I couldn't bring myself to believe it. I didn't want to hear about it. I left out of that cabin running, not knowing why or where. I ran and ran until I was plumb wore out. I laid out there on the ground all the rest of the night. In the early morning it started raining, and I never even noticed. I had spent the whole time thinking back on the times when Ma was alive and we was all together.

We'd never had much of goods and such when we lived in the mountains back in Kentucky, but having a lot of "stuff" was something we didn't worry about up in the mountains, cause nobody had much, and having a good snug cabin with enough to eat and some clothes to wear made you on the same footing as your neighbors. We had a tight little log place on the side of some good mountain ground, right next to a year-round creek, and all around us was tall, thick trees. Most of those who had places around us were kinfolk in one way or another, and we had them to count on when troublesome times happened.

But after a time, Pa became shifty-footed and worrisome, until Ma just gave up and we started west. Ma died the first winter out, and Pa never got over it, kept blaming himself because she hadn't wanted to leave, and he felt like it was the grieving that'd made her so sick. We hadn't started with much hard money, and after awhile, what little we had just went for getting through each day. So we kept moving west, working a little here and there to keep us going. This morning, Pa had said this was going to be his last day; we'd be moving on in the morning. If only we'd left out this morning, instead of waiting another day.

I buried Pa on the top of the hill back of the cabin we'd been staying in. I piled rock's knee high over his grave, because I couldn't afford to spend the money for something lasting to make a marker out of. My Pa's body wouldn't get a headstone, but I sure didn't need something grand to make me remember him. My Pa was forever locked away inside me. "Lord," I bowed my head, "this was no way for such a good man to end. My Pa was a right good man, his heart was as big as his body. No one ever left our door that needed help that my Pa didn't do the best he could for'm. No one could ever say my Pa's word wasn't like gold. He set a heap of store by your Word, and lived by your golden word. Please make him welcome. I know my Ma will be right glad to see him, but I'll miss him powerful bad."

Everyone was really sorry and I know Weaver felt like it was mostly his fault. He asked me to stay the winter, but one thing Pa was strong on, and that was to be beholden to no one. I sold the team and wagon we was traveling in, but I kept Pa's rifle, my bedroll, and enough beans and such to make it for quite a while. So I thanked him kindly, I know he meant well, but he already had a cabin full of youngens and didn't need another sixteen-year-old settin' up to his table. Goodbyes have always been hard for me, even now when I didn't know them well. I left with a "see ya," and some feelings I didn't want to show, because they were nice folks and they had offered me a place in their home.

Now the men in my family ran big to bigger, mostly kind of well set, and I run purty much to be like the rest of'm, except Ma always said my hair was the blackest and my hands the biggest she'd ever seen. I know I already stood head and shoulders over most men I met, and most took me for grown. Ma taught me to read from the Bible, and she taught me numbers and figuring. My uncle taught me how to throw a knife, and how to fight with my fists or boots, he being the best at those things in our mountains. Pa taught me how to shoot and how to look at things. Like a scuffed up rock or leaves that's mashed down, or twigs and brush bent or broken. Tracks can tell a story if a body knows how to read them. All in all, I had enough learning to get by in a man's world.

After burying Pa, I tried to put everything out of my mind by paying heed to what was around me as I walked. I seen things I had only heard of. There was a steam-powered boat on the river, there was large flat boats moving goods, and people! There was more people that I could see with one look than on the whole mountain back home. There was wagons on that road as far as you could see. I met some real friendly folks, and I guess I gawked at just about everything. I walked the river road and let past things be past. Pa always said not to ponder on things that couldn't be changed, though saying and doing had been different things for Pa after Ma died.

"Time and events." Ma said that meant that anything could happen to anybody at any time, and that's the first thing I thought of when I saw the man up close to the river bank, floating face down in the river. I'd started out early that morning, to get a good start in the cool morning clouds before the heat of the day hit, and there that fellow lay, floating in the shallow water by the bank. He didn't have a pouch on him, nothing that said who he was. There was a bullet hole in the back of his coat that was circled with scorched marks, which made me think he'd been shot in the back from up close and dumped in the river, probably from off one of those river boats, robbed most likely, because he didn't have no money either. I figured he'd only been dead a few hours. He was a big man, almost as big as me, and hard to move. I buried him except for his six gun and gunbelt. It was a fancy rig, it must of been special built. The handle was so big it almost fit my hand, and the barrel was at least three inches longer than any I'd ever seen. I made a marker by tying two small limbs together like a cross, and I piled as many rocks over his grave as I could find, to keep the varmints away. Maybe someday somebody would want to know what had happened or where he was. I didn't have nothing to write on or write with, so I had to leave him in a stick-marked grave.

Sometimes picking one thing over another changes things forever for a man. Like saving that gunbelt. I've thought on that a lot since that day. If I'd never kept that gun, my life might of been as different as night is from day. I dried that rig out and greased the leather every day for a while until the oil soaked in and the stiffness from being watersoaked was gone. It was a well-built holster, being laced together with leather strings, all fancy, tooled up with engraving. It had a picture on it of a bear standing up, paws outstretched and teeth showing. Somebody sure had a way with leather. Anyhow when I walked into Kansas City thinking of staying on and getting a job, I was wearing that gun and belt. I thought I looked more growed up.

I started up toward town from the river bank. It was early afternoon and the sun was bearing down fierce, so I was kind of thinking bout some shade and some cool water. There was teams and wagons and people all over the streets. Men loading and off-loading the boats. There was more noise than I'd ever heard before in one place. The teamsters were cracking long whips over their teams, men shouting back and forth as they worked, wagon wheels creakin'. There was the call of shills outside the saloons and the sound of cattle in the stock pens. It actually looked like about half the country was headed west, and they were all leaving from Kansas City and every one of them had at least two barking, mangy dogs. I figured the best thing to do was to find a place to camp before I started looking for a job. I camped up close to the wagon trains. I unrolled my pack and went and bought some bacon and some coffee. I hadn't had any for a coon's age, and my mouth was really set for a change. There was a lot of folks camping out. For one thing, most of 'm was trying to use what money they had for supplies, and for another, the town was full. I hadn't scouted it out, but I'd wager there weren't no empty places inside the hotels and rooming houses.

I'd ate slow and enjoyed ever bite before I laid back agin' that big old tree I was using for shade. There was a feller camped up close to me. We were sharing the same shade. He had to be city folk. He had a round little hat and city-type shoes. They weren't walking or working boots but shoes like I figured you'd wear in the city. They were all dirty and run-over like the rest of his clothes, and you could see he'd seen better days and was from a far piece from here. He was eyein' my victuals that was left over. He didn't look like he'd et for a while, he was real thin and gaunt looking. "Care for some coffee?" I asked him, trying to be polite. I stuck out my hand and said, "Name's Josh Bonner."

He grabbed my hand and smiled. "My name is Ruben Steiner," and added, "Yes, I could use some coffee, thank you."

He sure didn't waste no time gettin' to my grub. "Been here long?" I asked.

"Two weeks," he says, between gulps of coffee. "I had thought to seek employment here, but it is taking much longer than I had anticipated."

I took a gander at him. I weren't sure what he said, he had such a mouthful of fancy words. I weren't gonna hold that agin' him, cause he 'peared to be friendly. He had red hair, a kind of long face with a solid chin, and looked kind of uppity, like a feller used to having it all his way. Anyway, he had sure as shooting seen better days. Well, the up-shot of it was he'd gone busted back east and to get those he owed off his back, he'd took a stage this far and was going to head out west. Not finding a job yet, and him being broke, he hadn't had the money for a meal or even a cup of coffee for over a day.

"Dig on in there, partner," I told him. "I got plenty, such as it is."

If'n he hadn't found work, could be I'd have a bad time of it myself, 'cause he sure had the book learnin'. Then again, maybe he wouldn't take a roustabout job on the boats or as a swamper. That thought made me feel better, so I up and asked him, "You particular in your work?"

"No." He shook his head. "I'm willing to work at anything." Well, that beat me, until I figured out that it was his city gitup that made folks shy away from him. That made sense. I'd bet that tomorrow I'd have no trouble gettin' work. I had to do just that. My stake was gettin' smaller. I stretched out on my bedroll sure in my mind that all would be well. I wouldn't have no trouble. At morning light I set out, plumb set on finding something. I checked everything from the boats to the livery stable, and everything in between. It looked like the town was overflowing with drifting folks and most of 'm huntin' work. That is exceptin' for the dirty, greasy mountain men and the Indians who were doing nothing but hangin' around and drinking. There was drifters hangin' around the corrals by the train depot where the Texas trail drivers brought the herds in. . . . Whores, gamblers, shills and buffalo hunters filled the streets. The worst kind of varmints mixed in with the best kind of folks.

For a feller "from the mountains" just come to town all this was a real eye opener. On the main street starting from the river up there was saloon after saloon, lining both sides of the street. Gambling dives and dance halls mixed in with stores, gunsmiths, tanners and boot makers. There was a lot of people in town from the wagon trains that were forming up. Most of them were busy getting their gear together, though some of 'm were just lollygagging along eyeballing the sights.

The sun was standing just past noon and gettin' hotter'n blazes and I still hadn't found any work. I stopped in front of the stage house and leaned up agin' the wall whilst thinking what to do. It was a puzzle. There weren't much to do about it right then. I needed to take time to think on it a spell. There was a saloon across the street and I had it in mind to sit down out of the sun. I stood in the door whilst my eyes got used to the darkness of the room. There was plenty of girls in there, all wearin' painted faces and decked out in low-cut gowns with lots of feathers and lace. My Ma would'a had a fit if she'd a'seen me lookin' at them women, and them showin' themselves like that. I think Pa would'a just grinned at me. Pa was not as easy stirred up about some things as Ma. Some of 'm looked me over, but I must not have looked rich enough to 'm. It was certain none of 'm come over to me when I walked to the bar.

"Beer, if you got it," I told the barkeep. There was a couple of down-in-the-heels hard-cases bellied up to the bar close by me, roustabouts off the river boats by the look of 'm. The one closest to me was about a head shorter'n me and had a belly that hung way over his belt. He stopped the barkeep. "Hold up there, Jake. I'm gonna buy this wet-eared cub a real drink." He turned toward me, his bloodshot, bleary eyes showed mean around the edges when he turned that flat blank stare on me. "Boy, if'n ya are gonna stand around where we're at and drink where there's real men, you gotta learn to drink like one." I could see I'd made a bad mistake coming in here, and there weren't no way out less'en I let him make a fool of me, and I sure weren't going to do that. I was of a mind to meet trouble head on. "If'n I'd a-wanted whiskey, I'd a-ordered one myself. I don't need no one ordering for me."

"You didn't have a proper upbringing, boy. You need some respect for the grown-ups." He hitched his pants with both hands, trying to pull them up over that belly, and took a step away from the bar. Well, I didn't have to be uncommon smart to size up where we were heading. I weren't about to be buffaloed by a varmint like him. So I hauled off and fetched him a clout that knocked him over a spittoon. That worked so well that I let fly at the other one, while he was still blinking wide-eyed at the one on the floor. I rolled my shoulder, putting my weight into it and came clear up on my toes. My fist covered most of the side of his face, and when I hit him, he turned clear round and lit face down. I knew he weren't gonna get up again for a while. There was so much noise around us that nobody paid no mind to us a-tall. I looked at the bartender and he shrugged his shoulders and motioned toward the door, like I should leave. I told him, "Forget the beer." I stepped around them that were on the floor. I was moving quick and trying not to attract attention. I was plumb happy to get out that door without someone else wanting to fight.

Well, I didn't see no use in hanging around this town, when there weren't no work. I had to wait on the boardwalk till a wagon passed before I could cross to the stagehouse. There was a stage coming in, and it was sure stirring up a cloud of dust. The driver must of touched up the team some before he got to town. They sure came in at a good pace, scattering dust behind them, heads high like they was on parade and enjoying it. Fact is, they were on parade. Seems like a good part of the folks had turned out, just to watch the stage come in. I hung around to watch. Some mighty fine-looking folks were getting off that stage.

Then she stepped off! That was the purtyest girl I'd ever seen. She was about chest high on me, long black hair curling out and around the purtyest blue bonnet that made a cloth frame around the clearest blue eyes and a heart-shaped face. Her lips were kinda soft-looking, full and not too wide. She was about fourteen and wearing a real purty blue and white dress that swirled around her tiny white shoes. There was a wide lace collar and white pinafore. She was with a short, square-built man about thirty-five who had helped her down from the stage. I figured he was her Pa. I knowed I was starin' but I couldn't help it. I'd never seen a girl as fine dressed or as purty as she was. I took in and stored in my head ever' part of how she looked. She saw me gawkin' and her eyes sparkled a mite, and then she smiled at me. I know it was at me. There I was, mouth all gaped open like I was catching flies and my eyes popping out.

When she smiled at me, I turned hot from the top of my head to my toes, sure as all get-out I was redder'n a beet. If a dragon or a tribe of Indians or outlaws had'a showed up, I would of waded right in and rescued her, and right then I was wishing for one or the other of 'm to show. I must of been a real spectacle because her Pa turned to see what she was smiling about, and when he saw me there making a pure fool out'n myself, he grinned a big old grin an' winked at me. "You want to help me carry these bags, boy?" he asked.

"Yes, sir," and I grabbed as much as I could tote. I'm sure I'd a-carried more but I'd of needed another arm. Some friends of theirs had invited them to come and stay with them, and had sent their boy to meet them and be their guide. He didn't show up till just as we were leaving. He was about my age, but lots smaller, and had a smart aleck look on his face, especially when he looked at her, which he did a lot. I didn't cotton to him a-tall. It was quite a piece to the house where they were going to stay at. And my arms was about to fall off by the time we got there, I was tired and hurting with my arms and hands full while that smart aleck didn't carry nothing and was skipping around like a little kid jabbering away at her the whole way till I couldn't even get a word in edge-wise. But there was no way I was going to let on that the load had been too much for me to carry without help.

The house didn't look like much, even by my standards, and I could tell she was disappointed. But she never let on none. Just as cool as anything, she lifted her skirt and walked in the house just like it was plumb satisfactory. I set their bags down inside the door and waited for her approval, but she'd already forgot about me in the middle of all those howdy's and such. I just backed out the door and nobody seemed to notice or care. By the time I got back to my camp, I was burning. I was so mad at myself for being such a fool, I kicked a big old rock and ruint my foot.

"I'm glad you did that," Ruben said from his side of the tree. "I've been mad at that rock ever since I got here."

"I sure wished you'd a-kicked it 'stead of me." I muddled through a grin despite my hurt toe.

"Any particular reason for that outburst of violence?" asked Ruben.

I sat down and pulled off my boot and rubbed my foot. "I was lollygagging along when the stage came in and I went plumb silly over a pretty face and pulled my arms a whole passel longer'n they ought to be from toten' her bags, and then she just walked off, nary a thankee or nothing."

Ruben laughed. "You're not the first to be used by a pretty girl. We've all been down that path."

"You find work?" I asked. I didn't want to talk about me being a fool anymore.

"Maybe. I talked to a storekeeper and he said to come back when he wasn't busy tomorrow, and we would discuss it." He brushed his clothes with his hands. "I wish I had something cleaner to wear."

I dug in my pocket and fished out three silver dollars. "Here, get your stuff fixed up."

He latched right onto the money, promising to pay it back as soon as he got any money, and he headed back to town.

We rolled out early the next morning, Ruben getting shined up to try for his job and me to keep on looking.

"How do I look?" asked Ruben. "Any better?"

"Some," I admitted. "Better'n yesterday."

Ruben was a lot cleaner and looked good. I was wearing my one and only shirt. It'd been made out of deerskin and was held together with rawhide laces. My boots were mountain boots, almost knee high and made of cowhide, with the soles pegged on with wooden pegs. The only thing store-bought I had was that oak-handled colt, and that fancy holster. We made a real odd-looking pair walking down the street.

Even though it was early, the saloons were going full blast. We were just walking up on the boardwalk when two men just kinda exploded out of a saloon. Grim-faced and flushed from whiskey, they faced up to one another. Without no talk, they went for their guns. It was over in the blink of an eye. They both were down in

the street. One was dead and the other'n was wallowing around
the bloody ground and screaming in pain. He'd been shot in the
gut, blood was pumping in spurts over his clothes and out on the
ground. He was making a noise like I'd heard a gut-shot cat make
one time, coming from way down inside, a desperate hoarse agony
that pleaded for help. Some men come out and carried him off
towards the doc's, and him screaming. The other one still laid
there. I looked at him as we walked by. He was about twenty or so,
wearing trail-riding gear, and a Texas-style hat lay in the dirt, not
far away. He'd been hit in the chest, and his life was over. I'd seen
all kinds of fights back in the mountains where I come from, usually between folks that had been at each other for years, but this
was likely between men that didn't even know each other. I made
up my mind right then that I was putting all else aside and learning to be better 'n anyone with a gun. I wasn't going to go out like
that. I looked at Ruben. He was cloud white and sick. "You gonna
make it?" I asked. Ruben just nodded and stumbled on toward
town. I could tell he hadn't seen such carrying on before. I left him
in front of the store and started on to the livery where I'd seen the
freight wagons come in, thinking I might get work unloading and
stacking freight. I'd only took a step or two when I heard a bunch
of shots. I looked and saw another man down with what looked
like a Texas trail drover standing over him. I could see this was
gonna be a humdinger of a day.

I got a job unloading freight all right and worked all day at it.
About midday, I shucked my shirt and rolled my hardware up in
it and laid it out of the way. "Better leave that thing off, boy,"
advised the teamster, "unless'n you're some kinda hand with that
thing."

I grinned back at him. "I aim to. I don't cotton to dying that-
a-way."

I made two dollars that day. I'd never heard tell of making two
dollars in a day for wages before. This sure was the out-doin'est
place I'd ever seen. I walked back to camp carrying my gun wrapped
up in my shirt, happy for the work and taking no chances with my

life. Ruben was already there, busy gathering up his gear. "You leaving out, Ruben?"

He straightened up and picked up his pack. "I got the job and there's a room goes with it. It'll be nice to sleep on a bed again, with clean sheets and a door to close out this pest hole. Josh, as soon as I can put together some traveling money, I'm leaving this hell-hole."

"It's pretty bad, that's certain," I told him, "but sometimes a man's got to stomach things that's plumb disagreeable."

Ruben looked grim. "I'm going in that store and not coming out until I'm on my way back to civilization." I held out my hand. "Luck," I said. "I hope things happen like you want."

I watched Ruben load up and walk away, and sudden like, I felt like I didn't want him to go. It kinda hit me hard, and for about the first time, I realized I didn't have no one close by to care about me. I had those back home in the mountains, but they was a long ways off. Lonesome is a bad feeling and I couldn't shake it that night.

Morning came, and with it the bright sunlight. I walked back to the livery for another day's work, and the world looked good to me again. There was a tack room in the stable on one side of the office, and beside that was a small, empty space that wasn't a room, but it was the corner of the stable on one side and the wall of the tack room on the other. "Boss," I said, "could I throw my bedroll down in the corner there?"

He looked at me kinda thoughtful like and took his time about answering. "I reckon son, for awhile anyway." Well, it weren't much, but it was inside and it was free, and those horses made better company than most men. I worked most days and my stake was growing bigger'n I had ever thought about.

Every night I got out my rig and practiced drawing my gun till my arm wore out. I'd think about what I was doing and make changes from time to time. I could hold a rock in my hand, let it fall, and draw, dry firing before it hit the ground. I think having spent all those hours and hours as a kid learning to draw and

throw a knife and throw it where I wanted it to go, must've helped
me a lot now to learn to draw a gun. Ever' night I cleaned that
pistol till it shined like a new dollar. The boss said I was gonna
wear it down to nothing just polishing it.

I decided it were time to see if I could hit anything. I eased off
by myself every morning with a fist full of cartridges and practiced
a spell. When I'd get to thinking about sleeping in, that picture
would pop in my mind, of that man laying in the dirt, then I'd get
up and go practice. I soon found out that the long barrel gave me
a lot more distance and I moved my targets further off.

What with eatin' a whole lot better and unloading freight every day, my shoulders and arms were getting bigger and bigger,
and my shirt was getting too small for me. I spent some time
buying a whole new outfit. I bought my Stetson hat off the shelf,
but I had my boots special made for me, and my clothes tailored
to fit. I stopped by the store Ruben was working at to show off
some. I felt proud as could be when Ruben nodded his head up
and down. If a smart feller like Ruben thought I looked good,
then I must have done good. I bought some things to work in and
walked back, plumb satisfied with myself. I knew I was looking a
lot more prosperous when one of the painted up fancy ladies who
was working as a shill in front of a saloon tried to lure me inside.
For a bit, I was tempted.

From a ways off she was a real looker, all gussied up in feathers
and high-heeled shoes with most of her legs showing clear up to
where it could be embarrassing. I stopped and looked a lot longer.
She weren't any older'n me. Not very pretty in the face, and it was
painted up a lot. She laughed at me. "You never seen a girl before,
honey? Or is it you never been in bed with one? There's first time
for everyone, and this could be yours. I'll tell you what, I'll go
upstairs with you myself and make sure you like your first time."
She twisted up to me and clutched my arm. "Would you like that,
honey? Would you like to do it with me?"

I moved on out of there, but I could hear her mocking laugh
following me. I was red-faced and getting mad. I might not know

everything, but somehow or another she didn't fit with my picture of what I wanted, and she had no right to make fun of me. A soiled dove like her just wanted my money, it weren't because she cared about me. But she couldn't spoil how proud I felt about my new duds. I was bathed and my hair was fresh cut. I was looking good and I felt it.

Sometimes things do work out just right. I was walking up by the bank when that girl whose luggage I'd carried stepped out the door of the bank with her Pa right behind her. Right then I was sure glad I'd walked away from that whore. Her and her Pa would have saw me being lured in there, and she never would have thought well of me.

She recognized me all right. So did her Pa. I could tell she was giving me quite a look over as I was walking up to them.

"Howdy," I says, just as cool as could be. She smiled real bright and her Pa stuck out his hand. "Young fellow, we didn't get a chance to thank you. In all that confusion of greeting friends, we lost track of our manners."

I shook his hand, but with those big blue eyes on me, all I could do was stammer, "It weren't nothing," but he never even let on he noticed I was rattled and red-faced. "My name is Mike McGuire," he says, "and this is my daughter, Ann."

I allowed as how pleased I was to meet'm. "My name's Josh Bonner." We made some small talk. I couldn't remember what was said. But I was high-stepping when I walked away from them, and the world looked good to me.

CHAPTER 2

A Conestoga wagon is almost always sixty feet long with its tall sides slantin' outward. It takes six horses to pull it and a lot of work to unload it. It's said that this year, ten thousand wagons went west and thousands of 'em passed through here. A lot of freight came and went by wagons and I helped load and unload a bunch of 'em. Working was about all that I did that first year. I saved money and put in some time every day practicing my shooting.

Ruben was still about my only friend, and what with the long hours we worked, we didn't see a whole bunch of each other, especially after he met Maude. I never saw Ann at all these days. Her Pa built a great big house up away from Front Street, and the rest of us weren't allowed to cross over to where the uppity folks lived. The marshal made that very clear and made it stick. Those that tried going anyway were run outta town or dead. Shootin's and knifin's and fights were common sights around the saloons along the river. Ever time I saw a man laying in his own blood crying and screaming, I turned sick inside. I was doing my dead-level best never to be one of those dying in the dirt.

There was a lot of folks that just didn't belong out here. Ruben was one of 'em, Maude was another, with her big eyes and her hair all done up in braids. She was a sight to behold. She was small, full-bodied, wearing a black and white checkered pinafore, and running full tilt toward me, tears streaming down her dimpled cheeks. "Josh, oh, Josh! Come quick! He's hurting Ruben. Make him quit!"

Well, I took out a-running to the store. I could see one of those trail hands holding Ruben up against the wall with his left hand and ploughin' him in the face with his fist. Ruben was hitting at him, but not doin' much damage. His face was plumb white, where it weren't bruised or tore, and I could tell he weren't gonna do much but get bad hurt. That Texas trail hand was grinning and pouring it on Ruben. There was a bunch of folks watching from outen the store and some more of them Texas cowhands was circling around yelling and laughing, like a wolf pack bringing down a doe. Maude was screaming and carrying on something fierce, so I reached in and grabbed that ranny by his britches and tossed him over the hitching rail into the street. He came up swearing something fierce and clawing for his gun, excepting it weren't there. It'd fell out when he went over the railing and I had my boot on it. His big lantern jaw was shoved out past his nose, and his face was kinda purple. "Kid," he hollered at me, "I'm gonna take your head off." With that, he lowered his head and charged right at me, trying for a quick head butt.

I stepped aside and brought my knee hard against his head. He fell a-rolling and come up like a coiled spring, but I was right on top of 'im and fetched him a boot hard against the side of his face. He fell forward and just laid there. "Boy, you best be packing some iron when he gets up, or high-tail it outta here afore he comes to, or he'll kill you," advised one of the drovers.

I glared at him. "I might not kill that easy."

I weren't wearing no six gun, but I had a knife in my boot, and with it, I could take the eye outta a tree knot at twenty paces in an eye blink, and I'd give any one of them bragging bullies a chance at his shooting iron if'n I had a knife in my hand, and I'd split him afore he'd cleared leather.

Maude moved in and dabbed at my face with her handkerchief. "You okay, Josh?" Then she tiptoed up and kissed me. "Thank you, oh thank you so much."

Ruben was slumped down on the boarded walk agin' the wall; he was plumb out of it. I picked him up and was some taken back at his weight. He was all skin and bones. He was as light as a feather. I put Ruben on his bed and left him and Maude alone whilst I pondered how to handle things if that Texas cowpoke come after me with a gun. There's not no back up in me, and I sure weren't scared if'n the fight was on even grounds, but I didn't hanker after no trouble with the law, and I didn't want to be known as a bad kid to have around.

I went back to the wagon yard and put on my gun. I weren't gonna go looking, but if'n he come, I was gonna do whatever I had to do. Still, I moved on around back of the place. There was no use inviting trouble.

"Boy, you in trouble?" It was my boss Bull Masters. "Not unless he comes up here a-looking for it."

"Your trouble will have to be on your own time and away from here. Get your gear together. I want you to ride the wagon to St. Joseph and take care of the off-loading for me." Well, I'd never been on one of the trips before, so I knew he was just getting me outta the way for a spell, but to tell the truth, I was eager to see St. Joseph, and plumb relieved to be outta there.

St. Joseph was even busier than Kansas City. My time was spent unloading the freight, but I could see the comin's and goin's, and wished I'd a-brought my good shirt with me. There was some fancy saloons like I'd only heard about, but hadn't seen yet. We camped all night in the wagon yard, but we done our eating in a regular eating place, and we ate steaks and pie. I was plumb ready to go on all the trips if'n we was gonna eat like that with Bull paying for it.

Ruben weren't there when we got back to Kansas City. He hadn't said anything to anybody; he just up and left. Maude was sure he'd be back, but I kept remembering what he'd told me once before about getting outta here as soon as he could. Still, I didn't see how he could bring hisself to go off and leave Maude. I sure couldn't if'n she was mine. I had thought a lot about the soft kiss she'd gave me, and cussed Ruben for being the kind of fool that would go away without her. I hadn't seen any more of that trail hand that had bullied Ruben, but Bull said he'd been telling it around town that he was gonna make me pay for dumping him in the dirt. He claimed I'd snuck up on him from behind. I guess it made him think better of himself if he could get folks to believe that. Anyhow, I was cleaning up the stalls and thinking on things when these two men and a boy rode in.

I could see they were tired and dirty, like men that'd come a long way. I looked 'em over, and the two men were in their twenties, one well over six-foot and the other'n just a little shorter. The boy was about twelve or thirteen, tall and lanky, broad at the shoulders and narrow at the hips. All of 'm were wearing guns low down with the low end of their holsters tied around their legs with leather strings. "Partner, can we put our horses up here?" asked the taller of the men.

"Sure can. Take the three end stalls, and turn the pack mules out in the corral if'n you want to. You can stash your packs in that room there on the end." I put my shovel down and held the lead on the mules whilst they tended their horses. The two men left the boy to rub down the animals and stepped over to the saloon for a drink.

Not being especially busy, I grabbed a brush and helped the boy, whose name was Tom. I was real curious about them on account of they all looked like gunslingers and I found out they were all brothers. The big one was called Cam, and the other'n was named Ransome. They were bringing a herd from their ranch in Texas. Tom had been bringing up the horses in the rear. One morning he'd woke up staring at several rifles pointing right in his face by some half-breed Indians. They'd set him afoot, and he'd walked all that day to catch up to his family. His Pa put him right back in the saddle and him and his brothers took out after the horses.

They bunked down in the stalls overnight, but when I left out at daybreak like usual for my practice, Ransome saw me unroll my gun and asked, "Going out to shoot some?"

"Yeah. I have to do it before the boss gets here."

"Care if I tag along?" he asked.

Well, I'd never had nobody watching before and didn't want to now, but I didn't see how to say no.

"Sure, be glad of the company." There weren't no nice way of telling him I'd rather practice without him a-watching. Well, him and Tom follered me out to where I set some boards up for targets. Tom took his turn, and I could see that he was fast, but when Ransome faced up to shoot, I must of blinked because I never even seen his draw, he was so fast.

I stepped up and did my best, but it was woeful, pitiful. "You're not bad," Ransome told me, "but your rig could use some help."

"Don't reckon you'd like to give me a hand?" I asked, hoping he would but not really expecting him to say yes.

"Sure. I'm apt to be here a few days. Cost you, though." He gave me one of those calculatin' looks like he were figuring how bad I was wantin' his help.

"How much you thinkin' on?"

"About five dollars a day," and he grinned at me. Five dollars was gunfighter's pay. I figured it was high, but I could see he knew what he was doing, and I decided to do it. I was glad to find somebody that would show me what to do.

I took the day off so's to get my money's worth, but all that happened that first day was I watched him remake my holster. He added a piece to make it fit further down on my leg so's to favor my reach better. He cut out some of the front, scraped the inside with a piece of glass, and fussed over it most of the day.

When he finished with the leather, he started filin' on my gun. He made that trigger real touchy, and took off the front part of the trigger guard and filed off the sight. He took my gun to the gunsmith, and came back with longer, thicker oak grips that set in the palm of my hand like they was tailor-made.

"There are two things to consider about point shooting," Ransome said. "The grip has to fit your hand and the trigger pull needs to be just right. Then you just line the barrel like you would point with your finger. After that, it's just practice and practice."

Four days they sat there, Cam and Tom in front of the stable, while me and Ransome worked on my shootin'. Bull was gettin' mad about me spending so much time away from my work, and I could see he was ready to skin me. He hired me to roustabout, not to practice shooting. But what I was doing was the most important thing in the world to me. I wanted to be the best there was at slinging a gun, but not because I wanted to be a gunfighter, but so's I could defend myself. I figured it could make the difference between living or dying.

I was walking back from practicing when I heard running horses, a lot of'm. Ransome heard them too, and lit out a-running, so I ran right behind Ransome.

There was about twenty horses being driven in by five cowboys, half-breed injuns by the look of 'em. It wasn't a brand I recognized; it was a slanted B on a rocker.

By the time I got back to the livery Bull had already opened the gate and the wranglers were driving them cayuses into the corral. Cam and Tom walked out and stood by me and Ransome, where we all could be seen, and the four of us was spread out in a half-circle facing the corral. I was standing on the end next to Tom. You could tell that the rustlers was some flabbergasted, because they hadn't expected to see the real owners of the horses they'd stole, and fearful now that they had been caught.

"What you boys want?" one asked.

"Don't talk foolish, Jake," said Ransome quietly. "You know what we want."

"You boys back up a little and let us get down?" asked Jake.

We backed away, and stood there watchful and waitin'. The five breeds swung outta their saddles and walked out. They was bunched together, but facing us. They was sweaty, and grimy dirty from the ride and the dust they'd kicked up. A couple of 'em was wiping their faces with their bandannas and one banged the dust off his hat by whacking it agin his knee a couple licks.

Cam looked around at his brothers and saw me standing there by Tom. "You don't belong in this?"

I knew I didn't belong in it. I didn't even want to be mixed up in it. But I weren't leaving, so I just shrugged my shoulders and stood there, trying not to show how scared I was.

"Can I leave?" laughed Jake. "I don't belong in this either."

"You'll be doing your laughing in hell before long," Ransom lashed out at him.

"We've known you boys a long spell, Cam. We're all home folks here, excepting him over yonder by Tom. We kin give back the cayuses. There ain't no need for us to kill each other over this. In a way, we helped ya out by driving them up here for ya." Jake had put on a big, good-natured grin and was trying his best to charm his way out of trouble.

"Too late for that, Jake. You stole our horses. If we don't do it here, we'd just have to do it later, cause you're naturally just a low-down thief."

Ransome busted in on their talk and hollered out, "Fill your hand, you half-breed, yellow-bellied skunk."

This weren't my put-in, but there's time when things happen you just can't walk away. I was shaking real bad on the inside. On the outside, I was sweating something fierce, and my hands had the shakes. I just didn't see how to get out without being a coward. That would be worse than death. Right then something strange happened. I could feel Pa standin' by me, and I got a real warm feeling all over, and the shakes stopped. Then I lost track of everything except the rustler standing in front of me.

We were drawing a lot of folks, and out of the corner of my eye I could see that Texas cowpoke that had hoorawed Ruben standing with the bunch he run with. They was standin' there watching us, being rowdy and carrying on like this was some kind of entertainment.

I don't remember how or who started it after Ransome yelled for 'em to draw. I felt it just before it all happened. I wasn't even mindful of drawing, but I remember hearing guns a-hammering and the man in front of me had his gun out but the barrel was tilted down toward the ground and he was falling forward on his face. I heard some shouting and swearing, then it was over. A couple of them were kicking and moaning, but none of our side took a hit. That Ransome was greased lightning. He'd shot two before the first one had his gun all the way out.

We was all standing there not saying nothing. I was reloading my gun, so was Tom. He was spinning the cylinder on his Colt and replacing the spent cartridges. We traded sickly grins. I remember wondering if'n this was his first time too, because both his brothers had checked to make sure he was all right almost before the smoke cleared.

The marshal came a-running, all flushed and bothered. "What's going on here?"

"We caught these rustlers with our horses," explained Cam.

"You're supposed to come and get me when things like that happen." The marshal was snorting fire. "We don't allow no six gun justice here."

"Sorry, Marshal, we woulda, but they drew on us."

"That's a fact, Marshal," put in Bull. "I saw it and it happened just that way.

The marshal looked over at me. "Ain't you the boy that jumped in the middle of that fight over at the mercantile the other day?"

"Yes, sir, but that weren't no fight. Ruben wouldn't know how to fight."

"If he can't take ker of hisself, he don't belong out here, and you keep getting in the middle of other folks' business, it's you that's gonna end up bad hurt or dead." He turned to Cam. "I've got to hit you boys for three dollars apiece for the burying. It's the law here. Folks are tired of paying the bill for those who come in here shooting and leave their dead for us to bury."

The wagon came and they loaded them up for Boot Hill while we fished up the three dollars a piece. Right then I remembered the Texans. I looked around, but they weren't in sight. I heard later that they'd gathered up their gear and left out right after the fight. I figured when they saw I had some fast-shooting friends that ranny wasn't near as insulted as he first thought he was.

Tom and his brothers didn't wait around, but gathered up their horses and headed out. I stood there with Bull watching them go. Ransome turned around and rode back to me. "Boy, if'n you're down our way, you're always welcome at our place." I didn't get to answer because he spurred his horse and they left out of there in a cloud of dust.

There was a clink, a sound like metal falling. Ransome had dropped a tobacco sack. I hollered at him real loud a couple of times, but he never turned around. I picked up the tobacco sack and in it was the money I'd paid him. I knew it was his way of saying thanks for standing with 'em, but I would have liked to be able to have told him thanks for all the help he gave me.

Bull shook his head and laughed. "Them Texas cowpokes are all the same. They come in a-whooping and hollering, and always leave out like the place was afire.

"Josh." Bull looked at me real serious. "You're real good with that gun. Take my advice, boy, and take that gun off. There's a lot of this trash would call you out just to make a name for themselves, and the more you kill, the more you are gonna have to fight."

I went right on back to work, but it weren't the same as it were before the fight. The hands I worked with walked around me, kinda keeping their distance. We used to do a lot of horsing around and laughin' and such, making the work seem like play. Now it had changed. Even Bull treated me different. There weren't nobody to talk to anymore, and I felt more alone than I had even when my Pa died. It was like I wasn't me no more, and now I was someone that people didn't horse around with or be friends with. Bull said it weren't because I'd killed that rustler, but because I showed them how fast I could be with a six gun, and now to them I was a dangerous man. And people didn't treat dangerous men the same as they treated other folks.

A couple of days later, I saw Ann and her Pa driving in their buggy. She saw me, but when I waved, she turned away. She acted like she didn't see me. I guess nice girls weren't supposed to know or wave at boys that were dangerous with a gun. This being dangerous was going to be hard to get used to.

Seemed like a lot of folks thought that just because I'd shown I was fast with a gun that I must be a no-account to go along with it. Grown men don't cry, but that night tears kinda rolled out in spite of trying to hold 'em back.

I realized more than ever, I didn't have anyone to care if I lived or died. Pa always said families can make it through anything by sticking together. I wished more than anything to have my family back.

Maude came looking for me that next day. "Josh, are you all right?"

"Sure, unless you count being powerful lonesome as not being all right. Ever since I got caught up in that gunfight, folks treat me like I had horns or something." She put her arms around my waist and hugged me. "Were you scared?" she asked.

"At first I was real scared, but when the time came, I didn't have time to think about it, everything happened so fast. Worst of it is that folks don't treat me the same anymore."

She tiptoed up and placed her arms around my neck and kissed me again, only this time it was longer, and I kissed her back. I wanted to kiss her again, but I didn't because inside I knew it hadn't been meant nothing, but her way of showing me she was still my friend.

Maude was the only one who didn't change toward me, and I spent more and more time with her. Problem was, I was seventeen, and she was old enough to want a man of her own. Still, I was jealous when she let one of the clerks at the bank start calling on her, and I could tell he didn't like me and her being friends. So when the marshal come by to tell me the stage was needing a guard and he had mentioned me, I didn't have no problem figuring who it was that was working to get me out of town, and who the marshal was really doing a favor for.

The stage ran from Kansas City to California. Two armed guards went with each stage. There was danger from both the outlaws and the Indians. Like the Indian massacre about thirty miles south of Carson City, the Paiutes had raided Williams Station and killed every man. There was a lot of Indian raids going on, and the eastern papers were full of details of the horror of the gory scalping of babies and women.

A lot of the stage customers were backing out from fear of attack, so the stage was putting on extra guards.

The stage had been running for a long time now to San Francisco. It had always been dangerous, but now it was worse.

My run was to Fort Laramie, then I caught the returning stage. My pay was to be sixty-five dollars a month and keep. Best of all, they issued me a new lever action Winchester 44.40. My partner's name was John, about twenty-five years old. He looked more like a teacher or an actor than a guard. He had a dignified air about him, except when he'd had too much to drink, and that was a daily happening. He kinda talked like he might have come from somewheres south. He kept to hisself most of the time. He usually kept a book in his pocket, and he'd set up on that seat and drink whiskey and quote poetry mile after mile. Or if we'd ask, he'd get a book out and read to us. I liked the stories best, never did get to where I cottoned to poetry. Months went by with nothing happening except a lot of riding, but that kind of luck didn't last.

This time on the return trip, we carried gold from the mines at Virginia City, a lot of gold. It was being shipped back east, under the special guard of two Pinkerton men. They slipped the gold on the stage durin' the night, the night before we left. Tryin' to keep the shipment a secret. With me and my partner, John, and the two Pinkertons, there was more hired protection than there was paying passengers.

The Pinkertons were supposed to look like regular passengers, but with their city suits and their round bowler hats, they looked just like what they were. There were two drummers with their sales goods, both young, and both talked a lot. I had to ride inside with them while John rode the box with the driver. I tried to stop listenin' to the bragging the drummers were slingin' at each other about money and women and such. I saw one of the Pinkertons roll his eyes up and the other one laughed so I knew they weren't partial to the drummers either.

We pushed along that way till we come to the Platte River. We had crossed the Platte about two hours past when we come to a sharp turn in the trail and come on a wagon that was layin' on its side plumb across our way. There weren't a soul around it, or no horses either. There were sharp two foot ridges along the trail and the woods was thick with trees on the sides, making turnouts impossible.

There weren't nothing to do except move the wagon. It looked like an ambush to me and I said so. One of the Pinkerton fellers gave me a sour grin and motioned for the drummers to get on the floor. They cowed down on the floor whilst the stage just sat there. John hadn't moved. Neither had the driver. I stuck my head out to see what was happening. John had both barrels of his scatter gun at the ready. One of the Pinkertons pulled me back in and we got our rifles ready at the windows where we were crouched down.

I heard the driver go "Tsk" to his team and we began backing up. We were set for trouble, and we got it! It started with rifle fire from the trees. John and the stage driver both died in the first volley of shots. I tried to see where the shooting was coming from, but they were too well hid. Our lead horses were down and the others were kicking and snorting and makin' a ruckus that was shaking the stage so bad I couldn't hold my aim steady anyhow. The Pinkertons were swearin' something fierce and looking for targets, same as me, but they couldn't see nothing either.

What with all the befuddlement and the coach jerking about like it was, I decided to get outta there. I kicked the door open and jumped out and rolled under the stage. Lead was hitting all around me, but when I rolled under the stage I was out of their line of fire, so they switched their aim back to the coach, but under the stage wasn't any better and I got plumb notional about havin' a wheel on top of me, I figured it'd be better to be up on the bank under some brush if I could get there without being seen. I crawled up behind a tree and waited a bit, and when there weren't no lead coming my way, I picked out some close brush and crawled under it. From there I crawled to the next one and kept at it, till I was quite a ways from the coach. I was in front of the stage a couple of hundred yards. I figured the hold-up men to be in back and off to the sides of the stage.

I pulled myself up behind a big thick oak to a low-hangin' limb to get a better field of fire. I saw one a-movin' and hit him dead center. Now I had their attention, but I was hid in the branches and leaves. After a spell another one tried his luck and tried to slip up on the coach. He hit the dirt with a bullet in his chest. Right then someone fired two quick signal shots and about ten of them owl-hoots rushed the stage coming from the back and both sides. I was in a good position to see 'em all. I opened up on them.

Seems like they was fixed on the stage and never spotted me. The stage was taking a lot of lead, splinters were a-flying, whole boards was being knocked loose around the top of the coach. I didn't see how anyone could still be alive in the stage, but they returned fire and between us, we did for about six of 'em, some of 'em was still alive, but all six of 'em was down. We drove 'em off; the skunks pulled back, using the trees for cover. I couldn't see 'em anymore, so's I slid down, and that's when I got hit, as soon as I moved. I took lead in my left shoulder and my left side.

The outlaws left out, horses a-running. They hadn't expected there to be anybody in the woods. Since they couldn't figure who was there or how many there might be, they run. They left their dead and wounded laying there. I was losing blood and staggered back to the coach hurtin' bad because the shock was wearin' off. The Pinkertons were shot up purty bad. Both of them drummers were dead. I took time to look after myself and the Pinkertons, but there wasn't much I could do for 'em. I bound up what was possible, and hoped for the best. I thought about seeing to the varmints layin' out in the trees, but I was hurt so bad I figured it best to leave 'em be. I was hurrying as fast as I could, in case what was left of that bunch doubled back to try again. I weren't in no shape for another shoot-out. I figured the best thing to do was hide the gold, so I clumb to the top of the stage and levered the boxes of gold over to the coach edge and shot the locks off and spilled the gold sacks to the ground. I was still bleeding, and I was hurting real bad now, but I carried a bunch of the sacks of gold to the trees. I covered them sacks with rocks and brush.

I was plumb tuckered out by that time and I needed rest, but I took time to brush out any signs of what I'd been able to get done. Then I took my rifle and eased back to that tree I had hid in, but I couldn't pull myself up this time, so I contented myself with just plain hidin' in close under the brush. I'd have to rest awhile before I could hide the rest of the sacks.

Sure 'nuf, them owl-hoots came riding back before I could get the rest of the gold hid. I stayed put where I was hid, but I could hear 'em swearing and fussing over the gold that had been left by the stage. I heard two shots spaced a little apart. That must of been the finish of the Pinkertons. Somehow, some day, I'd make them pay for that. I swore that as long as I lived I'd be looking for them, and they would know why they died.

I was wishing I'd had time to hide more of the gold whilst I crawled out to where I could see 'em. I had lots of time to make sure I'd recognize them if I ever saw 'em again. There was one real small, slender outlaw I had a hard time figuring out. I decided it must be a small boy, but I couldn't figure out why they'd bring a small boy with them. Then the little varmint turned sideways to me and I discovered it was a woman, a well turned-out woman! Her hat covered her face where I couldn't see it, but I could hear her voice. I was flabbergasted at the sight of a woman being there with them outlaws, and not only taking part in what they was doing, but giving orders to 'em.

I don't know when I passed out, but I must have laid there for hours. When I come to, I was at Fort Kearney, and I was laid up there three whole weeks. I caught a stage back to Kansas City. I hadn't expected a parade, but I did expect some concern or at least a polite howdy. What I got was the boot. We'd failed as far as the line was concerned.

The Pinkertons were concerned about what happened to their guards, especially after I told them about the way they was shot by the holdup gang. They was mad, and said they'd have plenty of men after this bunch. After they asked if I recognized any of the varmints, they was done with me. Funny thing, they never even asked if I'd managed to save any of the gold. I guessed they just thought the robbers had it all. They shouldn't have fired me until they knew fer sure. I sure was mad enough not to tell them nothing that was gonna be any help to 'em.

Well, I still had my gear and I kept the Winchester. They never asked for it back and I never brought it up. What I needed now was a horse. I had some unfinished business to tend to. There was some hold-up men that had a bullet coming to 'em, and I had to clear up my name.

There weren't much use in going back and looking for tracks where the hold up happened. The posse had already tramped out what tracks there were. Question was, where would you go if you were on the run and didn't want your tracks followed? You'd swing back to a well-traveled road to cover your tracks and head for somewhere where ya could get your wounds taken care of, where you could be lost in the crowd. Since I'd recognized two of 'em as being ones that hung around Kansas City, my best guess was they'd hit the road back to their stomping grounds. I was going back to where I'd started from. It'd been some time now, and I'd be glad to see Maude again.

CHAPTER 3

The sun was shining. The sky was blue without a cloud in sight. I had my back agin a tree, shaded by its long limbs that hung clear out over the river. Limbs that were fully covered with big wide green leaves. The slow-moving current of the wide river shimmered in the heat. Even the riverboat men who were used to the heat were moving uncommonly slow today.

Even though I was setting still in the shade, large drops of sweat rolled down my face and my shirt was soaked with sweat from top to bottom. I threw a pebble flat so it skipped across the water and watched it ripple out and fade away. The river was busy as usual. There was a lot of folks moving about but not a hide nor hair of the men I was looking for. I figured if'n they was going to show, they'd been here by now. Question was, what was I going to do now?

The gold was on my mind. I should've told 'em about the gold when I first had the chance. Now they were going to think I had meant to keep it for myself from the start. If I hadn't been so all-fired het up about getting fired, I'd of used better judgment. Now there weren't no good way of telling them about it. I'd thought to be able to bring the varmints in that tried to rob the stage. I could even see myself bringing 'em in and everyone taking on and apologizing and being real sorry for the way they acted and such, even asking me to hire back on. I guess I was thinking like a kid, wantin' to be the hero.

I'd been thinking about Maude a lot and the first thing I had done was to go looking for her. But she'd left Kansas City and gone back east to be with her sister or something. Nobody seemed to know just where and if that bank clerk that'd been courting her knew where she was, he wasn't about to tell me. She hadn't left no letter or nothing, so I figured she hadn't been too interested in keeping in touch with me. I sure missed her, though. I had seen Ann a time or two, but she always acted like she hadn't seen me. I don't know why I should care what a little girl that I'd only spoke to once thought about me, but I did. What was even more kid-like, I daydreamed about becoming a real big man in Kansas City, and Ann and her Pa having to look up to me.

I reckoned the best thing to do was go on west like me and Pa had started. I didn't have no reason to stay here, and sure didn't have any friends to hold me back. I rolled my bedroll up and saddled up and left right then. I didn't tell nobody I was leaving, and nobody noticed when I rode out. I did look around as I rode out. I wished things were different, but there weren't no use in crying over spilt milk.

I saw one of Bull's wagons on the road ahead and hurried to catch up to it. I knew the teamster, and he grinned at me when I rode up alongside. "Howdy, kid. You headed out?"

"Heading on out west," I told him.

"Kinda late in the year to be headed very far west, ain't it?" he asked, whilst leaning over the side and spitting a long stream of tobacco juice.

"I hadn't thought how far I might go right off, I just had a hankerin' to get started."

"Tie that cayuse on back of the wagon and set awhile."

"Reckon I will, for a ways anyhow." I welcomed the chance to get shut of that saddle for a while.

He peered sideways at me. "Ain't seen much of you of late."

"Been laid up some."

"Heard some of it," he nodded.

"Wasn't that much to it, except we lost the shipment."

"I reckon they was a mite upset."

"You might say that. They fired me so fast we never even got around to saying howdy."

"Would ya know any of them jaspers that throwed down on you if you saw 'em again?"

I got a little hitch in my neck when he asked that. There weren't no reason to be leery of him that I knew of, but something about the way he asked it make me uneasy. I decided not to tell much. "No, we were too busy trying to keep on living to pay particular attention to what they looked like."

He gave me one of those knowing looks folks give you when they've been through something similar. "Know what'cha mean, times do happen when you're too busy to be looking at faces."

"We had passengers hollering, both Pinkertons was full of holes, and so much gunsmoke it were hard to breathe, and I had two holes in me. To tell the truth, I didn't care what they looked like, I just wanted 'em to clear out."

"How'd you get away?"

"They left, and I was hid out purty good. Then I passed out. When I came to, I was at the fort. Near as I can figure, they doubled back and took the money later."

"How many was left?"

"Don't rightly know. Maybe four or five that we could see. Might've been more back in the trees we couldn't see."

"Don't reckon you'd know 'em again if ya saw 'em?"

When he asked that, I knew I was right not to have told him I recognized any of them.

I looked off to the side so's not to show any feelings. "No, I reckon not. They was in the trees."

"Not likely we'll ever know now, is there?" He was frownin' like he were thinking serious thoughts.

"Not now," I answered. "Whoever has it sure ain't gonna tell nobody."

He let out a snort of derision. "I reckon not. Man would be a fool to tell anyone he had that much gold."

"Gold ain't much good if'n ya can't spend it—and if someone starts spending lots of gold, that ain't never had nothing before, everyone will know where the gold went."

"Knowing and proving are different things," he answered gruffly.

"Way I hear it, the Pinkertons don't wait for proof. They just send in one of their pet gunslingers and have anyone shot that they think is suspicious."

He reared back angrily. "Folks are gonna get enough of their high-handed ways and put an end to the Pinkertons one of these times. You mark my words, people are tired of being stomped on just because they can hire killers!"

Suddenly he glared at me. "Fast as you are, they'd dry gulch you."

"I don't have anything to worry about," I said. "They know I was laid up purt near death, and had no chance at hauling off their gold. It'd take a wagon or stage to haul purt near five hundred pounds of gold."

"Or some pack mules." He was squintin' like he was thinkin' hard.

"Well, they knowed I couldn't have had no pack animals with me, so I ain't worried none that they suspect me."

He nodded his head like he could see the sense of that.

"I'm gonna pull up here and rest the team, maybe make some grub. You're plumb welcome to stay if you want."

"I reckon to keep going. I figure to make some time on west before the weather gets bad."

I rode on up the road for about a mile till the road made a turn and I was outta his sight, then I pulled back in the trees and rode a ways off the wagon road, back to where I could watch him without him seeing me.

I follered him to Lawrence and watched him offload his wagon. He headed for a saloon and I tried to stay outta the open spaces and still keep him in sight. He met up kinda accidental like with a curly-haired jasper, square-jawed and broad-shouldered. He looked like one of those lady killers, the kind silly women go for when curly hair means more to 'em than if he's a good man or not. He had that cocky, sleazy look to him that I hate.

That night, a rider come in and sat at the bar with them. He looked like a regular range hand but so did most of the robbers at the stage hold-up. All three of 'em drifted casual like to the boardwalk that lined the front of the stores on Main Street. They smoked their makings and talked some. I was wishing I could hear what was being said, but I couldn't make out nothing. They didn't take long, then the curly-haired jasper saddled up and rode out with me shadowin' him. I figured I'd follow him. He was probably the best bet to find the rest of the gang. At least I'd see who he passed the message on to.

I stayed in the trees by the side of the trail and hoped this weren't gonna be a long trail. I'd left my bedroll back to the livery stable. But it weren't but a hour later that he took off on a side trail and ended up back in the brush behind some boulders. There them dry-gulchin' owl-hoots had a camp. Both them varmints from Kansas City that I'd seen when the stage was held up was just setting there. They was swillin' whiskey and laughing and carryin' on like they hadn't a care in the world. I recognized the others too; they'd all been at the holdup. I sloped out of there fast, back to the marshal's office.

In about an hour I was riding with five silent, grim-faced, heavily-armed men back to where I found their camp. We slipped off our horses and sneaked in to where we had them covered. When we stepped out where they could see us, they didn't move or fight at all.

"What's this all about, Marshal?" asked the curly-haired one.

"You men are under arrest. This man here says that he saw you at a stage robbery when he was riding shotgun for the stage."

There was some quick looks at one another, then one of 'em said, "Where was that holdup, Marshal?"

"Along the trail by the Platte."

"Man must be wrong or sump'en, cause we've been riding with a trail herd all the way from Texas till last week."

"If you can prove that, ya got no trouble," said the marshal. "But I got ta take you in. This man swore out a complaint against ya."

A tall, lean, horse-faced, mean-looking gent stood to his feet. "I want ta meet that lying snake that's telling lies on us."

I stepped forward. "I swore to it."

"I think ya made a honest mistake, boy," the curly-haired one said. "I believe ya can see that now, can't you? Ya got old Ringo here all riled up, and I know ya didn't mean to do that, did you?"

"I ain't made no mistake. Ya was the ones that dry-gulched us, all right."

"Boy, you're a liar and a no-good, yellow-bellied snake," Ringo shouted at me, his face contorted and purple with rage.

I was watching his eyes, and when he was through trying to scare me, he went for his iron. He never even cleared leather. He clawed at his chest for awhile, while blood ran outta his mouth, and then he just slumped forward nose-first right in the dirt. I stood there, gun in my hand, the stench of powder smoke tasting rough and dry in my throat. I felt strangely distant from all this, like it weren't real. Or like I'd been watching it happen from off a ways.

Not one of the men I'd rode out with had moved a muscle or made a sound. Not one had backed me when he pulled his iron. It was clear that even with the law by him, a man killed his own snakes. Now, if he'd tried to run, they'd have shot him, but in a man-to-man challenge, even a outlaw weren't interfered with out here.

I faced the rest of 'em. "Anyone else?"

"Reckon not," the curly-haired one said. The others stood there looking at their feet.

"Then let's move on out," the marshal said. "Boy, you killed him, you put him on his horse."

The trial was to be in St. Joseph, so I got a room there at the hotel, had a bath and a shave. I felt a whole lot better now because the stage line would have to own up that I had done my job. As soon as they had these outlaws in jail, they'd own up to where the gold was, and everyone was going to allow that I was a man to reckon with.

It was all over town—the capture, the gun fight, and every-thing. I guess the varmint I shot had the reputation of killing fifteen men in stand-up gun fights. When I stepped out of the hotel, it looked to me like I set everyone a-talking. I thought it was because I'd brought in the gang that held up the stage, and maybe I was younger than they would expect a man to be who'd done such a thing. But purty soon I got the idea it was because I'd outdrew Ringo, who had a reputation in these parts as a real bad man.

The day of the trial came and I was glad to get on with it. The judge set up there in his robe real proper like. For me, this was a real stirring sight. I'd never seen a real judge or been in a court before, and it set a lump in my throat and made me real fidgety. The marshal and all his prisoners were right in front of the judge, while I set on the first bench with the lawyer. Some of the bigwigs from the stage line were watching from the back of the room. They hadn't said they was sorry, or even spoke to me yet, but I was looking forward to it.

"Call your witness," the judge said.

I got right up there fast. The clerk held out the Bible and I was told to put my hand on it. "Swear to tell the truth?"

"Yes, sir, I do. Them's the bushwhacking, no-good varmints over there that shot up the stage."

The judge pounded the bench with a mallet and hollered, "Shut up," at the courtroom because they was all a-laughing. Then he told me, "Wait till you're asked to say something, boy. Just answer the questions when they ask you something."

"Well, it sure seems silly to me. I was there and they wasn't. How will they know what to ask?"

The judge leaned over the bench and told me real careful and slow. "Boy, just do as I say and don't say nothing till you're asked."

Then he beckoned to the lawyer and told him to start.

"What's your name, boy?"

"My name's Josh Bonner."

"You was a guard on the Butterfield stage that was held up?"

"Yes, sir, I was."

"Are there any of the men here who robbed the stage?"

"Yes, sir, they sure is."

"Can you point them out to the judge, please?"

"That's them over there that the marshal has got."

"Now listen, boy, and don't make a mistake. Is them the hold-up men?"

"Yes, sir. I saw 'em plain as day. If'n my arm hadn't had a bullet in it, they wouldn't be here."

There was some laughter and a couple of cat calls.

The judge kinda cleared his throat. "Just answer the question, boy. Don't add anything else."

Well, then the lawyer had the marshal tell the judge about the capture and the shooting of Ringo. The room got real quiet while he told about how I outdrew Ringo, and then that was all for us. I did see some of them that had been doing the catcalls and making fun of me for not knowing how to act in court get up and leave.

Then their lawyer asked the marshall if he had found any of the stolen gold on 'em, and he had to admit he hadn't. Then their lawyer fished out a telegram that he said was from the Texas trail driver these honest, hard-working men were working for at the time of the robbery and that all these men were on a trail drive when the robbery took place.

I jumped right up. "Judge, that's a blame lie. I seen 'em there clear as daylight."

He hit the bench again. "Boy, set down. I've already heard from you."

Then he let 'em go. He said there weren't enough evidence to hang 'em.

Well, I was mad. He as good as said I was a-lyin' and I weren't going to take that from nobody, and I said so. The lawyer told me to leave it go. The judge wasn't sayin' I wasn't telling the truth, just that there had to be more evidence. Just like the Bible said, "In the mouths of two or more witnesses shall a thing be established." And there weren't two witnesses agin them, but there was more proof on their side.

Well, I weren't gonna argue with the Bible. My Pa would turn over in his grave for sure if I done such a thing. I couldn' figure why the lawyer and the sheriff wasn't as mad as I was. Even the stage bigwigs didn't seem too upset. Then it hit me—they was more interested in where the gold was than who did it. They was gonna watch them and see if they led them to the gold.

I saw them snakes all bunched up in front of the saloon, but when they saw me walking toward them they got on their horses and rode right out of town. There must not of been any of 'em that wanted to fight me right then. But by that time, I didn't care about the loot they'd took or them. It wasn't what was right that moved this world, but who had the gold. I sold my horses and gear and caught the stage to Denver. For no particular reason, except that I heard it was booming and a man might make it big there.

Denver was booming and big and loud and boisterous. New hotels and fancy gilded gambling parlors. Everything glittered and shined from the signs outside to the inside. The saloon girls strutted in their fancy spangled dresses, and their shills was trying to sell 'em to each and all that was in hearing distance. Most saloons even had pianos and singers for entertainment, and everything cost a heap of money. I got me a room in one of the biggest hotels and went looking for a tailor to make me a suit. I got new boots, took a bath, and had my hair cut.

I was new from top to bottom, except for my gun that I wore tied down and ready. I reckon I looked green as grass. The desk clerk where I was staying told me I should leave my gun off and to keep any money I might have to myself. I listened real polite and thanked him for his advice. I went back to my room and shucked my holster and gun, then I went out and bought me a small hideaway that fit in my pocket. I stood in front of a store window where I could see my reflection. I looked pretty good in my new black suit, white shirt, and black tie. My hair was combed and my new boots shined, but I still needed something to finish it off. I finally figured it out. I needed a gold chain with a gold pocket watch. That took almost the last of my money, but I bought me one, and then I eyed myself one more time. I was totally satisfied. I thought of Pa for some reason. I guess I'd have liked him to seen me dressed thataway.

It weren't long till I had wasted all my money. There was too many fancy eatin' places and too many pretty saloon girls to buy drinks for. I were in the worst shape I'd been in since Pa died, and I wished I'd never come to Denver. Of course, there hadn't been much money to start with, but before I got there I'd at least had a horse and saddle. What was worse, after a few days with not payin', the hotel clerk wanted to talk to me, but as I didn't have the money to pay with, I turned my back and pretended not to have seen him. I was in a real pickle. Besides that, I was hungry and could use a friend. I decided that I only had one friend, and it was in a holster in my room upstairs.

I went up and put on my old clothes. They were washed and ironed, and looked a whole lot better than they did when I first come here. I buckled on my gun. I didn't exactly know what to do, but I had to do something. I tried the stage office, but they didn't need anyone. In fact, he hinted he thought I was too young to be of any use. I ambled around town some and watched and looked.

That's when things finally took a turn my way. In the back of one of the gamblin' halls, I found a small leather pouch with some gold dust in it, probably spilled out of some drunk's pocket while he was bein' throwed out. I took it to the hotel, paid my bill and exchanged the dust for dollars. I had twenty dollars left, but that wouldn't buy much of a horse here in Denver. So I spent some time watching the gamblers, particularly the wheel, but it looked too risky to me. I walked around till I found a small stakes poker game, and waited till a chair was open, then I sat in the game.

"Put your cash up on the table, boy," the dealer said.

So I hauled out my twenty dollars. "Is that enough?"

"To start with anyhow." He tamped his pipes against the table and refilled it.

"We are playin' two bits in and pot limit," he added, as he lit up his pipe.

I anteed my two bits and got my first card. My uncle had taught me a lot about poker, mostly when my folks weren't around. It ain't the cards, he always said. Watch the players. The first card was face down and most of the players never even looked at it. I looked at mine by liftin' one corner. Everybody anteed another two bits. The next card was up and mine was highest, being a queen of clubs. I raised it to a dollar, since that made me a pair with one of the queens hid in the hole. The next card was a deuce of clubs and that left me showin' two clubs, but there's a lot of distance between a queen and a duce.

Then a couple of players "paired up" and the price of poker went up. I drew another queen on my last card, which left me showing a pair of queens with one in the hole. My uncle would have been tickled to death with this hand. All that was showin' on the table was pairs, and all of their hands were lower than my queens.

It was my ante, so I played it close, like I was worried about one of them having three of a kind. I put in two dollars. I was raised and raised again, till I had only a dollar or so left.

"Better start diggin' in your pocket, kid," the dealer said as he flipped over three nines.

"Not good enough." One of the others turned over three tens.

I quietly showed them my three queens and raked in the pot.

Somebody laughed quietly. "Always watch out for beginner's luck."

I surveyed my pile. There was at least a hundred dollars in it.

I smiled at the dealer. "Don't reckon I'll have to dig for more money yet."

Most of the players at my table were miners or cowpokes. The only professional was the dealer. I watched him, and no matter how the luck ran, he always seemed to win a little more than his share. I didn't figure him to be cheatin', just doing what a good player does, reading the players. I played till after dark and cashed in for over three hundred dollars. That was more money than had ever been mine before.

The next morning, I stopped at the bank and deposited two hundred dollars, and about two in the afternoon I went back to the same table.

"Back again, boy?" The dealer smiled. "I figured you to be sittin' on some fancy saddle and a new horse 'bout now."

"No sir," I replied. "This was too much fun to walk off and leave."

"It's only fun, boy, when you're winning. Take my advice and play it careful."

"Yes, sir, I will do that. I been watching you play and trying to take after the way you do it."

He looked at me real serious. "Don't play if what you lost is living money."

"No, sir, it ain't money I need to live on."

He got busy after that and we didn't talk much for the rest of the game. But I could see him watching me with a new interest, and I tried real hard to play using some poker sense. I won again that night, not because the cards were runnin' right, but because I judged the players right. When I cashed in that night, I knew two things: The dealer's name was Al, and second, I liked playin' poker and winning. When I made another deposit at the bank the next morning, I discovered I liked doin' that, too.

I went back to the tailor and had two more black suits made. I bought some more white shirts, and sought out a laundry. I was fast becomin' used to people doing things for me. I didn't see no harm in that; I could still do for myself, but it was nice to be done for, too. But one morning I strapped on my gun and made a practice draw, and discovered that I was slower than I used to be. That scared me, and after that I went out every morning and walked a long ways to keep myself in shape, and then I spent two hours early every afternoon practicin' my shooting. I had lots more money now and could buy cartridges by the case, which is what I did. My life was so filled up with what I was doing, I never felt lonesome, not even one little bit.

If Al hadn't missed a day at his table, my life might have gone on pretty much the same for quite a while. I was enough ahead to keep about five hundred dollars in the bank. In a small game, a player needs to play it close all the time and be content with small, consistent wins. I liked to take chances too much to be a consistent winner.

With Al's table closed, the only other game in the house besides the wheel was a bigger limit poker game. I didn't feel comfortable going to some other place. So I watched awhile from the bar till some miner went broke and his chair was open.

"Hey, kid." The dealer waved at me. "Want in?"

"Don't know. Might be too rich for me."

"Naw, not tonight. There's not no big players here tonight. Get in. It's a dollar ante, no limit."

"Well, I reckon I could play some, till it gets too rough, anyhow."

There was the dealer whose name was Buck, a rancher next to him named Pierce, a couple of miners with the handles Dynamite and Red, and me. I filled up chair number five.

We played five card stud for a couple of hours and I was doing right well. Pierce, the rancher, was losing almost every hand. There weren't nothing going his way. If he had three kings, someone else had three aces. He had a ranch a few miles east and south of Denver, a good one. He put it up for security when he ran out of ready cash. After a couple hours, he was gettin' impatient and wanted to change the game to five card draw. Well, no one cared what we played, so we switched to five card draw. There's more bluffing in five card draw, and I started playing reckless and winning big, which led me to be even more wild, and created some man-sized whopping big pots, most of which I won. I hadn't paid no heed to how much Pierce was losing till Buck said to him, "Pierce, you're getting in pretty deep. Are ya gonna be able to cover all this without losin' your place?"

"I ain't got no choice now. I've got to play till I win some back. Don't worry, my place is good for what I've got on tab and a lot more besides."

"Could be you'd be better off to quit now and try again some other day," Buck advised. "We ain't gonna press you for the money tonight, and I hate to see a man throw away all he has on a streak of bad luck."

"Ya mind your own business," snarled Pierce. "I didn't come here to have ya try to tell me what to do. Just take ker of yourself, and I'll do the same."

"Sorry, Mr. Pierce. I wasn't meaning no offense," and then he started passin' out the cards.

"I think the man was talking sense," I put in. "Ain't my business either, but some days are luckier than others, and this one don't seem to be your day."

"Shut your trap, boy, or I'll shut it for you. Ya got most of my money, and I aim to take it back and everything else ya got." Pierce was hoppin' mad. Then he shoved his chair back like he had intentions on makin' a big to-do out of it.

"Sit down, Pierce." Buck pushed him back in his chair. "Boy didn't mean no insult."

Pierce looked at me like he hated me, and I could tell that it wouldn't matter what was said, he wanted to break me.

"I ain't gonna tell ya again. I'll mind my business, and I don't need no smart aleck kid to give me advice."

Well, knowin' he was after my hide gave me a whole different slant on things. I sure quit feelin' sorry for him. Buck passed out five cards. I had the ten and jack of hearts, a two of diamonds, and a five of spades, and a ace of hearts. Buck opened with a dollar, Pierce jumped it to ten dollars, Red raised it to twenty. I looked at my pile of cash on the table; it were considerable. I decided it would be fun to buy this pot and take it away from Pierce, if he had anything, and he was bettin' like he had a good hand. So I raised it to fifty. Buck studied me cool-like and met my raise. I could tell he thought I was goin' after Pierce. Ya couldn't put much past Buck.

He dealt the cards. Pierce took one. Both the miners stood pat. I threw away the two of diamonds and the five of spades and drew the two and three of clubs. When things are goin' your way, push it, my uncle used to say, and things had sure been going my way, so I decided to bluff my way through.

"We'll just start at a hundred this time," Pierce said, givin' me one of those I've-got-you looks.

"Make it a hundred fifty," Red said.

I met the raise and Buck folded his hand. "Too much for me," he said.

"I meet your raise, and raise ya a hundred," Pierce said. Dynamite folded and Red met the raise.

I looked a long, steady look at Pierce. "Ya want all I've got?"

He laughed at me, and I knew I had him buffaloed. I knew he'd fold.

I pushed it all in and set back and looked at Pierce. Inside, I felt this fierce elation like a big cat at his kill. My uncle said there was winners and loosers, and I was a sure-enough winner!

Then he met my raise with a sneer and a flourish. They all turned and watched me quiet like, The tension was thick enough to cut with a knife. I just sat there and felt powerful sick.

CHAPTER 4

The trip to the bank the next morning was to take out and not to put in. I was still some better off than when I came here, but I was sick way down inside. I'd been ridin' high. Pride was what it was, "unduly prideful," Pa would have said. They'd be pokin' fun at me now, and I sure wasn't going back in there to play poker for a while.

It was too late in the year to try going on west. It was already cold and snowing. I didn't want to stay here, so I figured on going to Dodge. I'd heard there was plenty of money being spent there. Between here and Kansas was wild country, country where ya have to stay mindful of everything about ya. It can be your friend or enemy, depending on your know-how. I had a knack for getting around in the woods. It starts with enough savvy to keep your eyes peeled and your ears open, and the right goods to do with. I could've made out with a lot less but it sure is nice to have hot coffee and bacon on a cold morning. It felt right to be on the trail again even if it was bitter cold. The only unfriendly Indians likely to be in these hills was Utes, and I didn't figure them to be moving around much in this weather.

We was moving slow and easy on a snow-covered trail. Ya could see your breath and that of your horse, and hear the crunch of horse's hooves caving in the frozen snow, with loud crunching sounds. There didn't seem to be much else moving. Even the critters had sense enough to stay abed this morning. In real cold weather ya don't go doing anything fast enough or hard enough to raise a sweat. So we was moving slow and quiet and being watchful when we come on some other tracks. There was four horses being rode close together, and what was most likely a pack animal being led behind. I figured it to be a mule. Being kinda watchful and heedful of the fact that not all folks was friendly, I drifted off to one side in the tree line.

From the shape of their tracks, they was taking it slow and easy theirselves. A running track would have thrown more snow away from the track. They would have been easy to foller in dry dirt, let alone snow. One horse was throwing its right front leg, and the left front shoe of another had wore bad on one side. I found where they'd stopped for a fire. It was still too early for me, so I kept on riding. I was getting real curious about these riders, I guess cause there weren't much else to take up my thoughts.

It was like a game we used to play back home, where one of us would make tracks and the rest would try to figure what was meant by the tracks and where they was going. There was none better than Pa when it came to tracking anything through the woods. He taught me a lot, but what he knew took a lifetime to get, and I don't savvy all of it yet.

Close to dark, I saw a big campfire up ahead and circled in the tree line around them. I stayed well hid in the trees and far enough away that the noises my horse made wouldn't reach 'em.

I was bent on passing them by and getting a fire of my own going because of the powerful cold, when I caught sight of a woman at their fire. I reined up under a tree and watched them. I was curious about what one woman was doing on a trail with three men.

That's when I took in that one of the men was tied up with his hands behind his back. They was eatin' and he weren't. He had his back agin a tree watchin' whilst they drank coffee and ate. It came on me that I weren't much better off than him. I hadn't ate either, and right then my stomack was settin' up a howl. It weren't my business anyhow, so I slipped on past 'em a ways and built me a little fire agin a rock and hid the flicker of the flames from reflecting on the snow by buildin' a frame of ferns over the fire. I swallowed everything right down and rolled up tight by the fire.

I don't reckon it was the morning sun that woke me, it was the screams that was coming from back down the trail. I rustled out of that bedroll fast and grabbed my rifle and backtracked as quick as I could. They had that poor feller that was tied up all stretched out with his boots off and that there woman was a-pushing a hot iron to his feet! The men was just standin' there a-watchin'. I hunkered down a mite behind a stump and eyed the woeful mess that pitiful old man was in. He was quiet now, and his head was all slack and hangin' to one side. I figured that cold-blooded, savage witch had done too much to him too quick. Too much pain will put a man out sudden like.

The thing is, how to help, without gettin' myself boxed in with no way out. There was no way to move around in this snow without making noise. I figured the best thing to do first was to part them from their horses. At least that way, if I did do enough to get him away, we'd have a start on 'em. Back in the mountains where I was from most men could hit what they was shootin' at. It was not only needed to feed your kin, but it was a matter of pride, seeing shootin' was just about all we did at any gathering. Turkey shoots, Sunday dinner on the church grounds, weddings . . . to be the best shot in our mountains was every man's aim, and such a man was every family's pride. My uncle was our family's pride, and almost even with him was Pa and me. So when I lined up on the lead rope that was holdin' their animals, I never even conisdered missing. By the time they heard the crack of my rifle, them horses of their had taken out running. I put some more lead right behind their heels just to keep 'em going. When I looked back to the camp, them folks was scrambling for cover. I stayed hunkered down behind that stump. I knowed they was trying to see where I was at, so I stayed still and watched. They weren't good at waitin'. It weren't long till I saw one move and then the other'n. I still couldn't place the woman, though. So I took aim on the one on my left. He had the least cover, and had a leg showin' plain. I hit him just below the knee and he hollered and rolled around yellin' for help. I could of killed him then—he was in the open—but I figured he wouldn't be no more help to 'em or danger to me.

I kept a sharp lookout, but I couldn't see either the one man that was left or the woman. I didn't believe they'd been able to join up together yet. Their horses was gone and their camp was under my rifle, so what would I do if I'd hit such a snag? I'd try circling around behind my enemy. So I figured to move back a ways close to where I'd left my horse and watch. Waitin' is a necessary part of the hunt. Any good hunter will tell you that, but there's a lot of men good with a gun that's lost out because they couldn't make themselves stay put. I watched and waited, but so did they, and meantime the old man was freezing down there cause the fire had gone low and I could see him twistin' in pain, but there weren't nothing I could do till I finished them other two.

The feller I'd hit in the leg had slipped away into the brush, and the moans comin' from the man they had been tormentin' was the only human sounds I could make out.

The wind was coming up and the tree branches was shedding some snow every time they was blown about. It weren't long till I was covered like a big old boulder in snow, but I was dressed as warm as could be and wasn't feeling the cold that much. They could move around without me knowin' but surprisin' enough, that woman slipped right out in front of me.

If she saw me at all, she probably thought I was a snow-covered rock or stump or sompt'n. She weren't more'n twenty yards away and with her back to me. I almost moved when I thought of something my Pa taught me about deer huntin'—how the buck would send the does out in the open first to see if there was any danger. Now these varmints knew I weren't likely to put lead in a woman. It could be she was trying to draw me out whilst he hung back to plug me. So I waited, and sure enough she turned and beckoned a "come on," like he was behind and higher up, so I waited whilst she slipped on out of sight. Only he never come, and after a while I finally figured that she was using that as a put-on, probably every time she moved—just to make anyone watchin' think someone was comin' right behind her, so I moved out in the direction she went, only I moved straight alongside the hill whilst she was slanting down the hill.

Sure enough, I caught sight of her sneakin' along in the brush and wavin' that come-on signal ever time she moved.

Now, I never shot a woman before, but when I thought about that hot iron she'd been usin', I pulled down on her dead center, but I just couldn't do it, so I dropped my sights down where the heel of her boot should be, and knocked her foot right out from under her.

Whilst she was still shocked and dazed, I ran the short distance betwixt us and before she could grasp what was happenin', I had her trussed up like a calf at brandin' time. It was a pretty good shot—I didn't take much of her hide at all.

She hissed at me—a snake noise—between clinched teeth. Her eyes glared out hate and poison, and she coiled and lashed about just like a sidewinder. She hadn't yelled or made any kind of noise, but I stuffed her bandanna in her mouth anyway. I judge I was too sure of myself, cause right then she swung her trussed up legs agin mine and knocked me catawaumpus in a snow bank.

While I was threshing around trying to get up, she was crow-hoppin' down the side of that hill. I finally got my feet under me and took out after her. I almost had her when a rifle barked, and I dove into a snow-covered bush, just barely bein' missed by a bullet. It chipped bark from a big old tree right by my head. Anyhow, by the time I collected myself whoever was doin' the shootin' had moved. I jumped clear of the bush and he fired again, but he missed and I saw where the muzzle flash come from.

I hit the ground rollin', his lead sprayin' snow ever place I'd just left. Till I got behind a tree, then I had my turn. I hit him—even though I couldn't see him—more by luck than skill, but sometimes bein' lucky is worth a lot of skill.

I saw him runnin' from tree to tree, and he was holdin' his side. I didn't get another shot because I heard her threshin' around. Time I looked at her and then looked back to see him, he weren't there anymore. She rolled behind a clump of brush and I couldn't see her no more. Thing was, what was I goin' to do now? I had a bad hurt old man, and I couldn't just go off and leave him. I had her trussed up like a Thanksgivin' turkey but I couldn't get to her without gettin' shot. If I had a lick of sense, I'd shuck it on out of here and call it a good try. But Pa always said I was more bulldog than human, and I knew I weren't leaving till I had had another try at getting that poor feller that was trussed up by the fire loose and free.

I thought about my animals and decided I'd better get back to them before I did much else. If'n they found my horse and pack mule, I might end up afoot myself. I slipped away as best I could, which ain't sayin' much. Every time I moved, I shook snow from whatever was close to me, and anybody that cared could see where I was going by watchin' the limbs and brush move as I crawled outta there. I looked back and could see I was leavin' a trail through the snow a blind man could foller. I'd had enough of crawlin' in snow, so I just stood up and walked. I figured if'n they shot me, they better kill me first try because I was through tryin' to sneak around when it weren't even possible to be quiet and unseen in all that snow. And I were some mad at this whole trouble 'n' mess I'd got myself mixed up in.

My animals were fine. I circled my camp and didn't see no tracks so I went on in to camp and stirred up the fire and put some coffee on. I was pretty well hid from view from any direction and high enough I could see my back trail. Which weren't hard in all that snow. I was settin' there sippin' my coffee when it started snowin' agin. It weren't long till the snow was fallin' so hard I couldn't see across my campfire. There weren't nothin' to do except dig in and wait it out. It snowed a lot that night and must of put another three inches of snow down.

When mornin' come, I didn't waste no time. I saddled my horse and loaded up my pack and rode right down the trail to their camp. Gun out and ready, I ran right in on 'em full speed, expectin' to shoot and be shot at. There weren't no one there. Not them—not the old man they had tied up. The woman had got away, too. I looked where I'd left her and there weren't a sign of nobody or anything. There weren't no trail, either, and I couldn't waste no more time. It was snowin' again and I wanted outta these hills. I left outta there feelin' like a whipped pup, but I had to git, if'n I wanted to or not.

The snow was fallin' so heavy I couldn't see anything and I could either hole up and wait, or try to keep goin' and maybe end up walkin' in circles and lost. My druthers were to keep goin'. I'd rather take a chance on dyin' walkin' in circles than be snowed in and die slow.

The horse I'd bought in Denver was raised in this country, and it come to me that if'n I couldn't see anything that I should give him free rein and see what he could do. He just stopped and stood there! I got off and tried to see if I could feel my way along, but there weren't no way. Plus I discovered I'd let the mule loose. I was tryin' to get aholt of him when he moved past us and took on down the trail. The horse stepped right out after the mule, and I just barely had time to grab the stirrup. I figured that I must be the biggest fool in the world a-hangin' on a horse while he followed a mule and none of us could see anything. The snow was halfway up to my knees and times were the horse dragged me more than I was able to walk. We went like this for what seemed like hours. There was icicles hangin' from my coat and it felt like that my face was a frozen mask. I lost any track of time and numbness covered me from head to toe. I was in between knowing and feeling, and not knowing or feeling, kind of a lost gray place in my head.

I don't know when I finally lost track of what was happenin' but when I woke up, I was in a small lean-to, I could see that much by just looking up. When I turned my head, I could see my animals standing close together in a corner. I was cold—but I was alive. I tried wiggling my toes, but I couldn't feel nothin'. I could move my legs and I could set up all right. I rolled over on my knees and looked around. It was still snowing, but we were inside. I didn't know how, and right then, I didn't have time to wonder about it. I busted up a board to start a small fire, then I got out my blankets and hung them up over the open side of that lean-to. That cut some of the draft out. The roof and walls looked snug enough, at least there weren't no big cracks or holes in 'em.

In a bit, I shucked my boots and socks and checked my feet. They felt numb, but didn't show no signs of being froze. I rubbed them with snow till the feeling come back in 'em. When the feeling did start comin' back, they hurt so bad I figured I knew exactly how that old man felt with the hot iron to his feet, except I didn't holler—even if'n I did want to. Little by little, the place warmed up enough that I took off my coat and unloaded my pack. After puttin' on fresh dry socks and some dry clothes, I set about rubbing the frost and ice off them animals. Silly as it sounds, I felt like kissing that blame mule—but I settled for giving it and my horse a double handful of grain.

That shed didn't have much left for bracing when we left the next morning, I'd tore off most of it for firewood during the night. But the snow had quit and I'd had a night's warmth and some hot coffee. I felt a whole lot better. I wondered how them varmints and that old man had made out. I figured there weren't much to be done about them now.

More'n that, I wondered how that mule got us to that shed and just exactly where we were at? The man I'd bought him from said he'd belonged to an old man that'd kicked the bucket in Denver that winter. Maybe he just found his way home. I walked around some. There were a few old corral poles leaning off at angles—part of an old gate a-hangin'. And aways back in the trees was a cabin. It was empty and hadn't been used for what looked like a long time. I bet if a body knew it, that there was a story could be told about that place. There were bullet holes in the walls—a lot of 'em, but not much else.

I started to step out of the cabin and bent over some to keep from bangin' my head on the doorframe—and that's what saved me! A bullet slammed into the side of the frame right where my head had been. I was on the floor and well inside the cabin by the time the next bullet hit. Whoever was shooting was off to the side, but I couldn't see him. I'd left off thinking about anything but getting on to Kansas, and had purt near paid for that stupidity with my life. Course, come to think on it, I weren't in great shape anyway. Here I was on the floor in a cabin that had no food, water, or even firewood, and near as I could tell from where I was, there was no way out except through that door. There wasn't even a window big enough to crawl out of.

I did what my Pa always said to do when it looked like there weren't nothin' you could do—don't get fidgety. Sit back and think on it a spell, it'll come to you. So I sat back and thought on it for a long while, and nothing at all come to me. So I took out my gun and took a running jump through that door, firing in all directions. Except there weren't no one shooting back at me. The reason bein' they had taken my animals and my pack and left me high and cold. I said "they" because there were two of 'em, and by the looks of their tracks, one of 'em was that woman. From near as I could tell, she'd done her best to kill me, whilst the feller with her got my pack together. They'd even emptied my coffee pot out on the ground and took it.

Now I don't get mad easy, but this were too much even for me. I turned up the collar of my coat and took off after 'em. If'n I lived to catch 'em, they was sure as shooting gonna die! One thing I figured would be to my advantage—they wouldn't be expecting me any more than I had been expecting them. I was some surprised at how thirsty a feller gets when it's real cold like that. Eatin' snow really don't do much for me, but I kept at it whilst I walked.

One good thing was that they weren't hurrying none, they was walking the horse whilst one rode and one walked. Then in about an hour, they'd trade off. I was getting tired, wore out and hungry and losing ground. I come on where they'd built a fire and had something to eat. That stirred some anger in me. I'd been walking with my head down and feeling sorry for myself till then, but I got mad all over again at the sight of where they'd stuffed themselves with my vittles, and me bein' so hungry I could hardly think of anything else.

I figured on walkin' up on 'em at night when they stopped to camp, but dark come and the moon come up, and it got colder and colder and they kept going. I was stumblin' now, I was so tired and weak from not eating. Pa would have said I'd gone soft in Denver from livin' too good. He'd of been right—and I was really paying for it now. I'd a need for some rest, and I decided to stop awhile. I picked a spot between two big boulders and cleared away the snow between 'em. I used my knife to cut some branches and build a shelter. With a fire going and a place to stretch out, it weren't long till I was asleep. The fire died down in a couple of hours, and the cold woke me up. I hurt all over, but I staggered back on the trail and in a few minutes, I warmed up enough that the stiffness wore off, but my stomach was still complaining.

The sun come up, and I was glad of the warmth it brought even if it weren't that much. Right after daybreak, I shot a rabbit and finally had some food in my stomach. I found where they'd stopped and rested a while, but it'd been sometime during the night because the ashes from their fire was cold. I was so tired I'd been stumbling along, barely able to keep going. I built a fire on their ashes and rested some. I wondered how long the horse would last with no rest. For that matter, how long would the mule stand this kind of treatment? I found the answer to that question a few miles later—the mule must of balked and refused to go any further. Mules have got plenty of sense. They know when they've had a-plenty. He was laying on the trail, they'd shot him right where he stood. The pack had been opened and stuff was strung everywhere, I guess while they picked out what they wanted to carry with them.

I had to fight back the tears I felt for that mule. In her plan to keep me afoot, she'd killed the best mule that'd ever set foot in this country. I'd planned on keeping that mule in high grass for the rest of his life, but his life was cut short to keep me walking, and there was going to be a time of getting even. I picked up a few things for a small pack of my own. I was glad to have the food and dry clothes. But time was going on, and I had more reason than ever to want to catch up with that witch.

At sundown, I built a fire and for the first time in a couple of days, ate a purty good meal. I hadn't meant to sleep, but I did and I must of slept for a while—lots longer than I'd a done on purpose. But as it turned out, it didn't matter. I'd just got ready to step back out on the trail when I saw a man riding toward me. He had his head down like he was trying to read the trail—probably trying to figure what a man was doin' on foot out here in the winter time. As for me, I was plumb glad to see him because it looked like he was leadin' a string of horses. I stepped out and waved my hand just so's he'd know I was friendly and stood there while he pulled up and looked me over carefully.

"Howdy," I said, with the best grin I could manage. "I'm real glad to see somebody, and real happy to see somebody with a horse."

I could see he had his rifle layin' across his saddle with the barrel pointed right at me and considering my recent experience out here, I didn't take no offense a-tall. "Howdy." He gave just a brief nod of his head, never once took his eyes off'n me. "How come you're afoot out here?"

Well, I could see this gent wasn't much on small talk, so I told him in as few words as I could what had happened to my animals.

"Tenderfoot!" he snorted contemptuously. "Man don't know enough to keep watch over his horse needs to walk."

Right about then, I kinda had the idea he was fixing to go on off and leave me standing here. Now, I'm not a contentious man, but if'n he tried, I was gonna do him some hurt. It might have been the look on my face, but he kinda grinned, at least it would pass for an effort at a grin. "Ya can throw your poke up on that black." With that, he pulled off the trail and swung out of his saddle. He went to stirring around the ashes and soon had a fire goin' with coffee boiling. I can tell you that that coffee was the best I'd ever tasted.

The man wasn't much of a talker, wasn't much of a listener either. So after a couple of lame tries at talking, I just shut up and rode. Before nightfall, we rode in on a boom town full of miners and such. I'd heard tell of such places, of course, but this was the first one I'd ever seen. All the buildings were new, there was lots of big tents, even though it were winter. The whole town was on one side of the road, if'n you could call a couple of frozen ruts a road. There was a stable and a hotel, of sorts, two saloons and a store made out of wood—then there was a dozen or more small cabins and a lot of tents. Some of the bigger tents were more saloons and places for trollops and such. It sure was a busy town, I guess because they couldn't get up in the hills with all that snow on 'em.

The only thing I was wantin' to see was the sheriff or marshall. When I asked the feller I rode in with where to find the marshall's office, he threw his head back and roared. I didn't see nothing funny about a simple question and said so. "Boy," he said, wipin' his eyes. "That's not only a simple question, it is, in fact, a simple tenderfoot question. There ain't no law in a boom town except what you're big enough to enforce your own self. But if you're figurin' on bracing that woman for stealin' your cayuse, then you'll have ta whip every hombre in town, because they care more about her than whether or not she stoled something."

I looked at him in surprise and shock. "Ya mean she's from this place?"

"If she's who she sounds like, and who I would guess she is, she's Nora, the queen of the Golden Belle, been here since the strike."

"Ya mean the miners won't care about that poor feller she was burning the feet off of?"

"Sure they would, if'n they believed it—but they won't. She's too important to 'em right now for entertainment. Later in the spring when the work starts again they might be willing to believe it, but not now. If fact, boy, they might just string you up if'n you were foolish enough to tell anyone."

"How am I gonna get my horse and gear back?" I asked.

"Just walk over there to the stable and take 'em. I'm sure she's through with 'em now anyways, and she's sure not afraid of anything ya might say."

That didn't fit with my notion of how I wanted this ta end. I'd been shot at, left afoot in the cold, starved and stolen from, and for the first time in my life, I was gonna hunt someone down and kill 'em because of the anger that was drivin' me. Always before, I'd killed because I was forced to, but not this time. This time I hated them with a fire that burned me from head to toe. So's I hitched at my pants and started lookin' for that varmint that'd been with her. I'd start with him and figure what to do about her later. I walked in the Golden Belle first because that's where she'd be and most likely that's where he'd be. First I opened my coat where I could get at my gun.

And that's where he was, walking around wearing two guns, actin' like everyone else was supposed to be afraid of him. He saw me, but his eyes just went right on by me like I wasn't there. I grinned to myself. He didn't even know what I looked like and had no way of knowing I was here, or that I knew why he was wearing that bandage around his ribs, so I walked up to the bar and ordered a coffee. The barkeep didn't look directly at me either; he just poured the coffee and moved on to serve the busy bar. The way he was working, he could be there all night and never know who he served.

I sipped at my hot coffee and watched for a sight of her. I don't know what I expected, a girl in pants wearin' two guns, I guess, but she come out wearing the most beautiful gown this side of Denver. Her hair was all done up in a pile, and if'n I hadn't knowed she was a she-demon, I'd a-thought she was plumb wonderful along with the rest of 'em. She saw me right off, and I could tell it because she gave a little twitch and started working through the crowd going towards that ranny that'd been out there with her.

Well, if'n I was gonna surprise him, I had to do it before she got to him, so I did the first thing that come to mind. I threw my cup of coffee at him. He whirled around, snarling, "Who's ready to die?"

I had my coat pulled back away from my gun, and he saw it. "You throw that cup at me, boy?"

I laughed, and that made him step a little back, and I could see he weren't used to someone not being scared of him.

"I been follerin' ya for some time now, horse thief." I threw that at him real loud. His face turned an ugly reddish purple, and his eyes were flashing like they was on fire. "I don't take being called that from nobody, whelp, even from a kid."

"Ya gonna talk me to death, or draw?" I pushed him. I wanted him to be unsettled and flustered. He sure nuf was getting shook. I knew he wanted to know who I was. "Either draw or beg," I shouted, blood hot with the desire to kill. I'd plumb passed the point where I even cared whether or not if'n I could discombobulate him and get an advantage.

He drew, and he were fast, but his shot went into the wall behind the bar. Maybe I did have him shook enough to miss on the first shot, but mine was dead center in his heart. Dead center being the right word, I guess, cause he sure nuf was dead. Part of what I'd set out ta do was done.

I looked at her. She was stunned, couldn't believe it, I guess. Neither could a lot of them. The place was a-buzz with things like, "Who'd a-thought?" and "I can't believe it."

Right then, two fellers rushed through the door getting out of there, and I got just enough look at 'em to see it were some of the outfit that'd been at the trial of the stage robbers. I wanted to chase 'em, but there was so many around me I couldn't get through. "Just who are you, boy? And what in thunder was that all about?" stormed an old miner, getting right up in my face. I could see he was beside hisself with all the excitement.

"I've seen him," shouted someone. "He was with that Texas outfit that shot up Indian Jake in Kansas City at the Livery there. Over some stoled horses."

"I didn't think the man lived that could take Gorman," another one put in. "I've seen a lot of 'em, from Curly Bill to the

Earps draw, but I ain't never seen nothing faster'n Gorman till now!"

I looked to see what happened to the woman, but she were gone. I did want to get her next, but you don't shoot a woman here in the west, no matter how bad ya'd like to take your revenge. I had to get somewhere and plan how I was gonna do what I'd swore to do.

It took a while to get past the back-slappers and well-wishers. Sometimes folks don't seem to have any better feelings or higher outlook than a pack of dogs. They reminded me of wolves bitin' on one of their own that'd been injured. Course, I reminded myself, I'm the one that shot him; I got no right to fault them. I was just feeling the letdown that comes after the fight is done, I told myself. I sure wasn't gonna be sorry for killing him now.

I stayed in what served for a hotel. There was one big room and about a hundred of us unrolled our bedrolls out on the floor wherever there was space for us, for the price of a dollar a night. Breakfast was fried potatoes and biscuits and cost two dollars. Coffee was a dollar more. I figured to get on out of there whilst I still had something left.

I sat and watched the Golden Belle all mornin' till she finally come out. She looked real hard up and down the town, but I were out of her line of sight. She walked around back of the place to the outhouse, and right then I got an idea. I got on my horse and rode around where I'd be off to one side when she come out. When she did, I threw my rope on her and quick as a wink was out of my saddle and had her hogtied and a bandanna in her mouth.

I looked around good but it didn't seem like I had been seen, so I throwed her over my horse and moved on out behind the town. At the edge of town, I threw my rope over a limb and put it around her neck, then I took the bandanna out of her mouth, but I had my hand around her throat just in case she tried to squawk. But she just stared at me whilst she made that hissin' snake sound she'd made up on the mountain.

"I'm gonna hang you, you poison she-snake." I wanted to see some fear or begging or something, but she just glared at me and hissed. "Ya want to pray or something?" I asked. "I wouldn't want to send anybody to meet their Maker without a chance to pray if'n there was time."

There wasn't no way she wanted to pray. All she wanted to do was tear my heart out, that much was plain to see.

I wanted to hang her high and watch her choke to death, but I just couldn't do it, so I left her feet on a stump and the rope around a limb over her head, and if she stood way high on her tiptoes, she wouldn't choke. I don't know how long it took 'em to find her. But I bet she sweated a lot, and I figured she'd never forget me! I found out that revenge wasn't that sweet after all, there was such a let-down feeling after I rode on—but I kept reminding myself of that old feller and her a-burnin' his feet.

There was still the feller that'd got his leg shot up there where we had our first set-to, but I hadn't seen anything of him since, and truth was, I hadn't seen his face or been close enough to know him if'n I saw him.

I rode on back to town and gathered up my stuff and rode out after those fellers I'd seen leaving out after the shooting. There weren't but two ways outta here. And one way was back toward Denver, and I was sure they weren't goin' there.

CHAPTER 5

Dodge City was boomin'. There were trail herds in from Texas, and there were Texas rannys everywhere. All of 'em had their pay from months on the trail, and a itch to spend it. The girls were pretty and plentiful, and the gamblin' games were everywhere. When I got there, the town was goin' strong around the clock. There was talk that there was a new marshal on the way to tame the town down, but right then it was wide open and goin' strong.

I stabled my horse and found a hotel. This time it were a real hotel and I had my own room. I had beans, cornbread and coffee and a hot bath, and lots of sleep. When I woke up, there was a big ruckus goin' on because another big herd of Texas longhorns was bein' drove in the stockyards. I drifted that way just to see the sight of a thousand or more head of half-wild cows with long, sharp horns being worked into loadin' pens. I'll say one thing, them boys knew how to work cattle.

I kept a sharp eye for them two that had been at the trial and had skedaddled when they saw me back at camp town. I kept movin' from place to place, shoulderin' through wall-to-wall cowboys standin' three deep at every bar. There wasn't even room for a good fight, though a few were tryin' it at every saloon.

Finally I found them. I stood back and watched. The last thing I wanted to do right now was to spook 'em. I wanted to watch them to see if there was any more of that bunch around. But I was most likely watchin' too close. I guess there is something to feelin' that you're being watched. One of 'em turned and looked me square in the eye. He nudged the other'n and they headed for the door. Well, the game was up. I could see I weren't gonna get anywhere this way, so I hurried through the crowd and got to the door right after they did. But they weren't in sight when I finally pushed out of the crowd and got outside.

Even at night Front Street was full, but this was still the early hours of night. The stars were out and the moon was just showin;, not enough to be much help seein'. Of course, the lanterns from the saloons and such helped a lot. Even so, it was pretty dark along the street and close up to the walls and back in between the buildings you couldn't see at all from the street. I figured they were layin' for me somewhere in the dark. I turned around and pushed my way back inside into the crowd. This was gonna be a long sleepless night for them fellers, if'n they was gonna lay for me. I grinned to myself as I went out through the back. I walked as quiet and careful as a Indian walkin' on dry leaves. I stood awhile before I moved to let my eyes adjust to the darkness, and walked close to the walls, so I wouldn't cast a shadow.

I set a chair agin the door with its back under the knob, and just to be careful, I shoved the bed over to the other wall. With my gun in my hand, I drifted off to a troubled, restless sleep.

When daylight come, I was glad to see the sun. I gave some thought to trailin' them fellers till they come up with the rest of their gang. I just didn't know how to go about it. Every time I saw them, they had spotted me and lit out for somewhere's else. I was havin' breakfast and lookin' out the window at the street when I saw 'em ride by headed out. They had their bedrolls on and a pack horse with a good-sized supply pack on it. Looked like they was outfitted for a long ride.

I decided I weren't ready to go trailin' off after them. It was cold out there on the trail, and I'd just got through with a long ride and the snow and bitter cold was still a fresh memory. Anyhow, chances were they'd already spent the gold or gambled it away. I figured I was on a wild goose chase and would be better off stayin' put and playin' some poker. Thinkin' of that reminded me that I needed to go by the livery and make arrangements for wintering my horse.

"I got lots of room," the stablehand said. "Two fellers just left that had planned on bein' here a spell."

"I think I saw 'em leave." I was real casual. "Why would they head out in this kind of weather?"

"Strange acting fellers." He rubbed at his whiskered face. "First they said they had to get to Montana, then later one said to the other'n that it was a bad time to be going to Nevada.

"Well, some folks are purely secretive about their business."

"I never asked 'em where they was going. There weren't no need to lie to me. I surely do hate a liar. If'n that's the way they are, I'm happy to see 'em go."

"I'm like that my own self," I put in. "The worst old rapscallion at home wouldn't lie to you, unless'n it were braggin' or story tellin'."

We talked some more about liars and low-life folks, and I kinda made up my mind to hold off going after 'em in this cold and snow. Besides, most likely they was expectin' me to come, so they was probably holed up somewhere layin' for me, ready ta blow me outta the saddle if'n I showed.

You can hear a lot when you're playin' poker if'n ya listen instead of talkin'. The story of Nora was bein' told everywhere. The story was some no-count jasper had tried to hang her and had nearly been caught at it. Leavin' her standin' on a stump, he'd run. Trouble was, no one knew why or what he looked like. I grinned to myself when I heard she'd been left with considerable rope burns on her neck. What was really funny was that some seven foot, two-gun, mean-lookin' hombre had outdrew and killed the fastest gun in this neck of the woods. Now, I'm not anywhere's close to seven foot and never thought of myself as mean-lookin' and wouldn't know how to use two guns if'n I had 'em. I was just as happy not to be singled out as the buckaroo that had done it.

Sometimes lookin' like a big, good-natured kid has good sides to it. Nobody took me very serious at the poker table, and I didn't fit their idea of a gunslinger. In fact, everybody called me "kid" and was friendly. Even those who come in mean and lookin' for trouble passed me by, favorin' some jasper who was as mean and ready as they was.

I'd been there a week or two and was feelin' real good about the town when some big mouth rode in from camp town and pointed me out as the one that'd killed Gorman. Braggin' how's he had been right up clost and saw it all—beats all how a feller would feel important because he saw somethin' happen. Right after that, men started whisperin' and noddin' when I come into a place. I could see one or two of 'em sizin' me up and thinkin' about calling me out.

I knew it were time to saddle up, but I put it off on account of the cold. But when the stage come in and this young feller wearin' two guns low down on his legs got off and I heard it were me he was lookin' for, I figured I'd leave come mornin'.

The next thing I knew, he was standing just inside the saloon doors all braced for a shoot-out. I hadn't figured on him findin' me so quick. There's been a gunslick in a buckskin coat over by the wall that had been watchin' all evenin', and I'd been keepin' an eye on him. Then the two gun totin' youngun come in. The buckskin gunman and me both saw him about the same time and he cut his eyes at me and shook his head, like we was in on a secret or something. I guess I didn't see the humor on it.

The two gun kid hollered out, "Who's Josh Bonner?"

Well, everybody in the place turned to watch, and those who stood nearest me moved away fast as could be.

I sure didn't want a shoot-out over nothin' and I don't know why I did it, but I just lifted my arm and waved him over to the bar. He stood there undecided and glarin' around the room. "Come over here feller, and have a drink on me," I suggested.

"I'm lookin' for this Bonner who's such a fast gun," he snarls, still all braced for trouble.

"Well," I says, "you can shoot somebody anytime, but there's no need to be in such a rush. Come over here and have a drink with us, and let us in on who you are and such. We want to get this all straight for the tellin' of it later."

After a little more lookin' around, he come over to me at the bar. I saw the feller in the buckskin coat laugh. So did the youngun who was huntin' me. He whirled on him. "What you laughing at? You there in the buckskin—you think I'm funny?"

"Nobody's laughing at you." I reached out and touched his shoulder to get his attention. "Come on and have a drink."

He was touchier than an old sore-tail bear, but he turned and lifted his glass. "I want to know if Josh Bonner is in here," he said to me. His eyes narrowed, and I could see he didn't trust me at all.

"Ya real good with that iron?" I asked, tryin' to get his mind loose from the only idea he had.

"You point out Bonner to me and I'll show you," he bragged.

"You mind if I make a little money on you?" I turned to the rest of the bar, not givin' him a chance to answer.

"I got ten dollars that says this feller can outshoot anyone in this room."

Well, them are bettin' words in just about any bar west of the Mississippi River. There are lots of good shots in every town who don't go around gettin' in gunfights, men that everybody in town knows can shoot and do their braggin' on.

Before he knew what was goin' on, we had him outside and targets set up and three of the town's best shots to shoot agin him. I had thirty dollars bet on him agin the townfolks. It was some contest—reminded me of back home at some of our gatherings. No one had gave me away; everyone seemed to think it were a good joke and acted like they was all in on it. There was some real good shots in that town. It finally come down to flipping silver dollars in the air because not one of 'em had missed a still target. I won my bets cause he hit three silver dollars in a row that I had threw for 'em.

I could see this youngun had never killed anyone. Most likely he'd been readin' too many dime story books and wanted to be somebody famous. With all the back-slappin' and takin' over on him, he was plumb happy with himself and he'd lost that look he'd come in with. "How'd I do?" He grinned at me.

I handed him half of what I'd won. "We done real good. You're the best I've seen in these parts." Every hand in the place had sized him up by now, and I could see everybody liked him.

Well, I figured to ease on outta there and get me gone when Buckskin said, "That's Bonner there besides you."

He turned on me. "You've been leadin' me down the garden path, hombre," he snarled, all red-faced, embarrassed-like. "Well, I'm about to take the fun outta it."

It were too late for talk, so I grabbed his gunhand and clouted him on his jaw. He folded like a limp quilt. I turned on Buckskin, "You want to see someone draw on me? You do it!"

Well, he hadn't seen me draw or shoot yet, and that's what he'd been after. I knew that, and he knew that I knew. He laughed and turned away and walked back in the bar. He wasn't afraid, I knew that too. He was just careful like any real gunhand would be.

"Don't you count him out, boy," an older, short, bearded, bandy-legged cowboy said to me. "I've seen him work and he's some kind of gunhand."

"Thanks." I nodded at him. "I ain't gonna take him lightly. All I want is to leave before I do have to shoot it out with some gunhand workin' on a reputation."

I went on back to my room to think awhile. There weren't no place to stay out of the way here in Dodge—and it would do no good to leave for somewhere's else anyway, because there'd just be someone else to deal with. It seemed to me that I was caught between a rock and a hard place. I wondered if'n I could do better just headin' back to where I come from—except I'd sure hate to go draggin' back there with my tail between my legs, Folks said we'd come draggin' back when we left. I wouldn't give nobody the pleasure of sayin' they told us so.

I stretched out on my bed and slept for a while—Pa would have thought it a shame to be asleep in the middle of the day, but I just couldn't think what to do and sleep just kinda come on me.

It was the poundin' on the door that woke me up. When I opened it, there stood that youngun with the two guns.

"You gonna hide in here, Bonner, or are ya gonna come on out in the street wheres I can show everybody I'm the best?"

I hit him, right on the jaw. I moved so fast he'd never seen it comin'. I guess he was expectin' to talk about it first and then walk out in the street like some kind of "knights of old" that was in the stories Ma used to tell. He sure had some learnin' to do. I'd hit him on the same side of his jaw that I'd punched on the first time, and it were sure swellin' up and turnin' blue. He was gonna have to eat on the other side of his mouth for a while. That is, if'n he could eat at all. I drug him on in the room and took his guns away from him and put them under my beddin'. I left him on the floor and laid back down on the bed to wait for him to wake up.

After while, he set up and rubbed his face. He looked up at me like my old dog used to look at me when he'd been whipped. He'd whimper and give me his best mournful-eyed expression. That was kinda the expression this kid had on his face.

"Ya hit me again!" He was plumb disgusted. "What kind of gunslick are you, anyhow?" He started gettin' red all over his face. "Ya lily-livered no-count coward, give me back my guns and get down to the street where we can finish this."

"Finish what?" I asked, tryin' to be reasonable.

"Finish what?" He stormed out, "Why, we're gonna finish what I come here for. I'm gonna put you down."

I layed back on my bed, and stared at him. "You'd best leave now!" I knew he wasn't big enough to take back his guns, and I figured he knew it.

He shifted some on his feet and finally blurted out, "I can't go back out there without my guns!"

I set up on the bed. "I tell you what, I ain't gonna waste my time with some kid that ain't even shot someone. I'll give you back your guns, but before you try me, ya got to go prove ya can stand up with someone with a name for being a gunhand." I figured that ought to fit in with his idea of how all this was supposed to work. I hadn't read any of those stories about the wild west that he must of been readin' but what I said probably fit right in there, because he nodded his head.

"All right, I can see that you'd not want to shoot it out with me, and me with no rep."

"Tell you what." I grinned at him. "You go back down to that saloon and put down that feller in the buckskin jacket and then we'll talk about what to do next."

I tossed him his guns, minus the cartridges, and he lit outta there like the place was on fire. I probably should have kept the guns and let him be shamed, but he was already gone and maybe this way would solve both problems.

I swung my feet off the bed and headed down to watch what was gonna happen. I was curious my own self, which one was the best. When I got there, everyone had already cleared the center of the room, and most was backed up agin the bar—Buckskin was back agin the end wall and gave me one of those I'll-get-you-for-this looks. The kid stood in the middle of the room, all braced and ready to go, standin' there waitin' for someone to say "go" I guess. Still playin' it out accordin' to his notion of the western gunfight. Still, he didn't look right, so I took another look at him, and sure enough there he was, all froze up, like some kind of grim statue. I figured that all of a sudden he figured it out that he could die here, and now he couldn't move to save his life. Buckskin saw it too and grinned, all ready to draw now that there weren't no danger to him. I don't know why I mixed in—I guess like everyone else that was there, it just didn't seem right.

"You don't want him," I shouted at Buckskin. "Ya want me."

He turned to look at me and I shot him.

Buckskin's gun was on the floor. He was holdin' his bloody hand with a shocked look on his face and the kid was still froze in his tracks and the room was as still as I've ever heard a barroom to be. I guess everyone was expectin' one thing, and when something different happened, it took them plumb by surprise. I stood there and got a lead-like feelin' in my gut. I'd hit him in the hand when I'd meant to kill him. I could get killed that-a-way. I sure-nuf couldn't believe I let myself get tangled up in this after I had it all worked out. But I couldn't bring myself to stand there and let him kill the kid. No doubt someone will do it anyway if'n he don't savvy up real quick, but I'd put him in a bind and I couldn't leave him there.

Outside on Front Street there was the sound of a runnin' horse and someone hollered, "He's runnin' outta town," meaning Buckskin. I never did hear his name spoke or if'n I did, I disremember it.

All of a sudden people were slappin' down money on the bar and tryin' to buy me drinks. The place was in a noisy uproar now, and with so many men around me, I lost track of the kid, but when I looked around for him he was gone. I don't know why I should have been, but I was uneasy about him. I shoved his trouble to the back of my mind and let the folks take on over me.

"He was gettin' ready to shoot that boy, and him too scared to move," one feller said to me. "I'm glad ya didn't let him do it." I heard that over and over; everyone seemed to think the same about that. I was a hero that night, and between the girls takin' on over me, and the pats on the back, I plumb forgot the kid.

The kid was settin' there on my bed when I got back to my room. I keep callin' him the kid because ever after that, folks most always called him that kid from the east, or that greenhorn kid. His real name was Obadiah Guillford. He didn't have on no guns.

"What ya doin' here, kid?" I asked. "Ya sure don't think to call me out now, do ya?" To save my soul, as Ma used to say, I couldn't figure what on earth he was doin' here.

"I don't know what to do," the kid says, misery just a-stickin' real plain out'n his eyes.

"Go home," I told him, just as blunt as I knew how.

"I ain't got a home," he whimpered. "I ain't never knowed no folks that was mine."

I was raised to shoulder my own saddle. I never in my whole born days would've let on to somebody else that I had a load I couldn't handle. In particular, to a hand that I'd come to kill. Of course, if'n he never had no folks, then he never had no raisin' and that might count for some of it. But his whimper sure brought out the worst in me.

"Boy," I said roughly. "You got to get hold of yourself. I ain't your friend. Ya came here to kill me. If'n ya can't walk with the grown men, ya best stay where the kids are." That last part was what my Pa used to tell me when I didn't act like he thought I should.

He got up real mad and stomped to the door. When he turned, his face was beet red. "Thanks for savin' my bacon," he shouted. "I won't bother ya no more." Then he slammed the door and stomped on down the hall.

I didn't fault the kid none. I'd had buck fever once when my Pa and my uncle with all my cousins was with me. I reckon I was as shamed as I was ever gonna be right then and there. I don't reckon he froze outta fear, but more because it weren't no game in his mind no more. It was right then he first got ahold of the notion he could die there and it took holt enough that he couldn't move.

Anyhow, Buckskin was gone and the kid weren't no problem no more. So I was feelin' real good about how it had all turned out. Buckskin was gone, the kid was outta the gun business, and I was a hero. Then I walked outside and there stood that woman and three of the meanest-lookin' gunslicks I ever seen. She was still all gussied up in female finery and pretty as I ever seen. If'n you didn't know she was mean and rotten inside, you'd swear she was a angel.

She pointed right at me and almost screamed, "There he is. Well, there I stood like a big knot on a log, flabbergasted, while they spread out in front of me. Folks sure moved out of the way in a hurry and there we stood— just me and them three boxin' me in, when outta nowhere this two gun kid shouldered through the crowd and stood beside me. "Looks like you could use some help," he says in his best book hero voice. I wanted to hit him, but I couldn't take my eyes off'n the ones in front of me.

"Kid, you're the biggest durn fool I ever did come across," I told him. "Get your tail outta my way before ya get me killed." I was downright mad. I didn't have time to worry with him and them too.

About that time, he drew, and a faster draw I never seen. I already knew he could shoot, and I quit thinking 'bout him and flashed my own iron, whilst I threw myself to the right, firin' at the one directly in front of me. I don't think any of 'em even shot at him. I hit the ground and kept rollin' tryin' to get behind the horse trough that was there to my right. They was all shootin' at me, most of 'em were hittin' right where I'd been, but I took one through the outer skin in my rear and another through the calf of my lower leg afore I made it behind the trough. Whilst I was rollin' and hidin', the kid was shootin'. They was all down, holdin' their arms and shoulders; they weren't shootin' anymore. And that she-devil wasn't nowhere to be seen. There stood the kid, legs spread, both guns leveled at 'em, and untouched, while I had blood runnin' down my backside where no brave man should ever be shot. To make it worse, he says real loud, "Ya can come out now, they're through shootin'."

Well, there are times for everything—Ma used to say it was in the Bible. . . . If'n there were a time for shame, that were set aside for me . . . this was most likely it.

The doc took care of the three hired guns that we had put down before he even looked at me. I figured I should have had first call on the doc, considerin' that they was would-be murderers. I felt foolish and mad whilst I stood there bleedin' down my backside and tryin' to come out of this as best I could so's not to be the laughin' stock of the town.

The kid, though, was makin' my life pitiful and wretched. . . . He didn't have a lick of sense! Struttin' around sayin', "See there. . . . I paid him back for pullin' my fat outta the fire. . . . didn't I?" The men were pattin' him on the shoulder, tellin' him how great he was, downright disgusting. All the time I'm standin' around with my backside agin the wall bleedin' whilst the doc took ker of them lowdown, no good bushwhackers that had tried to murder me. Anyhow, the sheriff had 'em and was waitin' to haul 'em off to jail. No one had even mentioned seein' the woman with them and I was spared answerin' lots of questions as to why she'd want me dead. That was something I really didn't want known . . . considerin' the stories that were goin' around.

Finally, Doc had me over to his place and fixed me up, only I weren't gonna set easy on a horse for awhile. Worst thing was, I weren't gonna rest easy around here anymore anyway, with that kid braggin' night and day how he'd cut down them would-be murderin' varmints and saved my bacon. Course, I knew lots of that talk was to make up for me havin' to take care of Buckskin for him, and everybody seein' it. Still, he were makin' me look like a fool, and I wished he'd just go away. But he was there first thing every mornin' runnin' and fetchin' things for me and talk, talk, talk. I never have figured out how to get rid of someone that's doin' things for you . . . all day long.

"I never figured when I come gunnin' for you, that we were gonna be partners," he'd say. In fact, he'd say that first thing in the mornin; and still be sayin' it the last thing at night. . . . I didn't want a partner. Partners rode with each other for years, always workin' together for the same ranch, dependin' on one another. "Backin' up his partner," was the favorite story that the kid read. He read it to me, he talked just like they talked in the story, and he sure nuf thought we was gonna ride together. I didn't see no way out without just comin' right out and tellin' him, and I couldn't do that. So when I finally got to where I could set a saddle—we rode out together! I tried gettin' off without him . . . but he stuck closer to me than a flea to a dog.

I'd made it through the worst time of my life, and all I had was a partner to show for it. A talkin' partner. . . . I tried to close my ears to him, but then he'd say, "You're not listening."

Of course I weren't listenin', I was trying as hard as I knew how not to listen to him. But he did have a guitar and could sing like nobody I'd ever heard. It sure beat his talkin'. I could listen all day to him sing . . . and did lots of days.

"Life is not meant to be fair," Pa would say when I come faultin' somethin' or somebody. "You got to do the best you can do and not worry about what the other feller has got or what the other feller can do." Still, when you're ridin' with a big, good-lookin' kid who can shoot the eye out of a needle and can sing like he could. . . . I guess I could learn to hate him. But everything he did fit in with them blame ten cent stories of the west that he always was readin'. It were like he weren't real. Just another part of one of them books.

"Where we headed?" he asked suddenly, raising his head and lettin' his guitar go quiet. It hung from the sling he had on it and was bouncing off his leg making a faint thump, thump sound as we rode.

"Kansas City." The thought jumped right out at me. I almost hollered out loud at the idea. I purt near laughed with excitement. I was going back to see if'n Ann was still there, and of course there was my friend Maude. All of a sudden, I realized I really wanted to be in Kansas City again.

CHAPTER 6

I should have never gone back to Kansas City. I wanted to see Ann, and I did, sooner'n I expected! He saw her as we were ridin' in. A grown-up, Ann, taller and more ladylike. She carried her head straight and proud and anybody could see she was quality. She still had a heart-shaped face. She still had her head covered by a hat, but her hair hung in long curls down her back. She was even prettier than ever, slim and well-formed, and graceful . . . and my heart hurt deep in my chest just from watchin' her.

But she didn't see me. . . . She saw the kid. Obadiah Guillford, he was ridin' right beside me. We both tipped our hats to Ann, who was standin' in front of the bank. She never even noticed me. . . . Our eyes never even met. She only saw the kid! There was a hate rose up in me that I'd known only once before . . . and that was when I'd shot that feller named Gorman. He smiled at her with his boyish grin, and she just stood there, her pretty blue eyes sparkling, boldly lookin' straight at him like she was invitin' him to get down and talk to her. Her Pa saw me though, and my face probably gave away my feelings, because he grabbed Ann by the arm and hurried her back into the bank—through the window I could see him gesturing with his hands and could see Ann put her handkerchief over her mouth. I didn't see more because we'd already rode by.

"Pretty girl." The kid's voice sounded puzzled. "You know her?"

"Met her once." I never looked his way, but stared straight up the road. My jaw was clenched tight and I didn't feel friendly.

"You like her?" he persisted.

I thought that that was the dumbest thing—out of a lot of dumb things—he'd ever asked.

But I just said, "Yes," and kept my head straight forward. "I'd never get in your way, you know. Partners don't horn in on each other." I recognized that sentiment from bein' right outta his favorite book. I didn't want Ann to see me if'n somebody else had to step aside. . . . I wanted her to see me because she'd druther look my way than at anyone else. Then my pride reared its ugly head. "She's not mine, I just met her once." The hurt had already struck its sharp pain into my very soul and nothin' would ever be able to remove it. All my secret dreams and all my private wants were somehow tied up in her and she'd cut the ground right out from under me.

We put our horses and pack mule up at Bull's livery stable. Bull didn't seem as glad to see me as I was to see him. So I just said a few howdys and such to the ones I knew, and got on up to Lucy's boardin' house. Lucy weren't much for fancy, but her table always set out the best eatin' there was in town, and it were clean. She didn't allow no swearin' or drunks. Maude had stayed here, before she had moved back east somewhere. I couldn't tell you how I felt, kinda lost, kinda like I did when Pa died. I just laid down on the bed and stared at the ceilin' cracks, thinkin' of nothin', just feelin' low.

I didn't pay no attention to where the kid went, he had a room of his own, and I expect he went right out to a saloon somewhere. The kid liked to be around folks, the more the better. Somehow I felt as tired as a plow-drawin' mule at the end of a very long day. For the second time in my life since I was growed to man size, I went to sleep in the middle of the day.

It was the commotion out in the street that woke me. There was a big cage setting on a wagon. Inside the cage was the biggest, meanest lookin' dog I'd ever seen. He would be waist high on a big man. That ugly-lookin' dog probably would weigh 150 pounds if'n you could get him on a scale. He was solid black from the tip of his nose to the tip of his tail. His chest was as broad as a big man's chest would be, and his head was so wide it wouldn't go in between the cage bars that were at least a foot apart. His lips were drawn back in a snarl, showin' long teeth capable of rippin' deep gashes with every slash. His green eyes flashed the fire of hate. Right now it looked like he hated just about everybody. His eyes met mine and I drew back without aimin' to. We kinda stared at each other, and for a little bit I could sense the anger and contempt he felt. I turned away from the window and hurried right out to see what was goin' on.

The cage was crowded around with the curious, and some that were mean along with bein' curious. They were the ones pokin' sticks through the bars just to see the dog bite the sticks in two with his big strong jaws. Some of them limbs were as big as small trees and still he would part them in pieces with just a snap of his strong jaws.

Then some drunk opened the door of his cage and tried to shove a big old mongrel in that had the misfortune to be standin' there. The mongrel was fightin' with all his might not to be shoved in there with that ugly brute and the drunk stumbled and fell while the crowd was cheerin' him on. . . . The big dog saw his chance and jumped through the cage door so quick no one could move to close the door.

Instantly, guns were flashin' and it sounded like a battle was being fought. The big hound was jumpin' side-to-side, bullets kicking up dust all around him. He was dodgin' through horses' legs and runnin' behind hitchin' poles, creatin' a big commotion whilst bein' shielded from the barrage of bullets that was going over, behind, and in front of him, whilst he was swappin' ends and dancing and dodging.

He was out of town and running hard down the river bank before the crowd could get movin'. Most just laughed and went about their business, but the feller that had brought him in and a few others who liked a chase went whoopin' off after him. I personally hoped he'd get away, and I pitied any who got in the way of them strong jaws.

I saw the kid standin' watchin' the goings on whilst standin' next to Ann's Pa, laughin' and talkin'. It were clear Ann's Pa was plumb taken with him. I figured it were time to shuck Kansas City and a partner. Him I hadn't needed anyway. I went through the hotel grabbin' my stuff on the way, and out the back door . . . down to the stable where I loaded my gear on the mule and saddled my horse.

I didn't have no particular direction, I just rode the riverbank as close as I could. Come nightfall, I was quite a ways upriver from where I'd started. I had a hurt inside, but I'd heal and it felt good to be by myself. I built a fire, made some pan biscuits and some coffee, and laid back with my back agin a big rock. The sky was clear and the stars were shinin' bright. I stared at the sky and let the world fade outta my thoughts. There was a rustling noise in the brush, and that big old dog I'd seen in the cage back in Kansas City drug hisself up to the other side of the fire. He'd been shot in his hind leg and had blood all over his hindquarters.

He stood watchin' me for a bit, his green eyes still flashing fire. Then he drug hisself over by the fire and laid down. I didn't move, I just kept my eyes on him. He didn't whine or whimper, but lay there and stared solid at me. I decided he wasn't going to try and bite me, so I tossed him a biscuit. He snagged it outta the air just like he was used to doing it all the time. I tossed another and another till I was empty of biscuits. He seemed to like every one of 'em. I thought about tryin' to see about his leg, but he growled when I moved so I just laid back and let him be.

Come mornin' I stirred around fixin' the fire and makin' something to eat and he just watched. I could tell he was too stiff to move. I tossed him some frying pan biscuits, which he seemed to like, and I poured him a drink into a small pan and shoved it to him using a stick. I pushed it right up to his nose and he drank it all. Probably had a fever, I figured.

I packed up my outfit and started on upriver. I really hoped the dog would get better, but when I looked back, he was just layin' there . . . not moving . . . watchin' me with eyes that seemed to say, "I could use some help." I rode a little farther, but he still couldn't move, though he was trying, dragging hisself with his powerful front legs. I got to worrying he was going to hurt hisself more by trying to follow me—so I turned back. I figured it wouldn't hurt none to wait a day or two to see if he could get on his feet. He opened the hole in his backside again by trying to get up and fresh blood was pourin' out.

This time he let me come close up and tend his wound. I think it must of been the biscuits—he acted like he wanted help, and . . . he didn't have a lot of druthers to pick from. For the next week, I shot rabbits and deer and caught fish to keep him fed. He might of been hurt, but he still could pack it away. He never took to pettin' or ear scratchin'. . . . I could tend his wound or feed him, but there weren't no partnership gonna go on here. After my ordeal with the kid, I could kinda get a handle on how he felt.

After the first day, he was hobbling around some. But it was a good week before he could lope a little. We traveled slow and easy for a couple of more weeks before he could chase down his own food. He stayed right with me till the day he caught his own rabbit, then he never come near me again till night come. Every night he'd come to camp and sleep up close, but durin' the day, he traveled a ways off, just keepin' me in sight.

That kinda suited me and it was right for him. We got along fine that way.

I had no idea where I was headed, if anywhere. I was short of money but didn't need much. I just wanted to be by myself. I got to thinkin' about that gold I'd hid when the stage had been robbed and right then I decided to go get it. I needed something to fix my mind on and I needed some money. I figured it were time to look after myself—maybe with enough money I would become some-body important and there would be those that would wish they'd put more stock in this old mountain boy. They'd know I was a bigger caliber man than they'd thought.

I took my time getting there, and that dog followed me all the way. He 'peared to be happy keeping his distance, except once when I came across some hunters' camp. . . . We didn't make our-selves known to them, but he come right up and stood between me and them, not growlin' or nothin', just watchin' close with them flashin' green eyes. That was a new feelin' for me—having a dog stand with me like that. I was beginning to put a different notion on having him around.

We camped right by where the stage had been robbed. It sure brought back some painful memories. I decided to get the gold and get on outta there without spending any more time there than I needed to. It sure made me uneasy being there. I found the rocks I'd covered them sacks of gold with and had 'em dug out pronto. I changed the gold from the mine company sacks to some I had used for provisions. By my figures there was clost to twenty thousand in them sacks.

That night, I dreamed Ma was standing there with a disappointed look on her face. She wasn't sayin' nothin', just lookin' at me.

When the sun come up, I shucked that camp as fast as I've ever packed a camp up before. I was some troubled by the dream. I reckoned it were something I ate, or maybe just being back in that place. I guess I was mad at the world and everybody in it, because right then I didn't care much about rights and wrongs, I was gonna do what I was gonna do, and them that didn't like it could step outta my way.

Lookin' back at the time since Pa'd been gone, I hadn't managed to finish nothing. I'd gave up on the stage robbery, I'd let them varmints get away with hurtin' that poor old feller out in the hills on my way to Dodge City. Worse thing was, I'd left Kansas City with my tail tucked between my legs because of a girl! I was gonna get things squared in my mind this time . . . what I was gonna do and how I was gonna do it . . . then I was gonna finish it.

I wouldn't know much about runnin' somethin' in town. The only thing I'd ever done in a town was work for someone else or play cards. Being a gambler was out; I weren't gonna risk the only stake I'd ever have on gambling. Besides, when it'd really counted, I'd lost. I didn't know much about ranchin'. Come to think of it,

I'd come to age twenty and didn't know much about anything that could make a man stand out in a place like Kansas City.

Me and that dog rode into Abilene, both of us ready to bristle up at any opportunity. Abilene weren't much, just a few ruts for a street, some board buildings, some tents set up as watering holes for those trailhands and buffalo hunters that had money to spend. There was a new railhead here and new corrals were lining the tracks with more being put up. There was a herd of Texas long-horns in some of the pens and a thousand or so waiting out on the grass outside of town. The noise and the stink from the cow pens was overpowering.

The dog was hanging in close to the horse and making it shy away from him, dancing sideways and prancing nervous like. A big old yellow, mangy, dirty, squalid-looking dog came to growl at Dog, but he decided agin it and tucked his tail and ran behind the unpainted board buildings. A Texas ranny with too much drink in him stumbled out in the street, and Dog growled at him. He reached for his gun, but then he looked up at my face and stumbled back to the tent he'd been drinking in.

A feller with a badge on stood by a place kinda like a outhouse with bars on it. It wasn't much of a jail; there was a small barred window near the high part of the wall. It would be hotter'n Billie blue blazes in there. That was one of Pa's sayings. He weren't al-lowed to say "Hell" around Ma. I knew down deep inside me someone would have to kill me before they would put me in a place like that.

There was a wagon drawn up by the mercantile store. I rode by it for a closer look. I'd never seen a wagon like that one before. It had iron axles and wide wheels, and there was a big box like a cupboard fastened at the tail end. On the side was a big water barrel with a spigot at the bottom. They was loading supplies in a big box hung beneath the wagon bed. I knew what it was; I just never seen a chuckwagon up close before.

I guess it was a natural thing for me to settle on buying cows in Texas and drive 'em to a railhead in Kansas. There had been big drives from Texas to railheads in western Kansas, and I'd heard that cows sold in Kansas for forty dollars had been bought in Texas for three to five dollars a head.

I wired The Lazy Rocking B in Lytle, Texas. I wanted to know if'n they would gather a thousand head for me. I told 'em to wire me back in Abilene. I camped near town, the other side away from the beeves, and stayed outta the saloons. I got a wire back from Cam saying they were bringin' a herd through and if'n I wanted to join up with 'em, I'd best hurry there with seven thousand dollars. I wired back I was on my way, and took the trail toward Kansas City.

I'd had time on my hands and got to thinkin' it weren't the kid's fault Ann liked him best. And we were partners. I guess I had let some of his storybook thinking about partners rub off on me.

Me and Dog got to Kansas City well up in the day and when we rode in, as luck would have it, I saw the kid leaning agin a pole in front of the stage office. He looked different, and I sat there on my horse a ways back watching him, tryin' ta figure what it was. When it hit me I had to look twice—he weren't wearin' no guns! He had his head down lookin' forlorn and forsaken like he'd lost his best friend, and he almost had, but he brightened right up when he saw me. "Where ya been?" he wanted to know right off. "I looked all over for you."

"I went out to take care of that dog." I didn't feel like a long drawn-out, tangled-up talk on where I'd been.

He looked at Dog setting to the off side of me, his tongue hanging out, his green eyes showin' some sparks and the ruff around his neck standin' up. Ever since we'd got to town, he'd moved over clost to me and hung in there tight by the horse like he was a colt on a mare. The horse was mighty skittish about him being stuck up close to us that way and pranced sideways some, kinda backin' away from him.

The kid got real excited. "That's the wild killer that was in the cage! By heavens, you've tamed him!"

"No." I swung down beside him. "He just kinda took up with me after I helped him out some."

Course, he had to hear all about the whole thing, so we sat on the bench in front of the stage office. He wouldn't go to a saloon or have nothin' to drink. For a feller that liked to be the plumb center hero of ever bunch that stood up to the bar in a saloon, this was a curious way to act. I didn't ask nothing—just waited till he got around to telling me why he was acting this way.

It were Ann and her Pa, he said. They didn't like him wearin' guns, and especially didn't want him going around where "them low-life trappers and hunters were hanging out with dirty, profane trailhands in the watering holes."

He hung his head and looked miserable, but he wouldn't go partners with me to Texas, even when I offered to loan him his half of the money to buy the cows with. He never even thought to ask where I'd got the money. Ann's Pa was going to train him in the bank—as soon as Ann learned him about account books and how to do figuring. I left him there, him a-settin' on the bench a-waitin' for Ann to have time for his lessons.

This was the fast gun that had been gonna make a name for himself, that was gonna ride around and right all the wrongs and rescue distressed maidens. He'd gave up his dreams, no matter how silly they were, for a little slip of a girl he'd just met. . . . It sure beat all how things changed. Time and events, Pa would say, only this time I said it and wondered at the power little girls had over otherwise growed men.

There weren't no reason for me to be in Kansas City. The place didn't feel the same to me anymore. It felt empty and lonesome, so I got my stuff together and said my goodbys and bought a ticket outta there!

Me and Dog rode the Kansas and Texas Railroad to the Red River close to Colbert's Ferry, which was as far as the rails went that year. Dog didn't want on the train and wouldn't let hisself be parted from me once I got him on there. The folks on the train didn't like Dog either, so's I rode in the caboose with him. I had to pay extra because the conductor didn't take to Dog much. I wouldn't have made him ride the train except I'd never rode one and the time for driving cows north to Kansas was getting late in the year. Cam's wire said to be there or be left and ride to catch up.

Wood smoke poured outta that engine stack and settled over everything, making it dirty and stinking us up to smell like smoke. The train caboose rocked back and forth so much I was scared we was going to tip over. Dog set there and growled at me a lot, just to let me know he weren't pleased with me. We ate jerky mostly, though the brakeman cooked on his stove and shared some with us. We stopped now and then for water and wood in the Indian Territory.

It was at one of these stops that I lost Dog. He jumped off the train and ran a little ways and stopped. I figured he was just findin' a spot to do what dogs have to do, but when he was finished, he looked back at me and stood there a while, like he was tryin' to make up his mind about something. Finally, he just walked off into the woods.

I hadn't seen the gray dog that had been hiding in the bushes. When Dog got close, she came to meet him, turning and twisting like bitches will do. They touched noses and he sniffed her all over. She bounced in front of him, like a puppy trying to get another one to play, then she'd run toward the woods, and then come back and bounce at him again. I could see she was trying to lead him off with her, and I yelled at him, but he never turned his head. He trotted away like he didn't even know me. I didn't know if I should be mad or sorry. I guess I was both. I felt like shooting that gray bitch, but you can't hold onto a wild thing like Dog by force. Come to think of it, he'd showed a lot of loyalty stickin' by me as long as he had!

Why Dog had taken up with me was a puzzle to me. He wasn't the kind to be grateful, and after he was better, he didn't need me. Maybe he just wanted to belong to somebody for a while. It's bad enough to be rejected by a little slip of a girl, but to feel bad because a dog had chose to be with his own kind over being with me was silly, but I felt bad anyhow. I'd never cared much for dogs except for the huntin' dogs we had used at home and they weren't pets. We admired a good dog and sometimes bet on a good dog, but we didn't pet a huntin' dog.

I hadn't petted Dog either, but then he hadn't seemed to want to be handled or petted. I watched to see if I could catch sight of him while the train was pulling out, kinda hoping a last hope that he'd come running when he heard the train leave, knowing he wouldn't, but still thinking maybe he might. I wished him luck and a long life. But I wished he hadn't left.

CHAPTER 7

From Dennison I cut over to Fort Worth, and from there across the Brazos River at Austin, where I turned southwest to San Antonio. I could see why the Texans were hanging around Kansas. I ain't never been hotter, dryer, seen more snakes, been bit by more flyin' things, saw more lizards and things I couldn't even name. I was just passin' through. I weren't gonna live here . . . ever!

San Antonio was a real old Spanish town. But it had a lot of new frame buildings. Feller name of Maverick had a lumberyard there and was doing big business. But I was kinda partial to the Spanish-style buildings.

I put up at the Menger Hotel. I went down to the barber shop and got a real bath. I must of shucked a foot of dirt and dust off'n me. What with being clean inside and out, I was rarin' to get started, but didn't see Tom or Cam, and they said one of 'em would meet me here. So I drifted on down to the Lockwood Saloon to listen to the talk. Feller can learn about a lot of things by listenin' in a place like Lockwood's. There was a newspaper reading room, so I sat over there and went through the papers. There was real big notices about buyin' cattle. Who to see or who to write to. Didn't see one from the Rocking Lazy B, though.

I was settin' there killin' time when that woman walked into the hotel lobby. Nora was here in Texas! First thing I did was get outta sight before she saw me and sicked some gunnies on me again. I kept her in sight whilst she walked through the room, head high, back straight, blue dress that almost swept the floor and a collar trimmed with white lace that stood straight up around her neck, folding back just enough to show all of her face and covering enough of her neck, so's not to show the rope burns. I grinned a little when I saw how she'd covered them rope burns. . . . She was purely the purtiest thing in this town, and she walked like she were the queen of the whole Texas territory. I knew her for a snake and still shook inside at the sight of her.

The fix I was in now was to stay outta sight till Cam and Tom got here and still see what she were up to. I hung around close enough to keep an eye on her and far enough back to keep outta her sight. She didn't stray very far from the hotel . . . seemed to be bidin' her time with a particular aim in mind.

I sure put in a wearisome day, hot, too. By the middle of the afternoon I sure needed a cold drink, but she wouldn't move away from where she was waiting. I waited and waited till night come and she went to her room. I got my cold drink and my supper before I went off to my room, but I slept longer than I figured to, and the sun was well up by the time I got down to breakfast. She weren't in sight, but I weren't worried none. She were most likely still in her room. But when she didn't show after the sun was well up, I asked the feller running the hotel about the "pretty lady."

"She's gone. A buggy came for her and her things early on this morning. . . . Don't be castin' eyes at her, boy. She's too much quality for the likes of ordinary folks."

"Well, I reckon that's so." I grinned at him. "But a feller can dream. Does she come here much?"

"Not so much. She been comin' here every summer last three-four years."

"She gone for good this time, or will she come back later on?"

"You plannin' on waitin' to see her?" My askin' about her seemed to tickle him.

"Might." I didn't like bein' made fun of, but I held onto my gumption and didn't ruin the only way I had of finding out about her.

"Then don't waste your time here, boy. I heard her tell the man that come for her things she were headed north and wouldn't be coming back this way."

Well, I sure was curious about what was goin' on, but I couldn't go chasin' off after her right now. Besides, Tom and Cam came in about then and we got busy getting things ready for the trail drive. I purt near forgot her.

Men don't usually ask personal questions of another man, and I weren't expecting Cam to ask me about where I got the money to buy cows with, but he did. He just come right out and asked, "Josh, afore we get started, where did that money you sent for the herd come from?"

I stared him straight in the eye and said, "I come by that money in a card game in Denver. I hope ya don't think I stole it."

"Nope, I sure didn't—but we're gonna have trouble enough getting a herd through without having surprises we ain't countin' on. I want everything out in the open and honest."

Well, I don't lie enough to feel real good about what I told him, but that money were my business and just mine. I probably should have just said that—but I took the easy way cause I didn't want no hitch in our gettin' a herd started north. Besides, the cattle had already been bought and it were too late anyhow.

We had fifteen hands, a chuckwagon, more beans and flour and coffee than I'd ever seen before. There was sides of bacon and kegs of molasses, sugar, salt, canned tomatoes, lard, and what all else I didn't ask. Cam had bought twenty new rifles and five hundred rounds of cartridges for every rifle.

"We going to war?" I asked, pointing to all the new guns. "I thought the hands brought their own guns."

"I don't want to depend on someone else's guns. They might be all right, and then again, they might be too short of money to buy good equipment."

I thought to myself he'd been pretty free about spending our money, but I were smart enough not to say it.

It didn't take long to find out I didn't know beans about trail driving, or for that matter about Texas longhorns. Cam was trail boss and Tom was riding point with another hand they'd brought from their ranch named "J.B." Most of them Texas hands didn't have rightful names—they was called by initials or by things like

"Shorty" and "Slim" or "String-Bean." I asked Tom, "What's a-matter? These people down here don't know how to spell or sumpt'n?"

"Why, sure they do." He got plumb indignant. "How come you would ask a crazy thing like that?"

"Well, I figured they must be short on learnin' because they couldn't spell them first names and just come up with J.D. or B.T. or something else like that."

Tom looked real put out for a while, then he laughed. "Don't ya let them boys hear ya say a thing like that. You'll have more fight on your hands than ya can handle."

I didn't see much of Tom as he were riding point and I was a flanker—eatin' lots of dust and tryin' hard to persuade them steers they wanted to keep together and movin' toward the Colorado River near Austin. Between ridin' flank and night hawkin', I was ready for the bedroll every time it was my turn. We all was tired to the bone ever night. I'd thought it would be a lot different than this, but I kept the thought of what a big man I would be in Kansas City when I'd made a lot of money, and the time passed better that way.

There's nothin' about drivin' two thousand head of beef that's likely to draw men to want to do it. They are the orneryest, mean-est critters with long horns afoot. Fact is, they stink—I mean, they really stink. Two thousand head of beef means a lot of them are relievin' themselves at any particular time. You got to be plumb careful which way the wind is blowin' and where your horse is walkin'. And when them critters is a-runnin', there's so much heat and stink comes from a big herd a man can get his face blistered from the heat and die from the stink. Then there's the dust and dirt and the constant bellowin' and the noise eight thousand hooves make when hittin' the ground under a fifteen hundred pound load. There's not the peace and quiet of the open range a feller might expect.

Then there's the snakes and wolves and the Indians and other varmints that want some or all your herd. Three days out and we've already had a stampede from a lightning and thunderstorm. That means you stay in the saddle most of the day and night if you're lucky enough to keep 'em bunched up kinda loose and runnin' together. Otherwise you might be days puttin' the herd back together again. So far, I've only learned how much I don't know about trail drivin'. But at night when the herd is bedded down and the night is clear and the boys are gathered 'round the fire swappin' stories or makin' music with their guitars, fiddles, and Jews harps, there's a frame of mind like nothin' else I've ever had for belonging somewhere.

About a week out, some scraggly-looking Indians—a few old men, squaws and some dirty underfed kids showed up beggin'. We cut out one of the bunch quitters Cam was fixin' to get rid of anyway. They seemed real pleased to get it. Since there was wild cows runnin' loose everywhere, I wondered why they didn't just gather up some to keep for when they needed them.

"Indians think different from us," Tom said, when I asked him about it. "They ain't got a handle on things now that the country's gettin' full of ranches. It's just easier to beg—and all the ramrods driving cattle through here gives them a beef or two."

We crossed the Colorado River with no special trouble—it was a sight to see two thousand head crossin' a river. Towards the tail end of the crossin', some riders rode up and watched us finish gettin' 'em across. They was back a ways from the herd, but they seemed real interested—maybe too interested. When I got a chance I asked Cam. "Did ya see them fellers a-watchin' us at the river?"

"I saw 'em." His face had a grim, hard set to it. "We'll keep our eyes peeled for trouble. That kinky-haired one is called Curly Bill, a bad one for sure."

"Ya think we got something to worry about?" I asked.

"Fifteen well-armed men from Texas is a lot for anyone to tackle." He swept his arm around in a half-circle toward the herd. "Especially the hands from our ranch."

Well, I weren't gonna argue with that. Them were some savvy boys he'd brought with him.

I half expected to see them fellers again when we crossed the

Brazos River—but they must have found easier pickings—we didn't see them again till we got to Fort Worth. I went in town with Cam to buy supplies and got an eye full right off. That woman was there and sidin' her was Curly Bill and his bunch. I was bunched with Cam and Tom and some of our hands from the herd, so I weren't much worried—howsomever, I didn't see nothin' to show that she knowed me, and I was pleased she didn't.

Fort Worth was a place where the hands could unwind and have some fun. It had big saloons, dance halls, sportin' women and a two-gunned marshal named Long-Haired Jim. He kinda slacked off and let the hands have their fun as long as property didn't get hurt none. We advanced everybody ten dollars as they took their turn going to town. We kept the herd on good grass out a ways from town and let 'em rest there for a few days.

I hadn't seen that woman since the first day and had quit expectin' trouble. Fact was I was havin' a good time with the boys when she walked in the saloon with the one called Curly Bill. I knew right off she'd been lettin' me get to where I'd let my guard down. She weren't wearin' a dress this time. She was dressed like a man. No self-respectin' woman would wear pants—but she not only wore 'em, she flaunted them by wearin' a man's shirt and hat.

That feller called Curly Bill hollered out. "I'm a-lookin' for that skunk named Bonner."

I sure got unpopular in a hurry—them hands moved back from me so fast you'd thought I had the plague. He saw me then and braced himself square in front of me. "You gonna go outside with me, or do I have to drag you out?" He stood there, feet spread out wide and his hands over his guns. His face was all drawed up in a sneer like he was tryin' to scare me. It struck me she hadn't told all she knew about me, 'cause he sure was actin' like he was the bull of the woods. "Well," he asks, "are ya gonna show sand and go outside, or do I have to drag ya out?"

I shot him! He never even blinked or made a noise. He just stared at his bloody arm, his gun still in its holster. I think he really expected me to walk outside. "Hit him right in the gun arm!" someone shouted. "He hit him right in his gun arm, and he never even got his gun out."

"Fastest gun I ever seen," another shouted. After that there was so much confusion, I couldn't get to where that woman had been and she was gone. Someone helped Curly Bill outside, I reckon to find a doc.

Cam came and stood by me and said, real quiet like, "Someday you're gonna get killed shootin' for their hands like that. . . ." I didn't tell him I hadn't been shootin' for his arm.

Back at camp, there was a lot of back-slappin' and some good-natured joshin', but I knew that she was still out there somewhere, a-plannin' who knows what, and I were the target. One of the hands, I think they called him J.D., said, "They oughtta call Josh 'Sudden' because of the way he shucked his iron," and sure 'nough from that time on in I was stuck with "Sudden." Cam said that meant that they accepted me as one of 'em.

Tom came round by where I was and said, "Ya shoot for his arm that-a-way?" I shook my head yes, and he looked at me kinda funny, like he didn't know whether to believe me or not. "Man wants to kill you, ya don't give him more chances. Pa says don't draw on nobody lessen ya figure he needs killin' But if'n ya have to shoot, make sure he don't get up again."

I figured that was good advice, but when ya miss, what can ya say.

All of a sudden, I realized I'd lied again. Here I was, becomin' the kind of man I didn't like. I swore to myself that I weren't gonna beat around the bush again or try to look like I was sumptin' I weren't. I felt really low, so I rolled up in my bedroll and wished for sleep. But when I closed my eyes, I kept seein' that woman standin' there pointin' at me.

We headed north toward the Red River and the Indian Territory. That's where the hands earn their money, if'n the yarns we'd been told was so. I was more worried about where Nora was than I was about the herd cutters and Indians we'd been hearin' about. We did have something to worry about. There was riders shadowin' us from the time we left Fort Worth. We could see 'em ridin' back off a-ways, always watchin'—but never comin' in close. Cam handed out the new rifles and a belt full of shells to ever' man, but wouldn't let us go run one of them down. He said, "We don't have the time to mess with them and it wouldn't change anything."

We all took extra turns standin' guard and ridin' herd at night. . . . Durin' the day we had outriders out each side and scouts out front. We weren't gonna be caught short if'n we could help it.

Cam rode back to where I was and stopped me for a pow-wow. "Josh, I want you to fall back a little at a time, and when you get a chance, ya hole up till we're a ways past you. I want you to see if'n you can foller one of them jaspers back to his bunch and see how many there is and who's ramrodding 'em."

"Sure," I agreed. "First bunch of trees we get into I'll fall back."

He gave me a short nod and I could see he was plumb worried. "Ya be careful. We can't afford to lose a gun right now." With that he turned and rode off.

"It's sure nice to know they care so much about me," I muttered to myself, as I started lettin' my horse fall back towards the end of the herd. I took from then to sundown to fall back to where I was, well back from the herd. I dropped off and stayed still when we come on a small gully. I found some shade and slid down and waited a spell, then I crawled up on my belly behind a rock and looked real careful to see if'n I had been seen.

I reckon I'd been seen all right when a bullet slammed into the ground clost to my head. I heard the thunder of the rifle and the whine of the slug after the lead was already in the dirt. I'd already dropped back in the gully before the next shot. I hadn't been slick enough to fool the one that was trailin' us. I was tryin' to figure how I was gonna get outta this mess when I heard the poundin' of runnin' hoofs. He was leavin', and leavin' runnin', and I couldn't for the life of me think of a reason why. I edged on up the draw a little space and stuck my head up again to see which way he was ridin' and purt near lost my head. . . . That feller was almost a good shot!

Well, he'd set his horse a-runnin' to fool me into thinkin' he'd left, which was good enough to get him another shot, but now he was a-foot. He was thinkin' I weren't no better off than I was before . . . because the way he had it figured, I was still trapped in the gully. But I was better off. He didn't have no horse and I did have one. I swung low, injun-like, hangin' on way down the side of my horse, the off-side from him as we come out the shallow end of the gully. We were runnin' hard as we topped out where we could be seen. I didn't expect he'd shoot the horse. It was a natural way of thinkin' for a cowman, even a skunk of a rustler, to protect a horse.

When me and that black horse hit the top of the rim, I dropped off behind the first big rock we come on. It'd worked for him . . . maybe it'd work for me. Sure enough, he stood up swearin' plenty loud. A-thinkin' I'd got plumb away, he kicked at the ground and started walkin' like he was headed somewhere. I just took aim on his knee and knocked his leg out from under him. He grabbed at his leg with both hands, squirmin' around in shock and pain. It didn't come to him that he should be protectin' hisself till I was standin' over him and him a-starin' into my .44. "Well, now," I says to him. "You just keep your hands where they are, and ya might live."

Well, I hoped I weren't gonna go where he told me to go . . . and considerin' he'd just been tryin' to kill me, it weren't too smart of him to talk that-a-way, because I weren't in the best of moods. So I kicked him in the other leg, just to make my point. He couldn't seem to take that much hurtin' and curled up and passed out.

I stood over him a bit and wondered why I'd done that. That was a mean thing to do, and lately I'd been doin' things I'd never have done a few years back.

My horse hadn't run very far, and stood for me whilst I caught up to him. His horse weren't nowhere in sight, so I put that varmint face down back of my saddle and hauled him back to camp. It took a while for him to come to and Cam tried to question him, but no matter how bad he hurt, he wouldn't tell us nothin'. He hadn't got no smarter; he spit on Cam. He was still cussing us when we hung him.

We left him swinging so that them that were shadowing us would find him and maybe get the message that we weren't gonna lose our beef to them without a fight. But whatever they thought, they stayed with us . . . ridin' off to the side a ways, and watching us every day. It was gettin' on our nerves, and we was all a little jumpy. Especially when we passed a couple of graves that had a marker on 'em that said "Kilt by rustlers."

We was comin' clost to the Red River, and we knew that they was most likely gonna try for us there. Me'n Tom and J.D. and T.J. rode on ahead that night to the river crossing to set a trap of our own. The river was full up on its banks and real bad for quicksand in places. Before we knew to watch for bad spots, we purt near lost J.D.'s horse in quicksand. Time we got him pulled out, we was real careful where we stepped.

We scouted the crossin' real good on both sides of the river, and then we hid our camp where's we could see both sides real good. Before night, we had a lot of company! About twenty, near as I could tell, they camped about a mile from the river on the Indian territory side.

"What ya think, Sudden?" J.D. asks me. "Should I go tell Cam?"

"I figure ya should sneak outta here after dark. Me'n Tom and T.J. will go scout their camp. If'n Cam sends up about ten more men, we'll call on them afore sunup. You go see if Cam thinks that's the way to handle things and get right back here." I was gettin' that queasy feelin' again, like always when I was raring to get the thing done and scared at the same time.

Me'n Tom and T.J. waited until dark and near as we could tell, they didn't figure us to be there ahead of 'em, or else there was so many of 'em they just didn't care, because we didn't have no trouble slipping up on 'em when it got dark. They had some tents up for sleepin' and a chuck tent—not bad living conditions for outlaws. There was four night guards out, one on each side—just out far enough from the camp to keep an eye on the camp and see anyone ridin' towards them in time to rouse the others.

There weren't much of a way to slip up on the guards, so we made our way on back to the camp.

Cam and six others come in just afore sunup. We didn't waste time on words, we just showed 'em the way.

Some of'm looked 'em over and decided we'd best go ridin' in fast. We might get as far as halfway before we were seen. That would leave about four hundred yards to cover to the camp. Cam shook his head. "That's too far—they'll be up and ready long before we're there. They knew what they was about when they picked a place to camp—they probably been here before."

"What about goin' in on our bellies?" asked Tom.

"Same thing. There's no cover, they'd see us and be on us before we was halfway there." Cam looked bleak. "Anybody else got a idea?"

"There's some buffalo over west a couple miles. I saw 'em when we was scoutin' around." J.D. pointed west. "Why don't we stampede them this way and see what happens?"

Cam nodded. "Tomorrow night we'll run them buffalo right over the top of them. We'll go hold up the herd and let 'em rest today so they won't reach here too quick.

"We'll stampede them buffalo the Indian way," Cam said.

"What's the Indian way?" I asked.

"Burnin' buffalo hair that's been caught on the brush," I was told. "There's a plenty of hair left on the brush when a buffalo herd goes by—Indians gather up the hair and burn it. It makes the buffalo stampede."

We left a man hid to watch the rustlers, and Tom and J.D. rode out to sack up buffalo hair whilst the rest of us rode back to our camp to put on a show of actin' normal to fool the rustlers watchin' us. It makes a long day when the herd is grazin' and there's not a lot to do except wait. But then, it was a lot of waitin' for those cattle thieves, too.

We sat around and tried to look like a trail herd at rest, but my nerves was strung out like guitar strings. It was so hot the sweat was runnin' down my back with me setting in the shade, and the flies were buzzing all over us, great big, big horse flies that bite. Between swatting flies and trying to stay in the shade, I was plumb wore out. Them longhorns were feeling it too; they was stamping their hoofs, twitching their shoulders, switching their tails, and shaking their big long horns at the flies. A little breeze would have helped a whole lot to cool us down and blow the flies away. Of course, knowing that a fight was coming sure didn't help the nerves any either. I was glad when nighttime come.

When night was on us, we started moving toward the river. We had wrapped our horses' hoofs with big, thick squares of wool blanket to be as quiet as possible. Anything that might jingle or jangle was removed or tied down tightly. Every man and horse was just a silent shadow on a deathly still, breezeless prairie; not even as much as a lizard was moving. There wasn't even a cricket chirping, and not a leaf was stirring. There was just some ghostly dark shapes slipping silently through a still, dark night.

CHAPTER 8

We were extra careful at the river crossing because we'd already found out a man could lose his horse or his life in some of them sinkholes along the bank. Tom and J.D. split off to start the buffalo running this way while we got in position to guide 'em right straight to them varmints.

Ya could hear them critters coming a long way off. They shook the ground, and sounded like rumbling, rolling thunder. I kept lookin' at the rustler's camp for signs they was paying attention to what was happening, but no one was stirring. There was something wrong here; they should at least be poking their heads out of their tents asking the guards what was going on. Come to think of it, the guards weren't nowhere to be seen.

I rode over to where Cam was at, but he was already setting quiet in his saddle listening. "I think we've moved at the wrong time, Josh." He looked worried. "They should be stirring theirselves over there to see what the Sam Hill is going on."

Right about then, the buffalo come running hard and we didn't have time to worry about anything but pushing them on to the rustler's camp. For the next hour, there was runnin' buffalo, lots of noise, dust, confusion, and when it was over, there wasn't nothing left of them tents, camp goods or anything. Them buffalo just mashed everything flat. If them varmints were in their tents, they was all flatter than Cook's pancakes.

We rode in to take a look-see, and there wasn't a soul in that place but us—but there was about fifty Indians that was surrounding us. I looked all around, and there was Indians on all sides. I nudged Cam with my elbow. "Look at all them Redskins!" They was just setting on their horses, about five hundred yards out, watching us. "They got us boxed purty good," Cam declared, turning all around in every direction.

I was wondering what was next when I heard cattle bawling down at the river crossing. Cam cussed some quietly and then said outloud. "We've been took,
Josh—they got our herd."

First thing I thought of was them boys we'd left with the herd. Cam was thinking of them, too. "Them boys of ours must be dead, or they'd be shootin'."

We sat there, hemmed in by injuns, while them rustlers was gettin' ready to drive our cattle across the river. "I wonder what they're givin' them injuns to help 'em rustle our herd?" Cam swung outta his saddle. "Take cover, boys. Get your saddles down and dig in!"

It was gonna take a lot of the day to get that herd across. We couldn't move and the injuns didn't seem to be in any hurry to move either. "Why don't they come on in and take us?" I asked.

"Don't be in such a hurry to be scalped," answered Cam. "As for me, I'm plumb satisfied to let 'em just set and look at me."

"So am I." I was looking at injuns all about me. "But there has to be a reason they ain't in here right on top of us."

"Sure there is." T.J. moved over to where me and Cam was. "They don't want no noise to spook the herd while they's crossing the river."

Well, that made sense. They didn't want them Texas longhorns to get spooked and to start milling around in the middle of the river—they could lose a lotta beef and cowboys that way.

"Well, that'll buy us some time to think of somethin'," Tom speculated, while moving about like a restless pup.

All that day in the heat and dust and stink, we stayed there looking at them and they sat there looking at us. The only movement on our side was the horses switching their tails or stamping their feet to move the flies off of 'em.

But everwhere else there was lots of noise, cattle noises from the herd at the river, and the injuns were breakin' open a whiskey barrel whilst laughin' and hollerin' back and forth. "Well, I reckon that answers how they got the injuns to help 'em," Tom said quietly. "A barrel of rot-gut buys a whole pack of redskins."

Our boys were setting quiet, wondering about their friends, wondering when all them injuns were gonna pile down on us—how long we were gonna live. They sure wasn't gonna let us live to get our herd back. That much was certain. Whatever agreements them rustlers had with them redskins, it must of included our scalps and most likely about half of our herd.

The wind come up and the tall grass around us began to wave a little—cooling us with a right welcome breeze. I could see clouds startin' to darken up some—rain weren't far off. I looked over at Tom. He was still the busy one—now he had a small fire going, and that didn't make a whole lot of sense—how could he be hungry at a time like this? Then I watched him unwrap the blanket squares off the horses' hooves and wrap 'em around small rocks. All of a sudden, I got real interested. He started layin' them blanket-wrapped rocks in the fire, catching them blanket squares on fire. I caught onto what he was up to and went over to help him get it done before them drunk injuns knew what was happening. Purty soon all of us was throwin' them rock-loaded, burnin' blankets ever which way, and it didn't take long till we had grass burning high all around us. The flames were being pushed high and hard by the wind that was gettin' stronger.

It weren't till the smoke was high and heat was strong and the fire was almost on them that their whiskey-fogged minds seemed to realize they was in trouble. Not only was they in trouble, but they was about to lose their prize. Then we was on the receiving end of a lot of frustrated shooting—but they was too late. They couldn't rush us through the tall flames and grass smoke.

I laid down on the ground whilst bullets whined over my head. Not for long, though, because it weren't long till those that could run had to run to keep outta the fire. We were close enough to see through the swirling smoke and flames lots of 'em that were too drunk to move.

Then the smoke and the fire blocked our seein' anything except right in front of us—but over the crackle and snap of the range burnin' we could hear screams of fright and pain. With the smoke and fire and the screams of the injuns and the thundering hoofs of the herd stampedin' and further away the rumblin' and shakin' of the ground of the buffalo runnin', our little circle of calm seemed to be right in the middle of Hell.

We weren't that far from the river, and those Injuns between us and the river swam the river, and got away that way . Those on the off side of the river had to run ahead of the fire—a long ways.

We laid there till the clouds opened up and the rain come down so heavy ya couldn't see ten feet in front of ya. We couldn't cover up, move, or get out of the rain any way at all. But I for one weren't complainin'. I felt awful glad to be alive. We just had to set there, rain fallin' on us so heavy we couldn't see how to move, and no place to get outta the rain if'n we could move. Of course, the rustlers had lost the herd they was tryin' to steal. No tellin' how many of them outlaws was still alive, and there was bound to be a lotta dead injuns out there—not just dead drunk—I mean real dead injuns. But by now the fire was most likely out, and whatever was left of our herd was scattered so far we'd never get them back. . . . All in all, it'd been a purty bad day.

When the rain did let up, we couldn't get back across the river because the rain had filled the banks, and where we had crossed in a shallow, calm stream there was a swollen and ragin' river. There was no way to get to where our herd had been. We couldn't go bury our boys that'd died "fightin' for the brand." It was a purty whipped out bunch that sat there at the river's edge, no herd, friends dead and not able to get to 'em, and all around us as far as ya could see was blackened wet range, smellin' that particular disgusting way only a wet, burned-out range could smell.

That's why I was so amazed when Cam hollered out, "Let's go."

I guess it was the sudden noise after settin' in the middle of all that quiet and those somber thoughts that gave me such a start the

I purt near jumped clear outta my saddle. It must of been funny, because every one of them rannies was laughin', and the laughin' caught on till purty soon they was laughin' so hard tears were runinn' down their faces. There weren't no good reason to laugh that hard—we just did.

When we settled down some and they was through pokin' fun at me for bein' jumpy, I asked Cam: "Go where?"

"Go round up what we can find of them critters." He was so matter-of-fact about it, I was plumb astonished.

"The herd is gone," I told him, in clear, spaced-out words so he would wake up to the facts. They are gone!. We wouldn't find enough of 'em to have a good feed.

"You stay here if'n you want." Cam turned in his saddle. "But the rest of you work for me—and we're goin' to round up what we can find. We got a drive to finish." I couldn't believe him, but I fell in with the rest of 'em and we rode out together.

"Ma used to read me a story about this knight that went about doin' useless things like lowering his spear and running at windmills. I used to laugh at such a sight when I was a kid." I was just talkin' in general to nobody in particular.

Tom looked at me and shook his head like he couldn't understand what I was talkin' about. "Sudden," he says, "we got to finish the drive. Everything we got is tied up in them longhorns."

Well, I hadn't thought about it that way—I guess because it weren't my last nickel if'n we didn't make it. I hadn't thought on it enough to pick up on them havin' their last dollar bet on this drive.

We rode bunched up close that first couple miles. There was some bad things to look at left over from the fire. There's been some of that rustler bunch caught in front of the stampede, and what was left of them was scattered from place to place. We left them a-laying without burial. After all, our boys was still across the river unburied. "Leave 'em lay," Cam ordered.

There was what was left of some of the injuns scattered for a ways. We rode past a tree where there was two young injun boys laying across some high-up limbs, dead, but untouched by flames.

"I guess they figured to get away from the fire by climbing a tree." J.D. pointed at 'em as we rode by. Nobody said nothing back to him. We just turned our heads and rode by. He didn't give up. "Guess they didn't know the heat and smoke would get 'em."

Cam touched up his horse with his spurs. We looked straight ahead and rode on by.

We rode a long ways, till we was past the burned range to the point where the rain had put out the fire, and Cam pulled up. "We're gonna start our gather here. Tom, you take half the boys and start sweepin' west. Don't ride more'n a couple miles away from here. Spread out and drive 'em this way. Sudden, you take the rest and do the same to the east. Me 'n J.D. will set up a camp further up a couple miles for tonight." I did what I was told, but I figured it to be wasted time.

The first drive brought in about a hundred head. The next day we rode out further and north a couple miles, and drove in another big bunch. "How come them rustlers just rode off and left?" I asked Cam.

"The raid turned sour and they didn't get the easy time they was promised. Men like them don't want the hard work of doing a gather. Taken together with the fact they lost a lot of men, they didn't have the guts to stick it out."

The chuckwagon was destroyed and everything else with it, so we'd been eatin' buffalo meat with no salt, no biscuits, and worst of all, no coffee. Now, men will stand most any hardship except when there's no grub and no coffee. They was takin' on like dyin' yearlings, grumblin' about everything, when me and T.J. chanced on some folks whose wagon was broke down. The man was working hard to get his wagon up in the air enough to work on the axle. He had a old stump drug up by the wagon bed, and was using a small limb to lever it with. Trouble was, as soon as he lifted it some, it either shifted one direction or the other, or the limb broke.

We got down to help, and it weren't long till we had him a new axle whittled out and put on. It weren't like a new one, but it would do till he got to a blacksmith. Him and his old woman were so tickled to get the help, they let us have some salt and they shared their coffee with us. Of course, we gave them some cash money for it, and they acted plumb happy to get it. I know we were happy to get the sale and the coffee.

All in all, we lost a couple weeks of time, and about five hundred head of stock. We did a lot better than I ever thought we would, but Cam was mighty upset and out of sorts about the ones we lost.

We rested the herd for a few days in the Washita Valley before crossing at Rock Crossing. We camped at Walnut Creek. From there it was about ten miles to the South Canadian.

It was here we came on a small band of injuns with their squaws. They claimed we owed them ten cents a head for crossing their land. Their head man was old and bent at the shoulders . . . not at all like the tall warrior you'd think a chief should be. Most of the tribe seemed to be squaws and little kids, and a few old men. "Where are the young men?" Cam asked.

"Much sickness," we were told. "The young men go on huntin' trail—get sickness and die."

We settled on three old steers and got outta there in a hurry . . . just in case some of them might be sick.

At the North Canadian, we held up to rest for a day. Tom said it was because the hoofs of the cattle needed the time to heal. There was sure a bunch I didn't know about a trail herd. The only good thing here was the boys come on a army camp, and we come away with some bacon and flour, salt, coffee, and a few other things we put on a pack horse. I didn't know a lot about a trail herd, but the one thing I did know was that you hadn't ought to let anything happen to your chuckwagon or the cook.

What was to have been a thirty to forty day drive had already turned into forty days, and we still wasn't out of the Indian Territory. We still had the Cimarron River to cross, but we'd been told that we could expect buyers to start showing up anytime after we crossed into Kansas. Trouble was, we still had a long way to go.

At Deer Creek, we had to hold up because of the rain. It were raining so hard that we couldn't keep the cows bunched, and they spread out over half the country. Most of us just hunkered down and waited it out. . . . We couldn't get outta the rain and we didn't have any protection since our gear had been left with the chuckwagon.

Then right in the middle of all this misery, a band of Comanches rode in on us, let go with every arrow they had, and whilst we were duckin', they took every horse that wasn't being sat on. Here we sat . . . no fire, no hot coffee or food, and T.J. had an arrow right through his middle.

We couldn't get a fire going and anything we had for a bandage was soaking wet, and T.J. was spurtin' blood like a fountain. Cam said there weren't no need to try to pull the arrow, and T.J. was dead a few heartbeats later. The diggin' was easy, though, and we buried him deep, but we didn't leave a marker.

Tom moved off by hisself so we wouldn't see the tears in his eyes. Cam didn't have no tears, but his voice took on a hardness I recognized from that time in Kansas City.

Whirling toward me, he ordered, "Sudden, you get on their trail and stay there till they light somewhere, and then you hightail it back here or get word back here pronto."

It didn't take me long to put together a small pack. I turned my horse to leave and lifted my hand to the nine men standin' there. It occurred to me that there were six missing. . . . Most of them we didn't even know for sure what had happened to them. But since they hadn't caught up to us, we could figure that they was dead. I thought about six good men that was dead as I followed the muddy tracks. It was too much cost, no matter what the profit turned out to be, and the ways things was goin' it weren't gonna be much profit.

CHAPTER 9

A muddy trail made by thirty stolen horses and likely twenty or more Indians on injun ponies really ain't much trouble to follow. They didn't even take the trouble to leave a couple braves behind to watch their rear, in case they was followed. "They must be pretty sure of themselves," I muttered to myself. My horse picked up his ears at the sound of my voice. "It's all right, feller." I patted him on his neck. "I were just figurin' out things out loud." Pa would talk to hisself now and then, and Ma would laugh and say his head was befuddled. Then Pa would bristle up and say he was not, it just proved he was a thinkin' man. I had to drag my thoughts away from times past. It just made me want what could never be again.

The rain kept pourin' down and I kept follerin' their tracks. I was tryin' to stay close enough so the rain wouldn't wash away their tracks and make me lose them and still be far enough behind that I wouldn't ride right up on 'em and get myself killed. I put a good deal of importance on that last part! When you got that many horses sinkin' hoof deep in mud, it would take a lot of rain to lose 'em . . . but the rain was falling so hard it was washin' all of our tracks out behind me. Which meant that I was really on my own. Those with me wouldn't be able to know where I was till I got word to 'em.

There I was, head down agin a driving rainstorm, just able to see the ground in front of me every now and then, and froze clear to the bone. I was beginnin' to think this whole cattle drive was one big blunder! How could this be any worse? Then something slammed into my shoulder and knocked me clear off my horse into a big rain puddle. And quicker than a wink, it got worse. I was all wet from the rain, but now I was muddy to boot and blood was running down my shirt from the arrow in my shoulder.

I jerked my gun and rolled as best I could toward some brush cover. That gave me some slack, and before whoever had shot me could get to me, I was behind a stump. I could just barely make out their forms through the foggy mist and the downpour.

There were three injuns a-running at me, right through the mud, not making no noise except I remember hearin' the water splashing around their moccasins. The next thing was that I could make out the knives in their hands. They weren't actin' like they was expectin' no trouble. They weren't spread out like they should have done, or being careful at all. They must of thought they had me down and done, but when they was up clost to me they found out things was a whole lot different from what they thought they was.

I emptied my gun into 'em. Them big .44's torn big, ugly, bloody holes in 'em, and the best way I can say it is that all three of 'em went to their happy hunting ground running full-tilt at me. I got up, scared and mad at myself for being so reckless with my life. I shook what mud I could shake off whilst I ran to my horse, running because where there was three injuns, there was bound to be more. Anyway, even if there weren't, when those three didn't come back to the bunch they was with, they would come lookin' for 'em, and they would know someone was behind 'em.

The shoulder was startin' to hurt bad. I took my knife and cut the head off the arrow, and with all the courage I could gather up, I pulled the shaft out. Blood spurted all over the front of me. "Now I've really done it," I muttered to myself, whilst I tried to stop the blood with my soggy wet bandanna. I did the best I could as fast as I could. I had to hide those injuns and get away from here.

Dabbin' a rope on their feet, I took a turn around the saddlehorn and drug their carcasses over to the nearest thicket and hid them. They weren't more'n just boys. I'd been lucky they hadn't left battlewise braves behind instead. Next, I found where they'd tied their ponies and led them to the thicket and killed them. I hated to do such a thing. I admire a good pony. It went agin everything

I'd been taught or done, and I hurt down inside me when I had to do it. But if'n I didn't, they might go trottin' back to their camp and it wouldnt' be long till I was hip deep in injuns. I was gonna need time . . . as much time as I could get before they knew I was behind 'em.

One thing about almost bein' killed . . . it makes you quit being sorry for yourself because of events you can't help and start bein' careful. I really got watchful. I had been certain of not being found out, and almost got killed. . . . They was cocksure of havin' me down, and they died. I know Pa would have had something important to say about that, but he weren't here and I couldn't think what it might be. . . .

I kept my eyes peeled for any sign at all and went right on trackin' them. All the rest of that day and part of that night, they drove them horses in the rain, till finally they camped. I found me a overhang next to a rock that weren't too wet and tended to my shoulder. I poured whiskey on both sides of the shoulder to get it clean. The blood had stopped but it throbbed with the pain, and there weren't much I could do about that. I was so tired and I could tell I was running a fever. I finally did sleep some though, and that helped.

Mornin' come and they had stopped to eat. What they did was kill a buffalo and they all stood around it and ripped into it with their knives . . . gorging it down raw . . . blood all over their hands and faces, running down their bare chests. I was hid a ways back watching, and it made me sick watchin' them even when I was that far back.

They split up after that. About ten of them took the horses and headed north. The rest camped right there around the carcass of that buffalo. I swung wide around their camp and got back on the horses' trail. The rain had died down to a drizzle and I dug in my saddlebag for some jerky. I wanted some hot biscuits and bacon with coffee, but this was turning into a long trail, and it didn't look like there was gonna be any hot food anytime soon. I tried puttin' my pain outta my mind, but the more I tried the worse I felt.

But we just went a couple more hours and they drove them cayuses in a canyon that had four or five log shacks strung out and what passed for a general store and tavern, according to the sign nailed on the front. I didn't follow 'em in because I could see they had guards out watchin' all directions. I hadn't been seen yet, or they'd have already stirred up a hornet's nest of trouble for me.

I was figuring on going back for Cam and the boys when some cowpokes come out and started them horses on up the trail. Now I was tired, wet, cold and hungry, hurtin' and out of sorts, and so was my horse, and he snorted and shook his head at me when I started undoin' his reins from the brush I had him hitched to. Usually a little pettin' and soft talk will make things right with him, but not this time. He tried to take a hunk outta my sore shoulder, and if'n I'd a been a touch slower, I'd be missin' a chunk of my hide right now. So I took the time to come to an agreement with him. I hauled off and hit him right between the eyes with my fist. That sent a stab of pain clear up my arm, and I knew it hurt me more'n it did him, but it sat him back on his haunches for a bit, and he 'peared to be surprised and a lot more agreeable, so I figured he was ready to go. There weren't no more trouble between us and we stepped out at a purty fair pace after them rustlers.

There ain't much worse than a thunderstorm to ride in. The sky got dark and the wind come on strong, whipping the stingin' rain into my face, and the lightning would flash from way up in the air and come towards us in great jagging white streaks, ending up tearing up the trees and ripping at the ground. Then the thunder would crack like cannons and rumble and roar across the sky, making my poor old horse tremble and shake, or that might of been me shaking so' bad from the fever I had I shook the horse under me. No matter which way it was, we rode a long ways in it.

There weren't no way them horses were worth the aggravation and trouble I'd already been through. If'n I felt that way with them being my horses, how on earth could anybody in their right minds go through this to steal a few horses? I sure had a lot less respect for the thinking power of them outlaws than when we first started. There was something wrong with them fellers. If they was doing this because they was too lazy to work, like Cam said they was, what would they be like if'n they wasn't so lazy?

Anyhow, before daybreak, they holed up at a ranch we come on. They corralled the horses and went inside with a bunch of "Howdy's" and "come on in's" loud enough and clear enough I could hear 'em from way back where I was.

Now, it were still cold and raining, and they was in where it was warm, eatin' breakfast and having hot coffee, whilst I was still wet and cold and feverish and in a lot of pain outside. They was the crooks, and they was inside! It just weren't the way things should be. I rode through the woods till their barn was betwixt me and the house, then I rode up to the back of the barn and pulled some boards loose. The storm was so bad they couldn't hear the noise I made, and it weren't long till me and Horse were inside and dry. He at least got some grain and a rubdown. I ate some more jerky. All the horses were out in the corral. They'd been in such a hurry to get themselves inside, they hadn't tended to the horses, so we had the barn to ourselves. I got in my saddlebags and changed into what was almost dry clothes. I found a bandanna and wiped my wound down with whiskey again. That seemed to ease the pain some. I was so tired, I just dug in the hay and drifted off to sleep. I figured that them fellers would want some sleep too, and I was too worn-out to care about what would happen next.

I should have cared more.

There's something galling about being woke up with a sharp kick in the side. I ain't called "Sudden" for nothing, cause I come up clawing for my gun, only it weren't there. What was there, was two yahoos with my gun pointed at me.

My first thought was why my horse hadn't even whinnied. I glanced at him, and he was standing there with his head turned toward me, munching on hay, watching us like he didn't have a worry in the world. I had counted on there being noise enough to wake me, if'n one of them hands come stomping in the barn.

Either they weren't the noisy kind or I slept harder than I'd counted on.

They tied my hands and prodded me in the direction of the house with their boots. I wasn't going to forget them fellers, not in the next hundred years. My Pa used to say, "Be careful of the thing you're stepping on . . . it may come around to be his turn and you'll get bit." If and when my turn comes, them fellers are for certain gonna get a bad bite!

Them varmints I'd been chasing all night was still abed, and these that had me tied up was trying to keep the noise down, so's them rustlers could finish their sleep. They shoved me down in a corner and said for me to shut up and be still. So naturally I let out a war whoop, loud enough to wake the dead.

The sleeping weren't asleep no more. They was grabbing their guns and jumping and rolling, looking for someone to shoot. When they had time to settle down, they figured I'd do. One of 'em had me by the hair and was draggin' me toward the door, and I was gettin' real sorry I'd let my ornery bone get the best of my good sense. Now, I've been in some bad spots from time to time, and what I'd learned from those experiences told me this had all the makings of being another one! I had it in mind some outside help would be nice when the door opened and that female varmint Nora walked in. She took one look at me an grinned from ear to ear. I thought she was gonna split her face plumb in two. This was not what I had in mind when I was thinking outside help!

That Nora sure had a vengeful spirit. I ended up standing on a rotting stump, clear out in the woods, rain running all over me, with a wet rope around my neck, on my tiptoes so I could just barely breathe, and worried about my future. I partly blamed my ornery, good-for-nothing, sorry horse for this. Of all the times to pick not to throw a complete senseless fit when strangers got close to him, this had been the wrong time! My toes were wearing out, and the middle of my feet were hurtin' bad. I wasn't gonna last long like this.

"Well, I'll be a son-of-a-gun." There was this surprised, excited clamor behind me and someone was crashing through the brush toward where I was. I couldn't turn around, but I knew that voice. It almost cost me my neck, because I turned halfway and my feet slipped down a inch or so on the stump. I was stretched past breathing when the kid jumped up and cut the rope.

I couldn't talk for a while, but when I could, I asked, "What in the world are you doing here? How'd you find me?"

The kid was still jolted from coming on me when he hadn't been expecting to. "I weren't looking for you, but it sure is a good thing I come along, ain't it?" He stopped talking and went to pounding me on the back. "I thought you looked funny behind the water trough back in Colorado, but this is a whole lot better," and he went to laughing.

Well, I didn't see much funny about being hung up on a stump, but I was glad to see anybody right then, but in particular, I was glad to see somebody that could use a gun!

"What are you doing here?" I asked again.

"I'm trailin' Nora. She come to Kansas City and took Ann to go away with her. I been trailing her because I don't know where she took Ann!"

"What does Nora have to do with Ann? How on earth did she come to know Ann to start with?"

The kid had a desperate tone to his voice. "It turns out that Nora is Ann's Ma, who ran away to the west when Ann was a baby. I guess the real reason Ann and her Pa come west was because they wanted to find her Ma."

"Are you saying Nora is McGuire's wife, and she's out here running with down-at-the-heels rustlers with him owning a bank?" I was flabbergasted. I'd heard of stupidity, but this topped anything I'd ever heard about.

"I guess she left years ago when Ann was only a baby and they didn't have as much then. McGuire was working as a bank clerk when she left."

"Didn't ya tell them about Nora? How could ya let Ann go with that woman?"

"I told 'em, but it was like she wasn't listening. She'd found her Ma, and everything I said was wrong, and everything Nora said was gospel."

"And so now she's found her Ma. What does Nora want with her?"

"I don't know. Her Pa says there ain't much he can do if Ann wants to go to Nora. And now that Ann's grown up and real pretty, he thinks Nora wants to be her Ma again."

"What about you and Ann? Ain't ya still gettin' married?"

There was pure misery on the kid's face. "They just took out and Ann never said no farewells to me, or said where they was goin' or when she'd be back, or nothing."

"How about you?" He switched from talkin' about Ann to wondering about me. "Nora must of found ya off guard for you to be in this mess. That woman sure knows how to get even, don't she?"

I told him of the cattle drive and the rustled horses while we got his horse. I had to go get my saddle and a horse, so I slipped back up to the barn and took my saddle back. I was glad to see the rifle was still in the boot. I was plumb sorry they had my six gun, it was special built and I didn't even know who made it. The kid kept some laudanum and pieces of cloth in his saddlebag in case of trouble and we fixed my shoulder again. I weren't too clear-headed, but I didn't hurt no more.

"What about Nora? You just gonna go off without findin' out where Ann is?"

"Josh, when they find our you're loose, she'll be crazy wild because you got away and they'll search this whole place, inside and out, and the best thing we can do right now is to not be here."

"All we have to do," I explained, being as patient as I could, "is go up there and block the doors so they can't get out."

"Josh, if you block the doors, how are we going to get to Nora?"

"We just set fire to the cabin, and if'n she talks, we take her with us, and if she don't, we leave her."

He stared at me like he weren't sure I meant it. "Josh, I ain't a injun and I ain't gonna have nothing to do with a thing like that . . . and you ain't gonna do it either, not while I'm with you."

I could see he meant it, so I saddled Horse and we rode out of there, as quiet as we could. "Kid, when varmints like that are after your hide, it's kill or get killed, and to pass up a chance to kill them all at once just might be something we'll be sorry for."

He got stubborn on me. His jaw was set like flint. "I ain't a injun and I don't burn people."

I thought of the grass fire we'd set when there weren't no other way out. "You'd be surprised how quick you'd do things you don't commonly do when the spot you're in calls for uncommon doings."

To my way of thinkin', ya killed your enemy before he could get to you. Otherwise, somewhere further along he might get a chance at you, and he sure wasn't gonna be bothered about how he did it. I didn't say no more because I knew he didn't see my way and there weren't no need to set a thing like that between us.

"Josh, you've changed. You're meaner than you was when we first met. If you'd been as mean as this when we first met, you'd have let that gun hand kill me back there in Colorado."

I didn't bother to answer. If'n he couldn't see the difference there weren't no way to make him see it. Then I got to thinkin' about it. I guess in some ways I was different. I wouldn't call it meaner, just more likely to live. "What about Ann? How ya gonna get back on her trail, now that you've run from Nora?"

"I never would find her if I'd of let you kill Nora along with them rustlers."

Well, that much was right, and that gave me a thought.

"She might of sent some of them hands a-trailin' us, and if'n they found us gone before the rain washed away our tracks, they might be on our trail right now! If'n we move off the trail a ways and double back to the house, we could lose them and find Nora and follow her to Ann."

I could see him lookin' at the wet trees and brush we'd have to ride through. Nobody likes wet leaves in the face and wet brush scrubbing agin his legs, but we wasn't gonna get no wetter any-way. Finally he nodded and pulled off the trail up in the brush. We rode till we was out of sight of the trail and started back. We got lucky and come on a old trail that had some brush across it, but it was not as bad as it would have been if'n there weren't no trail at all.

There weren't nobody on our trail and the tracks were gone now anyway. But the trail we'd found come out higher up the hill and behind the house. No one had used this trail in a long time, and I figured they didn't know about it, so we was probably safe up here for a while. We hunkered down and covered up from the rain as best we could.

"Reckon it rains all the time here?" the kid asked.

"I reckon it's like anywhere else." I looked at him a-settin' there all miserable and woeful. "One thing bad is the herd is prob-ably still at Deer Creek. We need a break in the weather."

"We need a shelter," he grumbled.

So I got my knife out and built us a shelter the way we built one back in the mountains I come from, a three-sided frame of small limbs laced over with big ferns. It didn't make us dry, but we were out of the rain. We couldn't of got no wetter anyhow, but the kid seemed to like it better.

Down at the ranch house, the rustlers fed the horses and got wood from the wood shed, but other than that, they didn't stir around any. We watched for a while, then the kid gets up and leaves. I said, "Where are you going?" but he was already gone before I got it said.

When he come back, he'd been to their wood shed and had an armload of dry wood, so we had a small fire, some coffee and bis-cuits from his supplies, and life was more bearable. I still had to take our horses back, and the kid still needed to find Ann, and I owed Nora some small act of vengeance to satisfy my soul, but for now, we were gettin' dryer and warmer. So the kid's idea turned out to be a good one.

It did quit rainin' and the sun come out in the afternoon. It was too wet to move around, the mud was ankle deep. So we sat and kept the fire goin' and watched the house. They stayed in except to feed the horses and to get wood for the fire. We had a dry spot to lay our bedrolls that night, and the next day was sunshine and warmth. It was still muddy, but the ground was dryin' up at a purty good pace. It was good enough that about midday, Nora and those with her saddled up and left. She didn't go down to where they'd had me tied up on that stump. From where I was, she looked like she could bite nails in two, she was that mad. I took that to mean she'd already found out that I weren't hangin' around that rope anymore! The kid left right behind them. I wanted to go with him, but I had a herd to tend to and some stoled horses to take back. The rustlers was still in the house.

Them no-count varmints were in there playin' cards. I could hear 'em clear up where I was, on account they was drinkin' and fightin' over the cards. When night come, I slipped down and used some of their fence poles to wedge agin the doors. I braced them good, so's they weren't goin' to get them open from in there. There weren't no windows in the ends and only one in the front, and one in the back, and they were small and up high clost to the roof. They hadn't been put in to see out of, but to let fresh air in. The place was built like a fort, but even forts have their drawbacks.

They had quieted down in there. I guess they'd had too much whiskey and needed sleep. One of 'em rattled the door trying to get out to the outhouse. When the door wouldn't open, I heard him stumble to the other door, swearin' about stickin' doors when a man was in a hurry. When that door wouldn't open there was some laughin' and some help from a couple of the other hands. When they'd tried both doors, they got real serious about gettin' out. . . . They was calling the rest to come help. . . . They was tryin' to use a ram. It must of been the table because I heard some feller givin' 'em fits when the table broke up. I waited awhile, then I hollered through the door, "Y'all havin' a problem?"

Someone said, "It's that jasper we had tied up out there." There was general swearin', and suddenly I think they realized they was in trouble. "Hey, cowboy, what ya aimin' to do?"

"Why, I reckon to burn the place down," I answered. "That's what ya do with varmints when ya got them holed up, ain't it?"

"Aw, come on, feller." There was this sudden reasonable pacifying tone of voice from inside. "Ya can't mean that you'd do that."

'What I think is that ya better toss your guns out."

"That's just one man out there," I heard one of 'em snarl. "Let's just send someone out there to take care of him."

"I figure that's your trouble," I hollered at 'em. "Ya can't get outside."

There was some low talkin' going on in there, and then one of 'em hollered out, "Hey, you out there!"

I didn't answer. I just waited to see what they'd do next.

"Hey, out there," he kept on. "Can we talk?"

"You're talkin' now, as much as I want to hear."

"Can we talk face to face? Maybe we could make a deal where we could all come out on this."

"We ain't doing nothin' till them guns of your'n hit the ground out here."

They was talkin' and arguing for a while, till I got tired of waitin' so I took a pole and tied a small sack of bullets to it, and then I pushed it up till it hung over the chimney. I drug the pole again the chimney top till I scraped the bag off, so it would fall down in the fire.

There was lots of bullets flyin' in there, and some bad cussin' goin' on. I don't think I was real well liked by them fellers, They must have stacked some stuff together to stand on, because it weren't long till there was a shooter at both them little windows.

I couldn't go where they could see me from the windows now. That cut off the barn that was on one side covered by the window and the hillside where I had made the shelter on the other side. That left the woodshed on the end where I was, so I backed up to the woodshed. There was also a dugout; most ranches used a dugout to store things they needed to keep cool. I poked around into everything I could find and found two barrels of gunpowder and a barrel of shot.

I had to deal with these fellers before I could get on with takin' the horses back and the gunpowder looked like a way of gettin' it done. I thought on what I was gonna do for a bit. I weren't no killer, but when there weren't no other way that I could see to get our horses back and get myself out alive, I couldn't see why I shouldn't blow them out of there. After all, I had gave them a chance to throw their guns out and give up.

I dug in under the house for a long ways. I knew they could hear me diggin', but they hadn't figured out yet what I was doing. I could hear 'em talkin', and they was worried but not enough to give up. The ground was wet enough to be easy diggin' and it didn't take long to dig as far as I wanted to go. I set a barrel of powder and made a long fuse. I was ready, but I thought I'd tell them first.

"Hey, you varmints in there."

"What you want?" one of 'em that was watching at the windows asked.

"You got two minutes to throw your guns out or I'm gonna blow the house up!"

They was cussin' and fussin', but no guns were comin' out, so I lit the fuse. I got back by the dugout and waited. Purty soon guns come a-flying out the windows on both sides. I pinched off the fuse and kicked the brace outta the way. "All right, you poor excuses for men, get your carcasses out here with your hands up."

They come out then, hands in the air and hangdog looks on their faces. "What ya gonna do with us now, cowboy?" asked one with a sneer. "Ya can't watch all of us." He had me there; I didn't know what to do with them.

"Take off your clothes," I ordered.

They looked at me like I'd lost my mind. "I ain't gonna do it," declared the one that's asked me what I was gonna do.

I shifted my aim at his leg. "Ya got a choice. I'll leave ya on the ground if'n ya don't."

They shucked their duds in a hurry and I made them throw them in the house.

I herded them over to the barn while I relit the fuse to blow the house.

"Hey! All our stuff is in there."

I never answered or let on I'd even heard what they was saying, and herded them in the tack room. It wouldn't keep 'em, but it would hold 'em long enough till I had the horses and was out of there. I watched the place go up with a bang. What didn't come apart, burned.

I hooked up a four horse team and stretched a lead rope to tie the horses to. I loaded the wagon with everything from their supplies I could find, and off we went like Cox's army, all strung out in a row. Team, wagon, and all them horses on a lead rope.

It'd been a sorry trip. Nora had Ann, and there weren't no tellin' where the kid was, or how that was gonna end. And them rope scratches around my neck still aggravated me enough I'd like to have that Nora for a few hours all to myself. I had to admit, she was some kind of enemy.

I set fire to the barn, too, just to leave them fellers with a challenge and no shelter after they'd broke out. I laughed out loud, and I ain't laughed in a long time, but a picture come to me of all them fellers, naked as Jay Birds, walking out of there in the mud and the rain, hiding from people, yet looking for help.

I turned the team toward where the herd ought to be headed and figured I'd meet up with them or find their tracks if'n I stayed straight as a string going northeast. Of a sudden I felt better. I could see better times a-comin. I sat up straighter and whipped up the team a little. I thought of a saying Ma used to have when we'd been through a bad time at home. "Being in the right, and the warmth of the morning sun, adds strength to the bones and courage to the heart." The sun was shinin' again and there weren't a problem I couldn't solve. Everything was gonna turn out fine after all.

CHAPTER 10

You can hear a herd of Texas longhorns a long ways before you get to it. Ya take a couple thousand beeves and each one pounds four hoofs on the ground with all the force of his heavy carcass when he walks, and then he lifts his head and bellows to everyone in ten miles he's had enough of this trail, and ya put all those thousands of bellowing complaints and thousands of tons of pounding hoofs together, and you don't need a guide to find the herd.

The return of the horses and a wagonload of food made things look a lot better for the hands. Just being back alive made things look better for me.

Cam just nodded at me. "Good going," he says, as he's going through the wagon to see what all I'd brought back.

"What took you so long?" Tom asked, setting there on his horse, both hands restin' on the saddlehorn.

I glanced at him, kinda put out by the tone of his question, like I'd been lollygaggin' along on purpose. "There was ten of them," I said, real slow, and drug the words out so he would know I didn't like the way he asked the question.

"No need to be touchy about it." He jerked his horse around to leave. "If we'd a-knowed there was ten of 'em, we'd a-sent the horse wrangler with you." With that he spurred his horse and headed towards the point. It were a good thing he left because I could hear him laughing. He knew he'd got me stirred up. Tom was always doin' that. He'd get ya riled and then leave out laughin'.

It weren't many days till we crossed the Cimarron where we was met by cattle buyers who wanted to dicker for the herd. Cam called me up to where the buyers had set up a tent. "Sudden, these fellers are offering us thirty dollars a head."

I looked straight at Cam, trying to read his intent. "Why out here? Why not wait till we get to Dodge?"

"Lot of buyers in Dodge," one of the buyers spoke up. "But the price won't go up, just more fellers trying to buy."

"I heard they was paying forty dollars a head in Dodge," I said to Cam. "If'n these fellers want the herd, they need to wait whilst one of us rides to Dodge to check on the price."

There was a tall, solid-looking gent in a buckskin coat that had been listening, and he put in, "I'll buy your herd here and now, and meet any offer you get in Dodge."

Cam stuck out his hand and grinned. "Ya bought our herd, Mister."

The buyer stood up and beckoned to some hands that were watching from the edge of the crowd. "These are my reps. We'll take over the herd here, so you can turn your boys loose. My reps will take a count, and we'll pay up in Dodge."

"Not quite," Cam answered. "We'll stay with our herd till we get there, and then we'll all take a count."

The buyer laughed. "I wouldn't even try to cheat you, mister. I just thought your hands could use a night in town after a hard drive."

"My hands work for me, and they'll go to town when I'm ready for 'em to go to town!" Cam's voice was hard and to the point. Anyone would know he meant what he said just by listening.

Now, I'd been lookin' forward to a bath and a steak, but I didn't let on to being disappointed. Cam turned to me. "Sudden, you can go on into town if'n you want and get that shoulder tended to by the doc. We can handle things from here on in."

"I reckon I'll wait for the rest of you." I grinned at 'em. "I would feel lost without ya."

"What he means is," laughed Tom, "he's afraid that woman will be in town a-waiting and he needs us to protect him!"

Well, he could not have said anything that would put a damper on me wantin' to go to town quicker than what he said. "I thought it were only proper that I should wait for the rest of 'em, because we'd rode the river together, and a good hand wouldn't leave his friends like that."

Well, that got a few chuckles. "Hey, Cam," Stringbean hollered. "Make me a offer like that, will ya? Someone needs to show this here would-be cowboy how a real trailhand would act."

Cam grinned at Stringbean. "He'll get those notions soon enough on his own, without a rapscallion like you teaching him. He's still a purty good old boy, and I'd like to think he didn't leave us no worse off than when we found him!" I didn't mind the jokes and the laughter; it sounded good, and there's a light-hearted feeling at trail's end—no matter how bad it was in-between.

The buyers had brought some jugs of whiskey, and Cam let the boys take a drink or two and then the guitars and the fiddles and Jew harps come out and the singing went on. Some of them old boys could sing as good as lots of them show folks working in the saloons. I felt like I belonged, and that made me feel better'n I felt in a long time. I leaned back agin the wagon wheel and liked to of grinned myself to death just listening and feeling good.

We did get forty-two dollars a head, and at fifteen hundred head, give or take a few, we had sixty-three thousand dollars to split after expenses. We set aside an extra sum for the families of the ones that'd died, and still had twenty-five thousand dollars apiece. I was gonna walk mine over to the bank, and Cam walked over with me.

"Sudden, if'n you're a mind to do this again, let us know, and we'll bring a big herd through, maybe six or seven thousand next time."

I nodded my head in agreement. "I'll be there. No telling how long a chance like this will last to make this much money on a drive. I'd like to get it while we can."

With the money in the bank and my wound looked at by a real doc, who said there weren't nothing he could do for it now, and it were all right anyhow, I felt like celebrating with the boys.

I was headed in the right direction to find them, but I come on some folks from home setting in one of the worst excuses for a wagon I ever seen. Of course, Lem Turns hadn't been worth much at home either. He never made much of a crop of anything except pretty girls, and he had a parcel of the prettiest younguns on our mountain.

I saw Lem before he saw me. "Howdy, Lem, been a long time since I saw folks from home." I stuck out my hand and Lem grabbed it and shook it like he was real glad to see me.

"Sorry to hear about your folks, Josh. We heard about your Ma that first winter ya was gone, but we didn't know about your Pa till we was at Kansas City."

He looked at me with a sly look. "I've heard you've done all right for yourself anyway. They say ya just brought in a big herd from Texas and made fifty thousand dollars." He shook his head in wonderment. "I didn't know there was that much money in the whole country."

I didn't doubt that none. Cash money was plumb scarce around our mountain, and a man might not see more'n twenty or thirty dollars in cash all year. "I had a partner, Lem, and we split whatever we got right down the middle." My curiosity was running high. "What you folks doing down this way, Lem?"

"Well, boy, we heard times was better this direction and gold could be had for the picking in Colorado."

"You got to be outfitted pretty good to make it through one of them Colorado winters." I couldn't help the shudder that shook my frame at the thought of the trip I'd had through there.

About then, his family started climbing out the wagon to say howdy. His oldest girl with them was about thirteen. Girls married young in our country, and the Turn girls growed up faster than any other girls on the mountain, so they married about as fast as they reached fourteen or fifteen. I didn't remember his oldest he had along with them, the others being married, but she was a sight to behold, not in a city way like Ann with pretty clothes and fine ways about her, but kinda busting out the seams in her

old dress that was a size or two too small. There was a air about her
that just made ya think of a female animal in heat.

I didn't figure she'd be with them very long out here where
even the ugly girls could get married, with a choice of fellers to
pick from. But she acted like she remembered me and took hold
on my arm and talked for a long time about things back home,
just like we'd shared a friendship back there. I put it down first to
her being so happy to see home folks, then it come on me that it
might be the money talk she'd heard.

Ever now and again, some of the boys would drift by and I'd call
them over and introduce them to Lem and his family. It didn't take
long till all the boys was gathered around to meet my old friends from
back home . . . only most of 'em was gathered round the girl.

Lem asked me if'n I could stake him to the gold fields. I didn't
want to but he was from home and they was setting there without
nothing to do and nowhere to do. So I priced a decent wagon,
some oxen, clothes, tools, etc. I paid out about a thousand dollars
and we made a written agreement for a fifty-fifty split on whatever
he found, which I figured would be nothing, he being so shiftless
the gold would have to roll right on top of him before he'd see it.

They rolled out of town to the disappointment of the crew. I
was plumb glad to see them go and hoped to goodness I'd not see
nobody else from home for a while.

Well, with the herd sold and Cam to take care of the rest of
things, I told him, "Cam, I've got to go find the kid."

Cam stuck out his hand and with a seldom-seen smile, said,
"Sudden, you sure liven up a trip. If'n ya run into more'n ya
expect, just holler and we'll come a-running."

We sat eye to eye for a bit. I knew that that was a real promise
from a man whose promise was unshakable. I just didn't know
what to do or say. I ended up lifting a farewell wave and turned my
horse and rode away, waving to the boys, and with lots of hollering
back and forth about "seeing you in Texas."

There's been a story going around about some youngster wearing two guns bracing a whole saloon of known bad men in Lawrence.

It's been one of the stories that go around because they were pokin' fun at him about being a little boy with guns when he'd filled both hands so fast they'd been took back by the suddenness of the draw, and how mean that baby face could look. It sounded like the kid, and I rode that way. If'n he was lookin' around there for Ann, chances were he's still be there.

I headed north toward Abilene, expecting to head on over to Lawrence from there. Except when I got to Abilene, I heard about the big bank robbery in Dodge. Now I was worried. I'd left a draft for my money with Cam, but what if he'd not left yet? Them varmints might have our money! I wired Cam, but didn't get no answer, except he weren't there. More'n likely he was on their trail. If they had our money, he would follow them till they died of old age before he quit.

Now I was betwixed and between. I didn't know whether to go on and find the kid or go and try to join up with Cam. I finally made up my mind over a piece of apple pie and a cup of coffee. I decided to go on and find the kid, figuring that it'd be late to try and join up with the posse.

I'd already bought supplies and had my gear together, and was gettin' on my horse when I saw this fancy buggy roll into town. Now, ya don't see a lot of fancy rigs out here, not like you do in St. Louis or Kansas City. But it reminded me of one like it that Nora had used in Texas.

She stepped out of that rig just as cool as ice, and stopped and waited for Ann. They stood there while their man gathered up their bags, two beautiful women dressed like you'd see in the city. Women didn't usually wear that kind of thing out here, because of the mud and dirt. Ya didn't find brick streets out here.

I rode right up on them before they'd had a chance to move. "Howdy, Ann." I sat there, trying to look as cool and collected as they did. She looked at me kinda like you'd look at someone you ain't seen for a long time.

When she did answer, it was not friendly. "Josh Bonner, isn't it? We met in Kansas City. Have you met my mother?"

I wanted to laugh, but I never blinked an eye. "We've met." I shifted my eyes to Nora and touched my hat brim. She looked right past me like I weren't there. "Ann, the kid has been looking for you." I smiled just like I was passing on the time of day or something. "He'll be here in a little while. I hope you're not leaving soon." I made up that last part just for Nora.

"You'll excuse us, Mr. Bonner." Nora took Ann's arm and marched away before she answered me. I sat there on my horse and watched them go into the hotel. Nora took the man they had with them to one side to speak with him. I didn't need to hear to know what she was telling him. I knew to expect trouble, lots of trouble.

I went to Western Union and wired the kid at Lawrence, just in case he was there. I made myself scarce and watched to see which way trouble was coming from.

After a couple hours, some real hard men began to ride in, grim-faced, hard-eyed gunnies. Those kind all have a hungry wolf look to 'em. They was good at not being too noticeable, but they was always watching the street and the hotel. They'd got here so quick, it must mean their camp or hideout weren't very far away. I recognized some of them from clear back to the stage hold-up. Some of them had been at the river crossing and been part of them rustlers that had took our herd. I'd bet money they was part of the same gang that had robbed the bank in Dodge.

Nora was involved in ever part of what had happened to me. If not the leader of that gang, she was at the center of what was going on. In my mind's eye, I could see her puttin' the hot iron to that old man's feet. I could see her standing there pointing at me, shouting, "Kill him," to those three gunnies me'n the kid put down. I could see her when she sicced Curly Bill on me. Now even our herd money might be gone, and I was as sure as could be she and her gang was the ones that done that.

Anger got ahold of me, it filled me up from my feet to my head. I wanted to squeeze her neck till the life drained out of her. Next time, I'd not back away when I had a chance to hang her.

I'd counted six of her hands that had rode in. I knew where each one was. What I needed was a plan. I wanted to get even, and this might be the place to start. I was watching them, figurin' out ways to get to 'em, when they commenced watching the east end of the street. I turned to see what they was looking at, when they started bunching up in the middle of the road in front of the hotel. It was the kid, riding in not knowing them gunhands was waiting for him, and I was the one that had brought them down on him by trying to shake up Nora. They was between me and the kid, so when I walked out on the street, I was behind them.

The kid saw me when I walked out on the street, and about the same time, he saw the gunslicks of Nora's, all bunched up and facing him. It didn't take him long to get off his horse. He walked over slow to the hitch rack and tied his horse.

Turning, he waved at me. "Howdy, Josh."

Talk about surprise, those men of Nora's turned and saw me behind them and they started hunting ways to get outta there. Fire from front and back is not what they wanted when they'd figured six to one was good odds.

The kid laughed recklessly. "Hey, you fellers, where ya going? Weren't ya waiting for me?" One or two of 'em stopped like they was gonna see it through, but whoever was in charge growled a order and they walked off with the rest of 'em. I kept moving back so that they stayed in between me'n the kid. I'd made up my mind to cut loose my dogs, whether they wanted it or not, when the marshal run in the middle of it with a couple of deputies with scatter guns. I wasn't buying into that.

"You get your hands in the air." The marshal pointed his sawed-off double barrel right at my middle. I got 'em right up there. I saw the kid had a scatter gun in his middle, a-standin' there with his hands up. We were the only ones; them gunnies of Nora's was a-walkin' away, talkin' with a deputy. I knew we was in big trouble!

"How come we're the ones you got corralled and them that was tryin' to way-lay the kid is walkin' away?"

I got prodded in the back hard with the barrel of his gun.

"You made your mistake when ya let them women get away from you. They made it to town to tell it, and now every man in this town will be there to help pull on the rope when they hang ya."

Well, it took a minute to get it in my head what he was talkin' about. "What was we suppose to have done? And when?"

"She says you two held up her and the girl, and that ya tried to get their clothes off, but they got away."

"And ya believe that? Without checking any part of her story?"

The kid was red from the neck up and mad. "I don't believe Ann would tell a story like that, and she'll never back up that kind of lie, even for Nora."

I sure hoped the kid was right. Because if'n Ann was to back up whatever lie Nora had made up, we'd swing before they ever had time to check out our side of it.

"Did the girl, Ann, tell you that story, Marshal, or just Nora?"

"We got the charges agin you from the women. You trying to say the girl won't back up her statement?"

"That's right. The girl is engaged to the kid here to get married, and her Ma is trying to keep 'em apart. Even hired some gunhands to kill him."

"That's right, Marshal," the kid put in. "Talk to Ann. I'll bet ya she don't even know about this deal Nora's trying to pull."

"Why would her Ma make charges if the girl won't back them up? That don't make sense."

"Because she plans on having the girl outta here by morning, and the longer you hold us, or if'n her hands could get a crowd stirred up to lynch us—both ways would work for her."

"We'll just go see about this." He pointed his finger in my face. "If the girl says you did it, I'll make you wish you hadn't tried a lie on me."

"Well, more than that, Marshal. I just sold a trail herd in Dodge. I rode in here today, and you saw the kid ride in from the east. Ya can even check the telegrams I sent out trying to locate the kid."

"That's right," put in the kid. "I was in Lawrence two days

ago. Ya could check her back trail, make her tell where she's been. A woman and a girl as pretty as they are will always be noticed."

He put me in the jail on a chain and took the kid to find Ann at the hotel. I sweated with all kinds of thoughts. Supposing Ann had changed and did say whatever Nora told her to? We'd be lynched by morning, and nobody would ever say they'd been wrong after that. It was just a bit till I heard them coming back, and the marshal was swearing and I could tell he was mad, I just didn't know who at. "They'd pulled out," the kid told me as they undid my chain.

"You can go. I got no one to testify against you. I told her to set tight till the judge got here. They've lit out and took all their things, lock, stock and barrel. It looks like she was just using us to keep the boy here."

"They ain't got much of a start on us, Josh. I don't figure they expected the marshal to check so quick."

We got our horses and started asking if anyone saw 'em leave. They was all gone—Nora, Ann, and the gunnies. "Must have been a big reason to pull all of 'em away like that," the kid said. "Nora would never have missed a chance to have them hands of hers steam up a lynch mob if she hadn't had something a whole lot more important to her to do."

"Like a lot of money from a bank robbery?"

"We'd best get moving. They're riding while we're talking."

We rode out in a hurry, but not running. It was bound to be a long trail.

CHAPTER 11

Norah had left her buggy and she and Ann were on horses. As near as I could figure, ever mile or so, two of 'em had been splitting off and leaving the road. I counted six had left. That left Nora, Ann, and that hardcase that had been with them all along. They probably figured on all of 'em circling around and joining up again. That kind of trick might of worked against most cowboys, but I'm from a mountain, where folks took pride in their sharpness at reading a trail. Pa used to say the knack for tracking was a gift from God. I been watching the tracks of the horse Ann was on and she was still in front of us. It was a older, smaller horse. Its shoes were wore more'n the others. Most likely it'd not been rode for some time, and hadn't needed shoeing till they needed a gentle easy horse for Ann, then they hadn't had time to do it.

I pulled up and waved the kid to stay back. "They stopped here," I told him.

I could see where Ann had got down and had got on double with Nora. Then another horse and rider had come from the brush by the side of the road and took the reins of Ann's horse, while Nora and Ann got off the road and into the brush. The new rider leading Ann's horse went on down the road with the other rider, whilst Nora and Ann doubled back through the brush. Somebody had even tried brushing out the extra tracks and then had throwed the limb they was using down in the bushes.

"If'n we'd come running down the road like they figured we'd have missed this." I grinned at the kid.

"If I'd been by myself, I'd of missed it." The kid was looking hard at the sign I'd pointed out to him. "So what now? Is Nora and Ann on the same horse by theirselves?"

"For right now, but my guess is one of them varmints is wait-ing for 'em not too far away."

The tracks led off the trail back in the brush and then turned back the way we'd come. I stopped. "Kid, there's bound to be some hardcase waitin' to ambush us, just in case we are still on their trail."

"How do we handle it?" The kid shook loose his guns and stood up in his stirrups to look all around. I grinned in spite of tryin' not to.

"You ride off to the side a ways, and stay about even with me, but keep watch ahead and I'll keep my eyes open. Whoever it is will most likely be on his belly behind something. Watch for brush or anything else that moves that don't look like it should."

I waited till he got in place and then we started. We didn't have to go far, I saw the kid pull up and wave at me. He pointed, but I couldn't see anybody, so I got down and walked over to him. Left by himself, Horse did what he always does . . . he walked on by himself. Sometimes I feel like shooting him, but today it was gonna work in our favor. "How do you get him to do that?" the kid whispered.

I shrugged and slipped into the brush whilst the kid walked his horse to keep pace with mine. I saw the bushwhacker when he edged his rifle over a stump he was behind. Whilst he was watch-ing my horse, I slipped up behind him and whipped him over the head with my gun. He fell without a sound.

"What do we do with him?" the kid wanted to know.

"We turn his horse loose and leave him."

"Shouldn't we tie him or take his gun or something?"

"No use to tie a dead man." I got up on my horse and we moved on.

"You sure he's dead?"

"If'n he ain't, he still won't be in no shape to follow us. He'll be lookin' for a doc to put his head back together."

"Reckon there'll be more bushwhackers?"

"There was nine of 'em when they left. Nora and Ann made

up two, that leaves seven. Two of 'em are on the road thinking that they are leaving false tracks for us."

"That leaves five, less that dead feller back there, so that makes four."

"One of those is bound to be with the women. I'd say they was hurrying on to somewhere. They'll figure on gettin' rid of us later."

The kid shook his head. "No, I think she'll use at least one more man to try and stop us."

We fussed over that a ways whilst we followed their tracks. "Ya know, kid, ya might be right. They ain't tried to hide their tracks or made any slippery moves. Could be they want us to chase them right into another trap."

We kept a close eye out for unexpected company, but nothin' happened all day. Come nightfall, we waited a bit for the moon to get up enough to light the way, and we got right back on their trail.

We found their new shooter, but he was rolled up in his bed, next to a small fire. There was a whiskey jug near him, and he was snoring loud enough to wake the dead. The kid laughed. "I don't reckon he was expecting us till daylight."

"Get a rope. There ain't no need to wake him. He can die easy, not thinkin' on it like some of his partners are goin' to."

"There ain't no need to kill everybody we come on. We don't even know for sure he belongs with them!"

"Well, if'n he don't, he's the most unlucky feller we'll come on today."

I threw a rope over a limb and was fixin' to hang him when I got a look at the kid's face. He was sick at the thought of hangin' this feller, and it showed all over his face. Pa always said when you're teamed up with a good mate ya got to give in to their ways now and again. Of course, he was talkin' about givin' in to Ma, but I figured a partner was about the same. So I asked, "What ya think?"

"I say we take his guns and his horse and leave him with his jug. He'll most likely be here till the jug gets empty."

We left him still asleep, but I knew inside we ought to hang him.

"We'll just meet up with him again and maybe next time he'll have the drop on us. Ya can bet your britches he won't think twice about what to do with us!"

"I swear, Josh, you're gettin' to be like a wild animal. Ya want to kill everybody. Don't a man's life mean anything to you anymore?"

Well, I didn't take to that, and I reckon he knew it, so we just rode on without talkin'. After awhile, he said, "How many men have ya killed, Josh?"

"Not countin' Indians?"

"Just those ya killed in a stand-up gunfight. I've heard it said you've done for twenty men."

"You can hear most anything if ya listen long enough. I ain't come anywhere's clost to that. There's a lot of varmints out here because there ain't no law to keep a halter on their kind. I ain't killed no one that ain't been the worst kind of animal and that ain't pulled a gun on me."

"You were ready to hang that man back there and him dead drunk."

"He was there to bushwhack us. He's the worst kind of them all, and hangin' him is what we should have done, and I'll tell ya something else, one of these times we'll have to kill him anyway."

"Maybe, but when we do, chances are he'll have a gun in his hand and it won't be murder."

I gave up. It weren't no good tryin' to argue with him. He couldn't see past them ideas he got from them dime heroes he was always readin' about. Truth was, he was a better man than those he read about.

Nora and her bunch led us right into Wichita. I was real leary of goin' into town, considering what she done to us last time. This town marshal might not be so quick to look past her and into the facts. The kid was set on seein' Ann if'n he could, so I set up camp and he rode into town. I was given out and the horses were tired.

This was as good a place as any to rest awhile, so I rolled up and slept. But first I circled my camp with dry limbs and twigs. I didn't want no surprises. I missed Dog—with him around, I never worried about being caught off guard.

I slept plumb through the night and well into the mornin' before I woke up. The kid weren't around, and it didn't look like he'd been there. I had some coffee and considered what to do. If'n Nora had pulled the same thing she'd done before, the kid was most likely in jail. If he'd walked into a ambush, he could be dead or shot up. If'n he found Ann and got her away, he might of had to go without coming back here. No matter which way it was, I couldn't help him by rushin' into town and puttin' myself in a box. So I put out my fire and found a spot I could stay hid in and still watch around me. I waited for dark to settle in and it were a long wait. There's nothin' worse than not knowing and havin' to leave it that way till ya can do better.

The afternoon wore on and on. I worked on my draw a couple of hours, but I was plumb sure I was as fast as I was ever gonna be. I found a couple of big rocks and did wrist and arm bends till I got tired of that. I oiled my holster and wished I had my gun back. I even took a brush and brushed my horse till he couldn't stand it no more and tried to bite me. First chance I get, I'm gonna get a decent horse that knows when he's well off, I told him. But I most likely won't—he's been mine so long now I wouldn't know how to get along with a good horse. Besides, there's not many horses as big and steady as he is. I finally put my back agin a big old tree and pulled my hat down over my eyes and slept till nightfall.

I rode straight into town. I figured there weren't much use trying to slip in. If'n they knew I was coming they'd be watchin' for me to try to put one over on 'em. And if they wasn't there or didn't know I was comin' it would be time wasted. The town was busy and horses lined with hitch racks till I was hard put to find a place to put mine.

There was a big Revival Tent set up and lots of wagons and buggies around it. A big sign out front had the preacher's name on it in big red letters. I laughed when I saw it. "Otis Bonner." He was kin of mine from back home. He used to make the best whiskey on our mountain. If'n him and his old woman hadn't drunk up so much of it, they'd be rich, or at least Pa used to say that a lot. His place was on the same creek as our's, but further up the mountain. My uncle used to slip up the creek and fill his jugs when Otis weren't lookin'. One day he was watchin' Otis plow his cornfield and thought it would be funny to fool with him. He hid under the creek bank and when Otis come to the end of his furrow he cupped his hands around his mouth and called out in his best, ghostly voice, "Otis." Old Otis never looked up, he just keeps on plowing. The next round my uncle hollers, "Otis." He did that a couple of times, and finally Otis stops and hollers back, "Who is it?"

"Go and preach my word, Otis." Uncle gave out his best eerie sound of a unearthly voice.

"I said, who is it?"

"Otis, go and preach."

If'n ya take my uncle's word, Otis fell right down there on the ground and repented, squallin' and bawlin' and takin' on for a hour or so. Anyways, Uncle come back laughin' his head off, tellin' Pa about it. It would have been all right exceptin' Ma heard it. She threatened to not let either one of 'em up to the table again if'n they ever told it. Otis was married to her cousin, and she weren't gonna have them be made fun of any more than they already was. Well, none of us told it, and Otis went right home, cleaned up, and had his first meetin' in the schoolhouse that very next night.

Folks come from all over the mountain to hear Otis tell how he'd been called. Next thing ya know, some town preacher heard about the meetings and come got Otis to preach in his church. They never come back. We heard about him from time to time. He'd got big in the preachin' business and had three wagons to haul his tent, wearin' city suits and shoes and everything. Every now and again, Uncle would shake his head and mutter, "He made the best corn liquor on the mountain and I ruined it." Then him and Pa would bust out laughin' till Ma heard them and would make them stop. She always claimed that if God was able to use a donkey to talk to a prophet, he must of used Uncle to get Otis to preach.

I figured the best place to keep away from Nora's bunch was to set in on Otis's revival. When it was over, I'd go out with the rest of the folks and have time to look around without standing out like a sore thumb. I'd be hid in the crowd. Cousin Ida played the fiddle and it was plumb sweet. I'd forgot how good she could play. I could see old Otis was doin' all right when they passed the bucket around for the offering. If'n that bucket of money was any kind of judgment about his preachin', he was a right good preacher.

I'm not the feller to see when it comes to pickin' a good preacher, but anybody could tell Otis was a crackerjack preachin' man. He'd always been one of the best storytellers on the mountain. He would tell some of the outdoinest things and make it sound like it were the Gospel truth. Men would set and drink from his jug and listen to his yarns by the hour when they should of been workin' on their fields. Now he was just as spellbinding as he'd ever been. Them folks settin' around me were as caught up in his preachin' as the men back home in the mountains had been at one of his yarns. If'n Pa were here, he'd shake his head like he couldn't figure it and say, "Time and events, boy, time and events," because neither Pa or my uncle figured Otis to account for much.

About then, Otis spotted me and waved right in the middle of his sermon, and then Cousin Ida got up and come back to set beside me. It were hard to remember her like she was when they'd been making whiskey. She was dressed so nice and smelt so purty, I figured Ma must of been right. Otis was doin' what he was supposed to be doing. Even if it took tomfoolery from my uncle to get him there.

I set in their wagon after the preachin' and after folks had left, and I told them about Ma and Pa. We caught up on old times, and talked about his preachin'. I was keepin' watch, but I didn't see anyone that I knew. I asked if'n they'd heard anything about a kid with two guns and they hadn't. It was hard to stop talkin' and get movin' because they was so hungry for any news at all about the folks back home, even though it'd been some time since I'd been there myself.

Finally I took my leave and went to get Horse, only he'd done one of his old tricks and picked his reins loose from off the hitch rack and wandered off. I had to go lookin' for him. I started by lookin' in the livery yard, on account of he'd most likely go where there was feed, and was thinkin' on gettin' a new horse when I walked smack dab into Nora and her bunch. She was settin' in a wagon with Ann. The kid was settin' on the back of the wagon all bandaged up, and his hands were tied. Ann's face and eyes were red from cryin' but Nora was settin' there lookin' all peaches and cream, like there weren't a bad thought in a hundred miles of her. . . . The kid was turned so he couldn't see me, but I knew he knew I was there.

I could see I'd been had. Horse hadn't walked away, they'd brought him down here, and like some witless jackass, I'd walked right into the middle of them. There were three gunslingers, one in front and one boxin' me on each side. I never stopped walkin' or said nothin' or even took time to look around. I saw what I'd done as soon as I walked in on 'em, and I threw myself forward to the ground. I hit the gunman in front right off. I kept rollin', but the varmint from the left got a bullet in my side. I got behind the feed bin. I had felt the slam of the lead and now the numbness set in. I knew I would of been done for if'n them fellers had been any kind of shots. A lot of that lead was hittin' all around me, but I only took one hit in the side, partly due to movin' so fast, but partly due to them being poor shots. Beats all how a man can use a gun to be a gunhand, and not be able to shoot straight!

I heard the wagon leave at a run, and there was no more lead coming my way, so I figured they'd left, and they were sure nuff gone. I got up and stumbled back to where Otis had his wagon.

"Land sakes, boy." Otis pulled me into the wagon. "Woman . . . Josh has been shot!"

They put me on a bed and Ida started cleanin' my side whilst Otis went for a doc.

"You're just like the rest of them worthless men," she fussed at me. "Ya can't even be let loose a minute without gettin' into a scrap."

"Here's the sawbones." Otis climbed in the wagon, followed by a feller that would look more at home swingin' a pick than being a doc.

His big hands pried at the hole in my side. "Ya done good, ma'am," he told Ida. "The lead went clear through him, and all ya need to do is keep a bandage on it."

I knew Ida knew that without needin' a doc to tell her, but Otis had been ready to do his best for me, and I put value on that. But I liked bein' took care of too. I told Otis about the kid and about Nora and Ann. Before I knew it, I'd told him about the gold and about everything else. He never said nothing much, except he said he knew I was just like my Pa, and for him that was enough to know that I'd make it come out all right. I figured that Uncle was wrong. There was a whole lot more to Otis than my uncle or Pa either one had knew about.

I had to get goin' before the trail got too cold to follow after them vermin. But before I left, I took down the places Otis and Ida was plannin' on goin' so I could keep track of 'em for when this was all over.

"Josh Bonner." Ida hugged me. "When ya get your friend back, you come stay with us a while."

"I'm gonna do that very thing," I promised. There was something good about being around them. It was like having folks again.

That many people in a bunch can't keep folks from noticin' them, and so I asked everyone I come on, and it didn't take long to get on their trail, cause folks out here like to talk, and the further ya get from lots of people, the more folks like to know something worthwhile tellin'. Mountain folk are different. The further ya are up in the mountains, the less jawin' goes on, and if'n ya are a stranger ya don't even get a howdy.

They was headed south back into Indian territory. I got to thinking, I bet they was headed back to that same ranch I had the run in at over the horses. I saw men travelin' in bunches now and then, usually trail riders headed back to Texas. Now and again, I'd come on a wagon or two headed for somewhere in the territory. There was lots of injun sign, and I kept a close eye out for injuns. They could be friendly or downright mean, dependin' on whatever day ya come on 'em.

So when I heard lots of shootin' goin' on ahead of me, I took a long slow look at what was goin' on. There was two wagons pulled up side by side, and folks under them layin' flat on their bellies shootin' at some injuns who was ridin' a big circle around them, all done up in paint and whoopin' it up loud. Looked like there was about six rifles under the wagon and maybe twenty injuns with bows or old guns that weren't worth shootin'. I got up on a hill and bellied down in the brush. When I unloaded my Winchester at 'em, them injuns left for easier pickins. They didn't know who all was up on the hill shootin' at 'em and they didn't wait to find out.

I rode on down to the wagons to see if'n everybody was all right. They weren't hurt none, and they hadn't lost no stock. I'd a rode on but they was missin' a girl. She'd been there when the shootin' started, but she was gone now.

"How big is she?" I asked.

"She's ten years old," her Ma answered. "I told her to hide, but I never thought she'd leave the wagons. I've always told her never to leave the wagons."

They was lookin' for tracks up clost to the wagons, so I started castin' back and forth further out. I found a pony track that was not with the others, so I followed it about a mile till it came to some small trees.

She was in a clump of chaparral. Her naked little body was crumpled and bloody. One of them braves had been hid over here with the girl instead of fightin' the settlers with the rest of his tribe.

I saw some leaves quiver and rustle about twenty yards further from me. When I looked in that direction, everthing got real still, so I knew I had that redskin, he hadn't got away yet. He couldn't wait me out, or he didn't think he was hid good enough. He'd had his pony layin' down, but now he got it up and was on his back and runnin'. He was so quick, I almost let him get a big start on me. This was one I wasn't gonna shoot. I wanted him alive.

He was fast, but Horse ran that little injun pony down in just a couple of jumps. When I got alongside and grabbed him, I found it was a injun boy, not much over thirteen or fourteen years old hisself. In my anger I didn't care how old he was. I'd kill a baby rattler if'n I found one, and this was the same thing.

I snatched him off the pony and cuffed him till he were still. Then I picked up the girl and brought them both to her Pa.

Her Ma took the girl and declared she still lived. The women took her to one of the wagons. "He hadn't had time to take her scalp yet," I told the men, "or she'd be dead now for sure."

"He's just a boy." One of the men nudged him with his boot as he lay where I'd dropped him.

"He was big enough to force my little girl, and she may die." Her Pa was cryin' and his fists were clenched while he shook with anger.

I didn't put into his business, but stood there and waited for them to decide how to kill the injun. In the end, we hung him and left him swingin' in the air for his own to find him. "I'd want to know what happened to my boy," one of 'em declared. "Let's leave him where they can tend to his body."

We left him hangin' and I rode on after wishin' them luck with the little girl. The last I saw of 'em, they was hitchin' up their teams. They was a lot more mindful of the dangers of this country than they had been, and one was on guard whilst they hitched the teams. They'd been lucky. I wondered how luck was holdin' for the kid right now.

CHAPTER 12

I kept thinkin' about them folks and their little girl. I hoped she made it through this, and I wondered if'n free land was worth what had happened to the girl. Then again, bad things can happen to a family most anywhere. Back in the mountains where I come from, there weren't no injun trouble anymore, but here was snakes and fevers and lots of other bad things that could happen. I guess a body just has to live his life and meet what comes his way the best he can.

I hadn't seen no sign of Nora's bunch for quite a while, but I was staying with what I thought was the right direction when I come on a place with three cabins and a outpost. It was set up with trade goods for the trail drivers comin' through, and for trade with the Indians. I stopped to see if'n there was any track of Nora.

Inside the trading post there was a makeshift bar of sorts, made up of a couple of barrels with a plank across the top of 'em. Two fellers were there having some whiskey. There was trade goods strung out over some more planks, and some squaws were fingerin' a bolt of brown cloth.

I asked for a drink and waited for a chance to be friendly, not wantin' to just walk in and start askin' questions. You get more answers if people take to you, and none at all if they don't like you. To let them get used to the sight of me, I walked around and picked out some supplies I could use. I come across some used six guns, all piled in a basket, and I figured it might not hurt to have a spare. I was picking them up and sortin' through 'em. I poked around some, not finding what I wanted, when, down close to the bottom of the basket, I found my own gun. I pulled it out and checked it over to be sure. It was my gun all right—the work

Ransom had put into making it just right for my hand hadn't been messed with. It was just as good as it was when it was took from me. I tried not to show the rush of excitement I felt. "How much for this here six-shooter?" I held it up for him to see.

"Same price for any of them, twelve dollars each." He come over to where I was.

"That's too much for a used gun." I squinted up my eyes and glared at him.

He didn't blink. "Take it or leave it. Ya can always take a week or so and ride to a town. There's so many close by!"

I passed over his sourness and the guffaws of the trail hands at the bar. I dug around in my pocket and got out twelve dollars for him. "Where'd this gun come from?"

"I don't ask. Feller wants to sell his gun, I don't care why. You want to try it out?"

"I reckon so." I loaded it up and walked to the door. The others come outside with me. I guess it's a natural thing to be curious about what kind of hand with a gun the other feller is. I shot at a tree limb and hit it, then I stuck a stick in the crotch of the tree and did my practice draw, firing as fast as I could. First I knocked the stick out of the tree, then I kicked it in the air and kept it there till I ran out of shells. It was purty good shooting if'n I do say so myself.

The storekeep clapped me on the shoulder like we was old friends or something. "I ain't seen good shootin' like that in a while. Fact is, I'm gonna have to have more money for that iron. I didn't know it was that good a pistol." I grinned at him on account of I knew he was funnin'.

Well, that kinda opened the door for some conversation, and after awhile I said something about seein' two of the prettiest women I'd ever seen in my life a few days back.

"That must of been them two that was here yesterday," one of the cowboys said.

"That woman was the best lookin' thing I ever saw," his partner agreed. "But she had enough hired guns that nobody was goin' to try talkin' to her."

"Must of been the same ones, all right." I grinned, friendly as I could be. "I fell in love right then, but I couldn't get close enough to tell her about it." Everybody laughed and we had another drink.

"She'll need all them guns if'n she's going south." I set my glass down. "I'm buyin' another'n for these gents." I lowered my voice so the squaws wouldn't hear. "I just had a run-in with some bucks on the warpath not two days back, and they was headed south when they left out."

Them two trail hands thanks me for buying and one of 'em added, "She weren't headed south down the trail, or we'd of volunteered to ride with 'em. They went west, and didn't act like they wanted company. But we're headed south and we appreciate the warning."

"Well, maybe I'll see 'em again. I'm headed west myself." I wished 'em luck and headed out, plumb glad I'd stopped there. I had my gun back. I'd never figured whoever had it might sell it, and I figured if'n I ever got it again it'd be when I took it off'n one of their dead bodies.

Now I figured I knew for sure they was headed back to that ranch. It was hard to believe luck like that. "Time and events," I said to Horse. "Time and events," but he never even picked up his ears or acted like he heard me talking to him. Someday I'm gonna get a horse that likes me. If'n I can find another'n that's as big as this'n, can run all day and walk all night and still be going when I need him. Thinking about him being so able to go the distance gave me a warm feeling for him, and I tried to scratch him behind his ear. He reached his head back and tried to bite my leg. That made me remember what he was really like, and I jerked his head up. There wouldn't be no more foolishness.

Towards nightfall, a buck deer jumped across in front of me, and before he knew what he'd done, he was meat for my supper. I gutted him out and skinned him. I was sorry not to be able to keep his hide, but I hung it up high on a limb to keep the animals off it. Maybe someone that could use it would find it. I built a small fire and was turnin' a haunch over it, the biscuits were cooking, the night was clear, and life was pretty good right then.

I had my back agin a friendly oak, keepin' my eyes off the fire and looking out into the dark night beyond my camp, when I saw firelight reflecting off of greenish yellow wolf eyes. I reached slow for my rifle, tryin' not to spook it. Then it growled. I knew it weren't no wolf with a growl like that.

"Come here, Dog." I snapped my finger. It whined and I could hear the tail thumpin' the ground. I snapped my finger again, and in it come, a-crawlin' on its belly, tail a-waggin', whinin' like it was hurt.

I got it up on its feet, and it was just a big old black puppy, purty well beat up. It'd been chewed on and bit so bad it had raw spots on its flank. There was no doubt about it, it was part wolf, and the other part had to belong to Dog.

I petted the poor thing. "Well, I don't know you, pup, but I know who your Pa was because ya look just like him." He licked my hand and scrunched up tight agin my legs. I cut off some good-sized chunks of deer and he made quick work of them. I knew I'd been missin' something because this pup seemed to fill a spot I didn't even know was here.

He layed right up agin me all night, sharin' my bedroll with me. We ate some deer chops before daylight, and he fell right in with me when I left. "Well," I told him, "I'm goin' to give ya a name and you should know I've never named a animal before." He liked bein' talked to and wiggled from the tip of his tail to his nose. I laughed out loud and the sound surprised me. I couldn't remember when I'd laughed last. "I'm gonna name you Prince 'cause your daddy is the king of all dogs."

We lazied along in the mornin' sun. Prince was stiff and sore in places, and I went slow to make it easy for him. We come on a dead wolf lyin' in the trail. A scroungy lookin' critter, the pelt was ragged and bloody, and his neck hung to one side like it'd been broke. Horse wouldn't go by it, so I got down to move it. There was a blood trail goin' up the hill, and another wolf lay dead a hundred yards or so on up the hill.

Prince whined and took off up the hill. I tried callin' him back, but he kept goin' as best as his little legs would carry him. I had to go get him. I couldn't leave him out here by hisself, he'd never live the week out. I followed the pup up the hill and to a small cave. It had to be the den Prince had come from.

The bitch was all wolf and she lay dead outside the den. She had two more dead pups laying by her. She'd fought till she gave all she had. Her pelt was torn so bad it was hard to see what she'd been. There was four more dead wolves scattered out in front of the den. This had been some scrap, and she'd put up a whopping big battle.

Then I heard a low growl ending in a snarl. I turned and looked in some brush beside the den, and there was Dog. He was ripped and almost torn in two. One hindquarter was severed till it hung loose in his skin. But his eyes still blazed with the fire of battle, even though he whimpered from pain.

I knelt down beside him, and he turned his eyes to me, beggin' with his eyes for help. I guess because I was able to help the last time he was hurt, he looked to me to do it again. I put my hand on his head, and for the first time in all the travels we'd had together, he licked my hand. I sat there and held his head and cried. I cried 'cause I couldn't help him. Prince pushed in beside me and licked Dog's face, whimperin' because he didn't understand why Dog didn't get up. I couldn't help him and he weren't gonna make it. All that could happen was he'd live long enough to suffer a lot. I did what I had to do for him. Dog never blinked when I pulled my gun and placed it to his head.

There's some things that stand out so far from the regular things that go on around ya that they're unforgettable. I'll always be able to see the wolves layin' dead around the den and Dog with his head in my hand.

I turned to the pup. "Prince, if'n you turn out to be even half the dog your Pa was, you'll be some kind of dog."

Here I was actin' crazy over a dog and me with miles to go and vermin to take care of. I pulled myself up on Horse. "I'm glad there weren't no one here ta see me being a fool over a dog," I said to Horse. He snorted and tried to buck a little, but I held his head up tight and we got through that foolishness and back to our trail. I was glad to know Dog's end and not left to wonder what happened to him.

I was glad to have his pup, too. "I guess I can call you King, now," I told him. He picked up his ears and tried to wag his tail, but his whole back half wiggled in the effort.

We had company right after we got started, two tall, rangy hombres that had Texas written all over 'em. Ya could tell from their hats to their spurs and their saddles that they was from Texas. They just kinda slid outta the brush onto the trail beside me. I never even knew they was there till they moved. They could have shot me from there and I'd have never knew what hit me. It was plumb unsettlin' to be caught off guard that way.

At first I thought it was some of Nora's men, but they never made no hostile moves and since they had me boxed, I didn't make any either.

"You fellers need something?"

"We're just ridin' through. We're friendly, if you are."

"The way ya got me boxed between you, I got no choice."

"That was the idea. We don't want guns going off by mistake."

"If'n ya didn't sneak up on a feller, there wouldn't be no chance of a mistake!"

The one on my left said, "They call me Clay, and he's Wyeth."

"My name's Bonner."

"We know who you are." This come from Wyeth.

"Didn't know ya had a friend, though. Is it safe to be around you with that killer running loose?"

"His name is King. If'n his Pa was here, you wouldn't have to ask a question like that. You'd have already been huntin' the high ground."

"Is that a dog or a wolf?"

"He's more wolf than dog, but there's enough dog in him to make him want to be with people."

I was tryin' to let my horse fall back a little so's I could be behind'm if'n they had gun play on their minds. But that feller Clay kept droppin' back with me. "That horse of yours must be tired." He grinned at me, a big grin, like he wanted me to know he was on to me. I reached over and shoved him clear outta his saddle.

By the time Wyeth had pulled up, I had them covered. "Ya hold still and you might live."

"Ohueee." Clay used his elbows to set up. "I'd heard they called you 'Sudden,' and I shoulda paid more attention."

Wyeth just set there with his hands on his saddle. "We don't mean ya no harm, Bonner."

"For men that don't mean me no harm, you sure got funny ways of gettin' acquainted."

"We're looking for a woman named Nora." Clay purt near hollered it at me.

I'd been hearin' some noise from the brush so I knew there was still someone out there. "Ya better hope that feller hidin' out there don't do nothin' foolish."

Wyeth says, quiet-like. "Sam, you come on in here." Then he tells me, "Sam could've killed you any time if that was what we were after."

Well, I had to admit that, so I holstered my gun. "What kinda notion made you sneak in on me?"

I could see the pup didn't take to these fellers. He was facin' Clay, who was still layin' on the ground. Ever time Clay would twitch, King would growl. Clay laughed and made a couple of grabs at King, who raked his hand with his sharp puppy teeth. Blood spurted, and I saw Clay's hand streak for his gun.

As I rolled off Horse I saw King grab his hand. I still hadn't placed the feller in the brush, but I had Wyeth right in front of me. I drew and fired as I rolled out of the saddle. I hit Wyeth dead center before he even knew the fight was on. As I hit the ground, I fired into Clay. There hadn't been nothin' from the one they called Sam, but I'd kept rollin' till I was in the brush.

"Hold on, Bonner. I want to talk," Sam called. "This wasn't supposed to come to shootin' and I need to talk to you."

I'd placed his voice about where he was at. I unloaded a couple of shots in his general direction. "I've heard that already."

"Bonner, Nora wants to talk to you. There wasn't supposed to be no shooting. That hammer-headed Clay has messed this all up."

"You come out where I can see you with your hands up and then we'll talk."

He walked out on the trail with his gun holstered and his hands spread out and empty. "I'm here. Come on out."

I stayed in the edge of the trees. "Speak your peace."

"Nora has your sidekick. He's comin' in with us, and Nora wants to talk to you."

"The last time I met Nora, it didn't turn out too well for me."

He chuckled. "She's got some memories of you, too, but Nora don't let feelings get in the way of business."

Clay stirred and groaned. I could see blood on his shoulder.

"You'd better tend to your sidekick over there. He's been hit in the shoulder."

"Let the dumb, thick-skulled nitwit lay there, as far as I'm concerned. He was supposed to get you to talk. He weren't to do nothing else."

"Where's this meetin' supposed to take place?"

"On down the trail here a piece. You'll stay on the trail, and Nora will be in the woods. Ya won't see each other, but ya can talk."

"You take your friend here and go tell Nora I'll be along shortly."

"I'm supposed to ride in with you."

"Nobody is going to ride in with me. If she wants to talk, tell her I'll be there in a little bit."

"I can't go back there without you. I was told to bring you."

"Well, then ya got a problem, cause I ain't going in that away."

He caught up Clay's bay and Wyeth's roan and sat there and watched, while Clay struggled as best he could to get up and clutch his shoulder at the same time whilst King was snappin' at his pants leg. "Ya get that hound under control, Bonner, or I'll kick his head in."

"You even make any kind of move on that dog, and I'll kill you. Ya got that?"

Sam swung down and helped Clay into the saddle. "Shut up, Clay, afore ya really do get killed."

"Yeah, well, he's got a lot to answer for. Wyeth never even went for his gun, and this bloodthirsty gunslick killed him without a warnin' at all."

"Wyeth would still be alive and you wouldn't be carryin' lead if you'd just done what Nora said to do."

They was still fussin' over who was to blame as they rode on down the trail. I thought on what Clay had said. Had I shot Wyeth and him, not even thinkin' on drawin' iron? Well, it was sure too late to worry about it now. Old Wyeth, wherever he was at now, would just have to put it down to travelin' in bad company. I patted King on his black head and he licked my hand. "I think we're goin' to be partners," I told him, and he cocked his head and listened just like he understood me. Fact is, I think he did.

I rode slow, lookin' for a side trail or even a break in the trees and brush where I could get off this trail. I didn't want to ride up on Nora on her terms. But she'd picked a good spot, and before I was ready, there was Sam settin' in the trail waitin' for me. He cupped his hands over his mouth and hollered, "He's here, Nora."

I heard some movin' around in the woods to the side of me. "Well, Bonner, you did come. I'd of bet money you were headed the other way by now."

"Let's just skip to what ya want with me, Nora."

"You're certainly not big on conversation, Bonner, but you are good with that gun. I think we should both be better off working together. I can't have you chasing me all over the territory, and you would be a lot richer working with me than chasing me."

"I'm a lot of things, Nora, but I'm not a rustler or a bank robber."

"I don't need you to be either, Josh. I just want you to go back to Kansas City and wait till you hear from me. I'm going to retire from this business, Josh, and take my daughter with me to a place where I won't be known as Nora and where we can be respectable."

"Why would ya need me?"

"Because you are the best around with a gun, and you are almost intelligent. At least you are cunning enough to keep me safe. Just in case someone does find me."

"And what do I get out of it?"

"Money, lots of money."

"What about the kid? He's purty quick with those shootin' irons of his?"

"He's not going with us. I have other plans for my daughter. But you can be rich, respectable, and never have done anything wrong."

"Exceptin' most of your gang is going to be huntin' us because you're planning on double-crossin' them and runnin' off with all the money?"

"Are you afraid, Josh?"

"What about Sam here? He's been listenin' to your whole plan?"

"You'll have to kill him. Do it now!"

I wasn't expectin' that, and neither was Sam. He glared at me and I was watchin' him close. I shook my head no, but he grabbed for his gun and I had to do it. I sat there on the trail, in the quiet of the woods, with powder smoke strong in the air. Another man down and dead because of Nora and her way of usin' men again' each other.

"You knew he'd do that, didn't ya, no matter if'n I agreed or not. Ya knew he'd have to go for it?"

"Oh, come on, Bonner. You're the one they call 'Sudden.' You're known as a hard man, Bonner. Wyeth should have remembered that, and maybe he'd still be alive. You've never worried about a man's life before, and you want to make me feel guilty over using Sam?"

I pulled my horse around to face where her voice was comin' from. "I'm not like you, Nora. I never will be. I'm comin' for the gold ya took off the stage I was ridin' guard on, and I'm comin' for the bank money ya took that had my herd money in it."

"So that's it. That's why you and that big Texas man and his crew are chasin' me. We got your herd money. How much was it, Bonner, fifty thousand or sixty thousand?"

I was caught up in what she said about Cam. "Where's Cam and his crew?"

"Oh, they're chasin' shadows across Kansas. I have some men leading them on. They think they're almost up to us. You are the real danger to me, but you could be the man I need to make my plan work. If you won't do it for me, think of Ann. You could make the difference in her living like she should, or being hunted down and killed by these animals. I'm willing to return your herd money and more, if you'll join me."

I hadn't been keepin' track of King since I'd been there. I'd been too busy, but now I looked for him, because we were leaving. "King, come on, King. Let's go, boy."

"Does that mean you're not comin' with me, Bonner?"

"That's right. I'm not comin' with ya, Nora. Leave my herd money on the trail. Leave the gold from the stage robbery and turn the kid loose, and I won't try to keep ya from goin' straight for Ann's sake."

"That's your final decision?"

"That's what it'll take to get me off your trail for good."

"All right, Bonner, you wait here for one hour, and the kid and the money from the bank will be on the trail ahead. The gold will be brought to you in Kansas City, and you'll be off my trail. Agreed?"

I slipped off my horse and was in the woods before she had a chance to signal for one of them varmints to bushwhack me. I heard King bark and Nora curse at him. He yelped like she'd kicked him, then there was a shot and I heard him makin' a yelpin' hurt sound like puppies make that have been hurt.

I ran toward the noise, but by the time I got here, Nora was gone. King lay there dying, his little legs kicking as his life went out of him. I could see the direction she'd took, and I crashed through the undergrowth and trees, not carin' if'n they heard me comin'.

I found where they'd been standin', and where they'd kept their horses. There hadn't been anybody sent out to bushwhack me that I could see. Had Nora been that sure I'd take her up on her offer?

I waited the hour like she said, feelin' like I was a hammerheaded idiot for doin' it. I buried the pup. We'd been together for two days, and I felt like I'd lost part of my family. There was a hate in me for Nora. If'n I'd added up all my losses, Nora was at the bottom of ever one of them. But if she kept her word, I'd keep mine, for Ann's sake. I followed them back onto the trail, but there weren't no bank money or kid either. There weren't no deal and I felt better for it. I'd lost King, but she'd lost two men, and maybe her plan to get rid of her gang.

CHAPTER 13

I kept goin' over the talk I had with Nora. She wanted to get away from how she was livin' and take Ann and get a new start. If'n she took all the gang's money with her, she'd be plumb rich, but she'd have the whole gang after her, and from what I could tell, that might be as many as forty or fifty men, or maybe more. Since they was spread out doing so many different jobs, it was hard to tell just how many men she did have.

One thing was certain—she did have feelings for Ann and wanted her away from that kind of life. Which meant she could be planning on goin' back east or maybe California. I bet San Francisco would be just right for her except she would need protection because it wouldn't take long for those she double-crossed to find her. That's what she wanted with me. I had a reputation as a fast gun and to get what she wanted. She'd make a pact with the old horned pitchfork himself. But I reckon now and then she'd look at them rope burns around her neck and hate me, and the first time she thought she could do without me, she'd get even.

On the other hand, there was Ann, and if a body was to take the offer he'd have a split of all that money and be around Ann all the time. In fact, once we were located, I could make any deal I wanted; she'd have no choice. If'n Ann weren't already in love with the kid, I'd give that some thought. But now that I've turned it down, she'll go straight to the kid.

Question is, what will he do? In his place, I'd do whatever she said, to get Ann, but the kid sees things all black or all white. There ain't no gray, there's no middle for him. If'n they gave him his guns and stood him in the middle of forty salty outlaws and said, "Join us or draw," they'd best be ready for the fight of their lives!

The kid is not Nora's kind of folks, so she'll have to look for a gunslinger that beats what she's got and is willing to die tryin' to protect her. Not likely she'd find what she wanted. There weren't but one way for her to go now—she'll head for back east. Which means she's got to go where all the loot is stashed. So she has got to be leading me straight to where I want to go, right to the loot. But she ain't gonna do that willingly; she'll use every man she's got to kill me first. In fact, she'll think that the more of them hardcases of hers I kill, the less there'll be to chase after her. So she'll be plumb happy with every one of them I have to kill, as long as one of 'em gets me before it's over.

I pulled up off the trail. I was a plumb ignorant fool to be running right into where she wanted me. If'n I cut southwest, I'd cross the Cimarron and the Canadian and hit the western cattle trail. Then I'd be in front of her and not walkin' blind into her hands. If'n she didn't show then, I'd know she was between me and where I was now. To get off'n the trail and headed that direction, I had to push through a lot of undergrowth and a thick stand of black jack oak. The trees were so close together, I had to cut my way through them. Most men will ride a long ways to keep from doing what I was doing, but when it means living or dying, it don't seem so bad. But it was days later before I broke free of the thickets, and I figured I'd lost all chance of getting ahead of them.

I made a stop at the tradin' store at Cedar Springs and bought supplies, but got no information. As I rode along, I stopped at the camps of the trail drivers, but there weren't hide nor hair showed of Nora's bunch. I was about to admit I'd made a mistake when I come on some drovers who told me about seeing them at Doans Crossing. That meant they weren't headed back to where I thought they was going, at least not right away, and they was way south of me, probably in Texas by now. I got on the trail headed south. They was ahead of me again, and I was gonna have to be watchful or they'd have my hide.

There was no way Nora had hauled all that gold to Texas. Wherever she had their loot stashed, it sure weren't that far away. She was set on leading me on a wild goose chase and giving herself time to get rid of part of her crew and me.

The trouble was, I didn't have no choice. I had to let her lead me to where she kept the spoils of her gang's holdups. But the more I thought on it, the more I was certain I ought to get off the trail. She was sure to have bushwhackers hid out and waiting, and I'd be a pure fool to blunder on down the trail into a set-up. I needed to think, so I rode off the trail and set up camp. I was gonna set right there till something come to me that would work. That was one of Pa's favorite sayings. When ya don't know what to do, set still till it comes to you.

I built a lean-to and put a rock pile around my fire to shield the light and waited. I didn't know just what I was waiting on, but there weren't no hurry now. I had Nora moving and she'd be easy to keep track of. I could pick up her trail anytime I wanted to. What I needed was a way to stay alive whilst I was following her.

You'd think that staying out and resting my horse would be just what I needed, but every snap of a twig, every time a bird flew, or even if Horse just raised his head to listen, I grabbed my gun and rolled down in a gulch I was camped by. I'd rolled down into that gulch so many times I'd wore a path from rolling down into it. I finally grabbed my bedroll and slipped back away from my camp and laid down in a little gully that was just barely deep enough to hide me. Then I slept.

I had time to think, but I couldn't hit on the outcome of where she'd end up. So I took a stick and tried to draw a map of all the places I knew she'd worked. She had to have information about where to hit. She had to have a hide-out to keep her hands hid. She had to have supplies. And most of all, she needed a secure place to keep what she stole. One of the big things was that she needed to get her gang out of sight in a hurry. The longer it took them to get back to a hide-out, the bigger chances they was taking. The more I studied her problems, the more I figured that she most likely had at least three hideaways. One big place where they could all come to hide, one special place where she could keep the outlaws that was wanted real bad right then, and a place where she could go with the loot and a few special men that would protect her. The one special place that was just for her would have to be kinda right in the middle of where she carried on her part of their deal. Some place where she could get the word on what to rob and who to send, and be able to do it fast.

I probably found one of her places when I followed the Injuns that'd rustled our horses to that small town that was hid away in the territory. That was the first place we'd come on first when I was following the horses. They'd had guards out, and I hadn't gone in, but I bet that was the general meeting place of the whole works. Then that other ranch where the kid had saved my neck was most likely where the men that was most wanted hid out. That left the place where she hid the stuff them owlhoots stole. That would be some place more in the middle of the territory where she sicced her pet varmints on banks and stages and stuff.

I studied my marks I'd drawed and the more I thought on it, the more I believed that her own hide-out was close by. If I stayed put instead of running off after her, she would get tired of her game and come right on back up this way. I picked out a hill and moved my camp to where it was high, and hid. I watched the comings and goings on the trail, and was surprised at how many folks were traveling up and down a cattle trail.

I laid there under a tree sweeping the valley with my eyeglass. I weren't seeing much. There weren't no trail herds in sight. There was a couple of covered wagons camped up by a small lake, more settlers headed for free land. This bunch looked like a family traveling together. Two young women come out of their wagon, carrying towels and extra clothes. It looked like they was headed for a bath in the lake. I grinned to myself. I bet they'd have a fit if'n they knew they was about to be watched. A older woman stuck her head out of the wagon and hollered at 'em, and one of the girls turned around and headed back toward camp. The other'n went on down toward the water, walking along toward a clump of trees she must of been planning on using for a screen.

I decided a bath was just what I needed right then, so I scooted around behind the hill and snuck through the woods right up to where she'd shucked her clothes. She was up to her neck in water and ducking her head up and down, rinsing her hair. I took off my boots and my shirt and was pretending to undo my britches when she saw me.

I heard a gasp of surprise and straightened up like I was flabbergasted my own self. "What in the world are you doing in my lake?" I hollered at her.

Well, she hadn't thought she might be in the wrong, and I could see the startled look on her face.

I couldn't tell how old she was exactly, but she was almost grown. All I could see was her eyes, and they was longer across the cheek than most eyes, and them big grey eyes was fixed solid on me. Her wet hair was brown and curly, and ever now and again, she'd fling her head back to sling it out of her face.

"I don't think this place belongs to anybody and you better get before my brothers find you here trying to peek at me."

I set down on a tree that'd been blown over. It'd been uprooted on one end, and the other end was in the water.

"Your brothers would just get hurt if you was silly enough to sic them on me. And you are on my property." I gathered up her clothes. "I'll just take these on up to your camp and let them know this is my lake."

"No, you won't! You bring my clothes right back here."

It was just some harmless fun up till then, and then I saw a wad of cottonmouth water moccasins slithering her way. I grabbed my iron and started blasting away. I did for three of 'em, but the others went under water. She saw 'em, but she stood there screaming and not moving. I jumped in and grabbed her. I was so scared, I jerked her out of the water and held her over my head outta the water. Them snakes was all around me, one of 'em struck my holster and I knew I was gonna be bit, then a bullet took the closest one, and he lost his head. I handed the girl to a man on the bank and started wading out. Bullets was churning up the water around me. Pieces of snakes was bobbing around my legs in a bloody mess.

I was plumb glad to get out of that fix without being bit or shot. There was three men and they was poking around in the water at the snakes, shooting any that still moved. I looked to see if'n the girl was all right and she was standing there sobbing. I quickly turned my eyes away, because she hadn't put no clothes on yet.

"What's the matter? Ain't this what you wanted to see? Ain't you wantin' to see me naked is what I almost died for?"

Her voice was low, so I was the only one that heard her. I turned back towards her. She was standing with her hands on her hips, her breasts heaving, and her legs apart like a woman about to pick a fight. She was tiny compared to my size. She was just tall enough to be almost chest high. She was beautiful, from the purty face to the small feet. There weren't nothing out of size with the rest of her. She was a picture with her wet curly brown hair and her wide gray eyes. Her mouth was turned down in a frown.

"Well?" she demanded. "You can see me now! Is looking at me worth dying for?" She was so beautiful, I couldn't breathe. I stood there fighting for ever breath I took, smothered by the sight of her nakedness, yet staring as hard as I could.

Finally, I got out, "I've faced death for a lot less, but me being here is what saved your life, little girl. You was ducking your head under water, and you'd have never seed them snakes or never have got out alive."

I guess it'd been the nearness of death that had set her off. As soon as I reminded her of how it was, her eyes softened, as she remembered the truth of it.

"I know, I was so scared I'm still shaking. But you was teasing me and I was so mad at you."

She put her clothes on right in front of all of us, just like it was the natural way to act, and no one seemed to think wrong of it.

But I saw that she was watching my eyes, as I was watching her. Her Pa and brothers was shaking my hand and thanking me for saving her life. They was talking, and I was trying to listen, but I could only see her. I felt funny. I wanted to stare at her, I wanted to always remember how she had looked standing there with her hands on her hips, all naked and her gray eyes fixed on mine. But her family was there talking to me, and I had to let on like how she looked hadn't mattered to me.

"I got to thank you again for Peggy's life, and I want you to come up to our camp with us." Her Pa was holding on to my arm like he was sure I was gonna try to get away.

"Ya gotta stay awhile." Her brothers was persuading me. "Whatever I did, you folks more than made up for, when you bailed me out of the middle of them snakes."

I looked at Peggy. She seemed to be back to being the girl I saw in the water. Except she was flirting with me.

"Well, are you satisfied?"

"Yes and no," I flirted right back. I was plumb surprised at how much at ease I felt with her.

"What do you mean, yes and no? Either you were satisfied or you weren't."

"I mean yes I was, and no because it's over and my memory ain't good enough."

"What the blazes are you two talking about?" Her brothers had stopped when we stopped walking, and now they wanted to know what we was laughing and carrying on about.

"It's nothing." Peggy shoved them on toward camp. "We were talking private."

She waited till they was out of hearing range. "If you got memory problems, you'll just have to come back and save my life again."

I ain't called "Sudden" for nothing. I made up my mind right then. "No, I ain't comin' back. I'm takin' you with me."

She had her hands clasped behind her back, and she was swinging the folds of her skirt side-to-side whilst walking backwards in front of me. Her gray eyes took a serious look at me. "We don't even know each other. Looking at me without any clothes on don't take the place of a courtship."

"Peggy, I don't have time for a regular courtship. Your folks are going on to places I can't go right now. If'n you think you might want me, we have to make up our minds while we're together right now. We'll maybe not ever come across each other again."

"Why can't you just go with us? If you really want me, you'll make the time for me."

By this time, we'd reached their camp, and it were plain to everybody what we were talking about. So I told them about the herd I'd brought up from Texas and the bank robbery and how I had to find the gang that did it to get my money back. I explained that I weren't a kid, and that I had other money but I had to back my partners. Then I told her I had a reputation as a gunslinger.

"What do folks call you?" her Pa wanted to know.

"Some call me 'Sudden,' and some call me by my real name, Josh Bonner."

I could tell they'd heard the stories.

"We've heard you've killed more'n twenty men and you hardly twenty years old."

"I ain't killed twenty men, but I have killed some robbers and back-shooters. I hope you ain't never heard that I killed someone that didn't face me, or someone that didn't need killing."

I expected Peggy to back away from me, but she took my arm and snuggled up close. "He saved my life, Pa, and I need a man that I can feel safe with. He ain't no coward, and you know you purely hate a coward, Pa. I'm sixteen and most girls are married by now. I ain't sure I could love him, but don't chase him away, just because he ain't a farm boy."

Her Ma stood and faced her family. "If she wants this boy, she can have him. But he is going to come to where we are going to settle, and she's going to have time to find out if she wants him or not."

Me and Peggy walked out by ourselves. We had more to talk about than I'd ever had to say before. But I didn't get much said.

She put her slender arms around my neck, and I picked her up in my arms and held her to my chest.

"You're squeezing me, Josh."

"I want to squeeze you right in next to my heart so I can carry you there forever."

"Silly, you can't squeeze me inside you. Besides, how would we do this?" And she kissed me, long and tender. I ain't never really been kissed before by a girl except Maude, who kissed me like a friend. This was different! I never knew how sweet a kiss was, or how tender arms around your neck could turn your head upside down.

She was so excited, she twirled around and around like she couldn't stand still. I think it was catching because I felt like doing a little dance myself. But it was getting dark, and it weren't smart to be where you couldn't see the ground with so many snakes around, so I took her back to the wagon.

I had a fire to build at my camp, and I stirred around, not willing to bunk down and sleep yet. I set some coffee on, not especially because I wanted it, but because it gave me something to do. I turned around to add a stick of wood to the fire, and there stood Nora. She appeared to be all by herself, but I figured there was men I couldn't see scattered around my camp. My heart sunk clear down to my toes. I'd been so busy with thoughts of Peggy I hadn't been watchful, and now I was as good as dead.

I wasn't gonna let it show. I was too proud to let on I'd been careless. "Howdy, Nora," I said, as calm as if I'd been expecting her. "I wondered if'n you was gonna come and show yourself or was you going to hide out there in the dark."

"You're bluffing, Josh," she laughed. "You're good at it, though. There's no way you heard me, and here you are letting on like you knew all the time."

"I ain't gonna argue with you, Nora. You want some coffee? I put it on just for you. I figured you to be tired by the time you got here."

She hadn't thought about the coffee, and she could see I was just making it.

"You're a cool one, Mr. Bonner." She cocked her purty head and looked kinda admiring at me. She was wearing a riding skirt like she'd use to ride side-saddle. Her shirt was frilly down the front and it had a lace stand-up collar. I bet everything she wore now had stand-up collars to hide them rope burns on her neck. There was a real strain on the buttons on the front of that shirt. For a little bit, I thought of Peggy in the lake and couldn't help thinking I'd like to be there when Nora took a dip in the water.

The folks always said whatever I was thinking showed plain on my face, and that's most likely so. Nora was watching my face, and I could see she was plumb tickled at me. "You think I'm pretty, Josh? Or are you in love with me?" I knew she wasn't serious, but I decided to act like I thought she was. I always heard that what was good for the goose was good for the gander, so I figured to do a little play-acting my own self. "Nora, I don't know how you know that. My Ma always said a woman could tell when a man loved her, and I guess that's so."

There was a shocked look and then she covered it so fast if'n I hadn't been watching I'd a-missed it.

"You're quite a man, Josh Bonner. If I said I didn't have feelings of admiration for you, I'd be lying, but you and I have not been on the same side of things, have we? Why would a man fall in love with someone he's been enemies with?"

I looked as much like a lovesick dog as I could manage. Inside I was grinning. This was starting to be fun. "Being at odds with each other don't make me blind, Nora. I've seen you all dressed up, and I've seen you like you are now. A man gets lonely on a trail and can get to wondering what it would be like if things were different. The next thing ya know, he's thinking crazy over someone when it don't make sense."

"Anyhow, you said you was changing things, that you was going to quit the old ways."

She stared at me awhile, but seemed to consider what I said as serious.

"You want to be my man, Josh? Are you going to change your

mind and help me after all?"

"Nora, I'm gonna help you get away from your bunch, I'm gonna do whatever needs doing to see to it you get away. I want to have a home in a nice place, go to church on Sundays, and be respectable. What do you want?"

Either she was the best actress in the whole world, or she was serious. "I want a home, I want respect, and if that means I got to put up with a man, he has to be a strong one. Frankly, Josh, there's not many men can do what you would have to do to get me clear of the gang and get my money out." Nora reached down behind her and picked up a bank bag and tossed it to me. "There's your herd money, Josh. You didn't chase me anymore after we had our talk and I promised it to you. You kept your word, and now I've kept mine."

"Not quite. There's still the kid."

"He's free. He got Ann, and he's gone back to Kansas City."

I couldn't believe she'd do that, but I didn't even have to ask how that come about. She just come straight out with it.

"Ann didn't want to stay with me, Josh. She wanted her mother for a while, but once she satisfied her curiosity about me and why I'd left her and her father, she wanted to leave. This is no life for her anyway."

For the first time since I saw her put that hot iron to that old man's feet, I almost felt sorry for her. There was real tears in her eyes.

"Has it been worth it, Nora?"

"Do you mean, has it been worth leaving my family and living the life I have, as compared to staying at home and being a good little wife, standing when I was told to stand, setting when I was told to set. I don't know, Josh. I want my daughter, but I would never be able to be what that man wanted me to be."

I couldn't believe I was having a serious talk with this woman. I've hated her as much as I've ever hated anyone. And now we were talking like we were old friends, and more than that, I could understand her feelings.

She must of been thinking the same things. "Strange, isn't it,

Josh? Here we are talking together after all this time. We became enemies because of circumstances, and now are we going to feel differently by choice?"

"What about now, Nora? You know how I feel."

"Josh, I can't imagine you expecting me to be a puppet for you."

The thought of Nora with strings on her hands and legs and moving to my pulls made me laugh. And the more I laughed, the harder I laughed, until tears was running and she was laughing as hard as I was.

I stopped laughing when Cam stepped into my camp. That was the second time I'd been caught without knowing someone was there. It was getting downright unsettling.

"I didn't hear ya ride up."

"You and the lady was having too good a time to be listening."

I felt like a kid being scolded. But I let it pass.

"We was waiting here for you and the boys. I knew you'd come by here soon enough."

"I guess you heard about the bank being robbed?"

"Yeah, I heard."

"I'd a-thought you'd a come a-running to help get it back. It was your money too. We could of used your help; we didn't have no luck a-tall. And they got clear away with it. All that work went for nothing, Josh. If'n you and your lady friend could've parted for a little bit so you could have helped, we might of got it back. As it is, we've run them right by you and you was too busy to notice! Now, how about you get your gear together and let's finish this thing!"

I shoved the bank bag out where he could see it. "There's the money, Cam. I don't know who you've been chasing, but our money is in them bags, safe as can be."

He got mad. He was mad clear to the bone. "You mean we been busting our butts chasing outlaws clear to Texas and back, we even run them right by here! Right by your fire, Sudden, and they're not a hour ahead of us. They had to run right through here while you sat here with your lady friend, and you had our money all the time."

Well, now I knew what game Nora was playing. She'd been running hard to get away, and when she saw my camp, it was like a gift from heaven, if she could get me to go along with her. She'd dropped away from her gang and come to my fire, hoping to use me.

"I didn't know how to get in touch with you, Cam. I tried. I figured the next best thing was to set here where you couldn't help finding me and wait for you."

He was counting the money. "There's seventy-five thousand dollars here."

"Yep. I think that ought to go a ways paying for some of the beef we lost because of them varmints waylaying us at the river."

The rest of the boys come on in and squatted around the fire. When they found I had already recovered the money, they had a thousand questions. I made up a long yarn while Nora got busy and made biscuits and some redeye gravy. It weren't long till everybody's tempers had settled down. In fact, now that he had the money back, old Cam was feeling purty good. Nora had a bottle of good whiskey in her saddlebag, and they was passing it around. "It sure beats bar whiskey," was the general feeling. Someone would take a drink and say, "It sure beats bar whiskey," and pass it on and then they would say the same thing.

"These boys have a limited vocabulary," Nora murmured in my ear. I grinned, but I knew they was tired, and their tempers were bound to be short, so I didn't make no jokes. You just don't make fun of tired Texas cowpokes and expect to come away without injury.

I could see Peggy's folks' campfire, and I was wondering how I was gonna work this out. I sure didn't want Peggy to see Nora, and I weren't finished with Nora yet.

"You want to split this now?" Cam tossed me the money bag. "I was planning on us making another drive or two. Things couldn't get no worse next time, and we might accidentally make some money."

I tossed him back the bag. "You take it and get a herd together. This next time, I'm going to send a couple of reps to take my place."

"Getting too much for you?" Tom poked fun at me.

"Nope, I'm taking the little woman and going into the banking business, probably back east somewhere."

"How you doing to do that? We've got your money."

"The great thing about a bank is folks come along and put money in it. We'll use their money."

Me and Cam struck hands on a deal and the boys started hunting places to bed down. I picked up Nora's hand and pulled her up. "Come on, Sugar, we're due for some sleep ourselves."

She smiled at me. I could see the wheels turning in her head, but there weren't nothing she could do without giving herself away, and she wouldn't want to do that with this bunch or there'd be a hanging before bedtime, and she knew it.

"The little woman?" She questioned me with raised eyebrows. "Is it time to stand up or set down?"

I put out my chest and said, "You'll do as I say, when I say, and as often as I say it." I was teasing and she knew it, but she stomped on my foot anyway.

We set our bedroll behind a big old boulder and we had all the privacy I needed. I pulled her down beside me and unbuttoned her shirt, slowly, button after button. I was taking my time, enjoying the position she was in. As each button was undone and the strain on the shirt got looser and looser, she showed more and more and I got so I was trembling with each button.

She misread the whole situation; she thought I really was in love with her. She was so used to using her beauty to make men want to do for her, she never questioned that a dumb mountain kid might be getting even with her. She put a hand on each side of my face and kissed me whilst I exposed her. Her beauty turned my head, and my revenge and power over her turned into plain old lust.

We was in the bedroll when she figured out I didn't know much about what we was doing. "You never done this before?" she whispered.

"No, I ain't even been kissed by someone who loves me," I lied. That brought up the image of Peggy, but I pushed her out of my thoughts. She got the strangest expression on her face, almost tender. "You mean I'm the first?"

"I never wanted a whore to be my first time. I know it makes me sound simple but I didn't have no one else and one of them girls weren't what I wanted."

She ran her fingers through my hair and hugged me with both of her arms, as tight as she could. I could tell I'd touched a warm spot and right that minute she was as close to loving me as she had ever loved anyone.

CHAPTER 14

When we finally did sleep, it was almost daylight. I slept as sound as I ever have. Only when I woke up, Nora was gone. I kicked myself for being a fool and was thinking she'd took the herd money again, but Cam still had the money. She'd left me a letter, though.

"Dear Josh, I have things that must be done. Last night was the first time I have ever felt like a woman, but I have things to think about and so do you. I am twelve years older than you. We can't choose our time, and I am not your age, and soon I will have wrinkles on my face and gray in my hair, and you might be sorry we were together. Please love me! I have never known real love. Be in Dodge City in three weeks. There will be something there I want you to have. Nora."

"What's up?"

I turned around and handed Cam the letter. He read it through.

"I saw her leave, Sudden. She knew I knew who she was, and she said to tell you when you saw her again, she wouldn't be Nora." He slapped me on the shoulder and said, "There's more than one of us in all of us. That's a saying I got from my Pa. Since you're always quoting your Pa, ya just as well hear what mine said."

I had to think about that one. I decided that fit Nora to a fare-the-well. I'd learned a lot from Nora, my "enemy" and I'd learned things a man should know from Nora, the lover. I'd seen Nora, the vixen, and Nora the queen. I wondered how many more Noras there was.

"What I wonder is what does she have for you in Dodge City. Prize or ambush?"

I shook my head in wonderment. "I truly don't know. I guess it could be either. Ya know, Cam, I was so sure a couple of days ago

I'd kill her on sight, I hated her so much. Now I don't know if I'm in love with her or not."

"You're not in love with her, Sudden. Or at least not the kind of love that makes a man a family man. She's no good. She might get away, and we hope she does, but if she got what was coming to her, she'd be on the end of a rope."

"Can folks change, Cam? Can a bad person become a good person?"

"I think what happens is that there is good and bad in all of us, and sometimes the good in us steps forward and says it's my turn now."

He got thoughtful. "Ya know, Ransom is like that. He's been hired out as a gunman and now he's riding with the rangers. But don't ever take him for granted that he's gonna do what's right."

I took that as the warning he meant it to be. And I took it as a sign we was more than partners, we was fast becoming the kind of friends you'd ride the river with. I watched 'em ride away towards Texas and there was satisfaction in knowing we'd soon have another five thousand longhorns headed this way.

I rode down to see Peggy at their camp and they was putting their stuff back in the wagons.

"Ya leaving so soon?"

"Got to," her Pa said. "If we're going to get to California this year, we got to get over the mountains before snow hits."

"Can I talk to Peggy?"

He grinned. "You're not going to give up, are you, boy?"

"No, sir. Did you see them fellers that left out early this morning? That was the partners I was telling you about. In a little while, there'll be five thousand head of longhorns headed this way."

"I take it they got their money back?"

"Yes, sir, they sure did, and a little more."

"Listen to me, boy, and if you want to marry my gal, I think you'd better ride along with us and let her get to know you. You better have the idea you think more of her than you do cows, or business, or anything else."

"I do want her more than anything else. How come she can't know if'n I'm the man she wants or not?"

He laughed and laughed till I was getting sore at him.

"Ma, come here!" he hollered and when she come, he told her. "This youngun wants to know how come that little slip of a girl don't know if she wants him or not."

"It's all right, boy, there's no secrets in a family like ours anyway. Did you know she's not sure if you really want her because you've fell for her, or if it's because you saw her naked and you're like a dog in heat?"

"Well, she's something to see all right, and I'm glad that she is purty, but I want her because I'm sure she's the one I want. I don't know why, I can't tell her any reasons why I want her. But I know she's the one I want."

"Are you coming with us?"

I felt so miserable. "I can't, I got to be in Dodge City in three weeks. Why can't you folks wait till next season to go to California?"

"We got to get over the mountain this year and get us a place staked out. I'm a-feared you're going to lose out, boy." Putting his hands to his mouth, he hollered out, "Peggy!"

And Peggy came a-running when she saw me. She ran till she got about four foot away, and jumped straight at me, and I grabbed her up in my arms. She's so tiny she's like holding a doll. Her arms hugged my neck whilst her big gray eyes searched my face. You going with us, Josh?"

What was I going to say after that? There weren't nothing I wouldn't do for her. "If'n nothing else will satisfy except I go with you, then I'm going."

I heard her Pa laughing to himself, and I knew he thought she had me wrapped around her little finger. I guess she did because I'd do anything to please her. I set her up on my horse and she rode with me up to my camp to help me pack up. I tried to tell her about Cam and the boys and the cattle drive, and how we was bringing more longhorns up the trail, but she didn't care about things like that. "Them's man things," she said. "Let's talk about the house we're going to build and what kind of furniture we're going to put in it, and whether or not we'd have a carriage and a carriage house."

I didn't care. If'n she wanted the moon, she could have it if she wanted it. I packed the camp stuff, the pots and pans. She was going to roll up my bedroll, but she was taking so long, I went to see why. I walked around the rock where me and Nora had put our bed the night before, away from prying eyes. There was Peggy, setting there on the blanket reading that blame letter Nora had left for me. I'd tossed it back on my bedroll after Cam had read it. There was real tears running down her cheeks. "I reckon you made a pure fool out of me, Mr. Bonner. You must of had a real good time fooling me about your instant love for me when all the time you had a woman up here in your camp!"

I could feel all my happiness just melting away and falling like hot lead in the pit of my gut. "I never had a woman up here all the time. No such thing. I never lied to you about my feelings. I don't take long times to figure things out. I met you and I knew right then you was the only girl in the whole wide world for me."

"Oh, come on, Sudden Bonner! I can smell perfume in these blankets. You had a woman here last night and here's the letter she left! She's too old for you, she says. Am I so young and simple you figured me to share your bedroll tonight?" Now tears were starting to gush outta her eyes and her cheeks were wet with tears. She was so beautiful she made my heart ache.

"Peggy, I swear you got this all backwards. Would you listen for just a minute? She wasn't here till I got back from your camp."

She jumped to her feet and wouldn't let me finish. "And that makes it different? I hate you, Josh Bonner. I hope you pay for this. I wasn't sure I could love you, but you acted like you was so sure you really loved me, I believed you! You made a fool of me," and away she ran, stumbling downhill, wiping both eyes with the backs of her hands. I would of chased after her, but I could see it wasn't gonna do no good. A few minutes ago, I'd had the whole world, and no one could've been as happy, and now my life was ruined. I would never love a girl like I loved Peggy right now. My heart had filled up my chest so full, I hurt. There was a weight pushing on my shoulders, and all I could think was I'd lost Peggy.

I sat down and buried my head on my knees and cried. Here I was a growed man, one that other men feared. A man that had substance and a business partner and I was crying like a little kid.

"You don't look like a real bad man right now," I heard scorn in his voice and before I even looked up and I knew it would be Peggy's Pa.

"I ain't a real bad man. I'm just a man, and right now I'm not sure of that."

"My little girl come back to camp bad hurt and crying. Ya want to tell me about that?"

And so I told him, through my own tears. I told him about Nora, about the robbery, about how it cost me my job. I told him about the old man in the mountains and how she'd took my horse and how I purt near died walking out. I ended up with the shot that killed my pup. Somehow, I managed to put it all together just the way it happened, including Ann and the kid.

"So for the first time, I finally had her where I could get even. She couldn't leave or let on, or the boys would've knew, and they'd a-hung her right then. I can't tell you how I felt. I had her trapped, she had to do as I wanted or die. I felt so much power over her for the first time since I'd had a rope around her neck and I was pushing her down to my will. Ever button I undid, and ever piece of her clothes I took off made me feel more and more power over her. I was getting even for ever hurt she'd gave me and ever'thing she'd took away from me. Till Peggy found out I was walking on top of the world."

He listened all the way through and didn't say anything right away. "I'm glad to know the truth, boy. I'd a-hated to leave, thinking I'd been so wrong about someone as I'd appeared to be about you. I can't say if ya was right or wrong to do it that way. That's between you and your conscience. I can tell you that there's a little girl down there that ain't never gonna see it like a man could see it. Twenty years from now, the memory of what happened would cross her mind and she'll get just as mad as she is right now. But after the sun sets tonight and the fire is burning low, you come down. I'm gonna tell her Ma how it was, how you didn't try to lie to me, and how I think she should at least listen. She might never like you again, but if her Ma tells her to, she'll at least listen all the way from start to finish."

"I'm thanking ya for that. You might not understand how I could be so in love with your girl and still do what I did, but it's true. When I saw Peggy, I found the only girl I'll ever love. I know that might sound like a little boy talking instead of a grown man, and I can't put into words how I know, but it's as true as if I'd a-been courting her all my life."

He got to his feet and looked at me a long time, standing quiet and just looking. I met his eyes and kept still. Finally he shook his head and turned away. I heard him mutter to hisself as he was walking back down the hill. "Lord, please help these kids. There ain't enough gumption between them to fill a thimble. They'll never be able to help themselves."

That sounded so much like what my Pa would've said, I had to smile, even when I didn't feel like smiling. I fretted and stewed and made up a hundred things in my head about what she might say if'n she really took the time to listen to me. And when it finally got to be time to go and see her, I was as spooky as a man might get.

She was standing with her hands behind her back with her back to the glowing ashes of the campfire. She didn't meet my eyes and I figured it must of took her Ma to tell her to do it, or she wouldn't of been there.

"Peggy, I couldn't stand it if'n you left hating me. Ya might not figure what happened to be right, and if'n ya don't want to see me again, I'll do what ya say, but please listen and try to put yourself in my boots for just awhile."

She nodded her head up and down, but wouldn't speak or look at me.

So I did the best I could. I started at the start and told it all, bit by bit, injury by injury, till I come to the part of having Nora under my complete control. I wanted to skip the hurtful part, but I was sure she'd already heard it all, so I explained as best I could in my poor way without enough of the right words to say it how I felt it.

"I was so full of this thing, Peggy, I never thought of how this would set with you. I would never have done nothing to hurt you if'n I'd a thought on it first. I was wrong doing what I did."

"I'm glad to hear the telling of all of it. At least I don't have to feel so much like a fool, but I do think if you loved me as much as you seem to feel you do, I'd of been first in your thoughts, no matter how galling her actions had been to you. I don't hate you, Josh. I never hated you this morning. But I don't know if I could love you; I don't make those same instant decisions like you do. If you want to come with us, or come to me when we get settled and let me get to know you, you can come."

She was so quiet and soft that when she finally met my eyes with her own large oval gray eyes, I saw a womanliness that was way beyond her sixteen years.

"Do ya want me to come now, Peggy? I will if ya want me to. Or I'll wait and come when you folks get settled."

"I'd just as soon have some time without looking at you ever day. I don't think it'll do you any good either way, Josh. This morning, I almost knocked you down by jumping in your arms, and I was ready to fall in love with you. You seemed like my knight on a white horse. I was ready to make you my hero and my husband. But I'm not ready for you now, Josh."

Without no goodbys or nothing else, not even a nod, she just turned back to her wagon. I loved her more ever time I saw her or got close to her, but I weren't gonna beg or grovel for nobody. If'n she saw what I'd done as a wall between us, then I'd just leave. It couldn't be took back, even if I wanted it to.

I left that very night. I didn't even wait to say goodbye to her family. I didn't want to be around people, so I camped and fished and stayed off the main trails till it come time for me to go to Dodge City. I didn't know what this was all about, but I kept my gun handy and hoped for the best. I checked into the Dodge House and found Nora already there. She was dressed to look like a little old lady, but I could see it was Nora and if she hadn't done that good a job fooling me, most anybody would be able to see who she was.

"Come on up to my room, Nora!"

"Well, I can see I didn't fool you. I hope nobody else saw through me like that."

"You shouldn't be out here where folks can see you. You're taking too big a chance someone will know you."

"Well, Josh, I missed you, too, and I've been well, thank you."

"I'm just worried because you shouldn't be here." She clung to me. "Josh, hold me, hold me tight." Well, that weren't hard to do. She had her arms around my neck hugging me, and her face buried agin my shoulder. Purty soon she started crying and I just held on, and then the crying turned into sobs, and her whole body was shaking.

"Ya going to tell me, or am I going to have to guess?"

"They got Ann."

"Them varmints you was trailing with, they the ones that you're saying has got Ann?"

Her head nodded up and down, but she couldn't' talk.

"You took the money, so they figure to force you to give it back by taking Ann?"

She sat up, wiping her eyes on my shirt. "They won't just give her back, Josh. They'll kill her as soon as they get the money."

"Why?"

"To get even; they'll kill me if they find me. I broke the code; I double-crossed them. They won't rest till they've got even."

"Do you know where they'll take her?"

"Sure, they're counting on that. They want me to come."

"Do they know about me?"

"They don't know about us, but they do know who you are and that you been chasin' us."

"Then I'll go get her. Me and the kid can get anybody out of anywhere."

She gave a bitter kind of laugh. "They have the kid. They took him with Ann. I don't know why you think that kid can do anything. He's just a dumb clod. Ann says he's dumb, and she has to tell him everything he's supposed to do."

"Well, she sure picked him, and him riding right beside me. She never even looked at me."

"She looked at you. She just looked at the kid more. Before she knew I knew who you was, she used to tell me about this big black-bearded man who worshipped the ground she walked on."

"How'd she know that?"

"How'd she know you thought she was the girl all other girls should be measured by? By your face. You show everything you're thinking on your face."

"What am I thinking right now?"

She rubbed the top of my head with her hand. "You're wishing, not thinking."

I sat holding her and thinking about the night we'd had together. I wondered if she'd really been as helpless as I had first figured she'd been.

She had been laying back on my arm, but turned at my question. "I made love to you because I needed you to protect me, and you knew that. But I loved you after we started because I just felt that way. Even though we've been enemies, I can love you because I know why you did what you did, and I believe you can love me even though you once wanted to kill me.

"Did you know I've never made love to anyone after I left Ann's father? I've only been with two men, you and him, and he used to beat me. My father gave me to him when I was thirteen, and he taught me everything by using a stick on me, or by slapping me. After Ann was old enough to be taken care of by her nurse, I ran away. By then, I was fifteen and I wasn't about to be used by any man ever again, so I stole to live. He put detectives out looking for me, so I come west.

"I found it was easy here because men respected a girl out here, and any man would come to her defense. I found out that I was beautiful, and that by a smile or a touch I could get all kinds of valuable information about gold shipments and banks and most anything of value. So I found some men that would steal for me, and I'd take care of business for them."

It was getting dark, and I sat rocking her, watching out the window. The moon come up and the night sky was lit with stars. Still I held her. I'd only had that one night to think on agin years of hating her. What was I doing here? Why now was I going to try to get Ann and the kid back whilst her bunch wanted her? A little while back I'd a hunted them down to give her to them. "Time and events" sure fit this spot I'd put myself in.

The morning sun hit her in the eyes and woke her. She smiled and kissed me. "I've never felt so safe as I do when you're with me."

"Then why did you run?"

"I left you a letter, Josh. I meant every word of it. It's too late for you and me. Josh, I've been thinking about things. When this is over, the quicker I get out of your life, the easier it'll be for both of us."

I stood up. "Time's wastin' Nora. Where's Ann?"

"I'm going with you and show you."

"No, you are not! Where is Ann?"

She drew me a map and I hadn't been very far off before when I was thinking about where she might have her special hide-out. It was in the high country in no man's land. In that part where the injun territory and Kansas and Colorado come together.

They had the kid, but come to think of it, one man might move around without being spotted better'n two could anyhow. I loaded a mule with provisions, but mostly with shells and a box of dynamite. The ones who might of noticed me would only think I was going mining. I went up through Colorado into the high country. I didn't even know how many men I was up against. But they would be looking for Nora to be coming, probably thinking she'd be bringing a lot of men with her. They wouldn't be watching very close for the sign one man might be making. So I weren't surprised when I come on her place without being found out.

I had to admire the cunning she had used when she had this place built. The back of the house was agin a vertical rock cliff that towered high and outward over the house itself. There weren't no way of getting at it from the back or from the top. If'n ya didn't know where it was, ya wouldn't see it even riding through the valley below. But from the house there would be a good field of fire to each side and the front. It was not going to be a easy place to get into. From what Nora had said, there was a tunnel running from the back of the house into what looked like a solid rock cliff, but the reason she'd picked that spot was because there was a cave in that part of the cliff that was covered by the house. And in the cave was a natural cleft that ran through the cliff and upward to the table top up above.

All I had to do was find a certain rock that covered the crevice or cranny or crack in the rock or whatever ya want to call it, and make myself crawl into it when I can't even stand to be in a small room, and crawl on my hands and knees for a half or mile or so, going through places where Nora said only a small child could get through in the absolute darkness of a place where light has never been and never will get to. And since I've done that, I'll come out in the house behind a big woodbox by the chimney that will move out of the way if'n I've got any strength left by then, and if'n the blame box is not too full of wood.

She didn't say but my guess is that all the loot from all her raids is stored in that hunk of rock as well, because she said she was the only living soul that knew of the tunnel. Makes you wonder what happened to the poor feller who built the house for her. Imagine his surprise at payday! He's probably stored in there, too. Nora was born a couple hundred years too late. She'd of made one of them tyrant kings a great queen. Ma used to read to us about the kings of olden times. I remember she read us a story about a king who built a secret place and then had all the workers and their families killed and stored in a chamber of his secret place.

Now, Nora would have been right at home with him. I think of her as she has been lately and I don't know the Nora who would kill as easily as the Nora who must of killed the man or men who built this place for her. Who knows, if the man had a wife, she might be in there with him. If I get up enough nerve to go in there, I'll look for 'em.

I was through looking the place over and was ready to back out of there when I felt this cold hard gun barrel stuck right in the back of my neck. There is such a sinking feeling when you think everything is fine and then find out it's not all fine. A hand reached down and removed my iron from me. "Just back out slow, hombre, and if ya want to live for a bit longer, be real quiet."

The lifespan he was talking about didn't sound real promising. "If'n ya won't get excited, I'll just do that very thing." That voice had sounded like I'd heard it before, but I couldn't place it, and without being invited, I weren't gonna turn my head.

"Josh?" Now he sounded like he might know me. "Josh, I thought you was in Texas with Cam and the boys."

"Kin I turn around? Ya sound like we might know each other, but I'm at a disadvantage here."

"Sure, turn around, but ya got some explaining to do."

"Well, howdy, Ransom. It's been awhile since I seen you. What in the world are you doing here?"

"I'm here with the Rangers. We got some people down there we're after. What are you doing here?"

"They got a little girl and a friend of mine down there that they took by force and they are holding till they get paid before they kill them, if'n they ain't already killed them." About that time, some more dangerous looking fellers come up, and Ransom told 'em who I was and what I was doing there. We did all the howdys and such and they asked me if I had a plan. I did. My plan was not to tell them about the loot or the way through the rock into the house.

"We'd best back away a piece and think this thing through," the ranger in charge said. And we did, we backed up a couple of miles and made camp.

I walked over by Ransom. "We got to do this thing in the dark—well, after the moon has started down and before daybreak." He nodded his agreement. "I reckon so. At least that might get us down close to the place, but how will we get in?"

"How about we ride just at daybreak, when they can see a little but not real good. We'll ride down there like we're being chased, and your friends can ride like they are chasing us, shooting ever which way except at us. Have 'em shine them ranger badges up real bright and wear 'em where they can be seen easy. Them varmints will think we belong to them, and they'll give us some cover fire, and when we get to the door, they'll just open it up, and we'll jump in!"

"I'd heard you was crazy, Josh, but I was hoping for your sake that ya wasn't too bad off. Now, I can see you ain't going to live long without help."

"That don't sound like a bad idea. In fact, I think that might work if the rest of us keep coming instead of turning back as you go inside, we'll have their attention split both ways."

We hadn't heard the ranger captain walk up, but he'd been listening, and liked the idea.

"It sounds like a short life and a sorry funeral to me," Ransom growled.

"Ya don't have to do it if you think there ain't no chance of making it. But if Josh is willing to try it, I'll go with him if you won't."

We talked on it every which way and didn't see no other chance of taking them. I was willing because of Ann and the kid. If'n I'd a-been Ransom, I wouldn't of went for no ranger badge or money. But he figured to go and we made our plans and hit the bedrolls. Come daylight, we was all mounted and waiting in the edge of the woods. Me'n Ransom lit out for the ranch house at full speed and right behind us rode six rangers, badges showing and shooting like a small war. Only thing was, we weren't more'n a part of the way there when some folks in the woods on the other side of the house opened up on us and they was serious. I could hear the whine of lead as it went by me and that weren't a pleasant sound. But then the varmints in the house started shooting, and danged if'n they weren't shooting at us, too.

"You had enough of this?" Ransom hollered at me, and we turned and rode down the valley out of range of all of 'em, and come 'round through the trees back to where we'd camped.

"That was a dandy idea, Josh. Ya got any more ways we might get killed real easy?" I could see Ransom was some upset. He had a hole in his leg and his roan had a couple of burn marks from close shots. I didn't have no marks at all on me or Horse. "If that don't beat all." Ransom sounded bitter. "It was his stupid idea and he ain't got a mark on him. I've a good notion to shoot him myself."

It was when he said he had a notion to shoot me his own self that I decided to let him rest by hisself for a while.

When the ranger captain come back and he'd been across to the other side and found out they was Pinkerton men over there with some of their pet gunslingers. They was on the trail of the gold from the stage robbery, and hadn't known we was over here, and thought the chase was the real thing. "It's too bad we didn't fool the outlaws. They must be smarter than the Pinkertons. At least they thought we were the real bad hombres."

Ransom was still outta sorts and it showed. He had a bandage on his leg, and it weren't serious, but it probably hurt. He groaned ever now and then, but I figured some of it was just to let me know it was my fault.

We had them hemmed in on this side, and the Pinkertons were on the other side and none of us could get to 'em, but they weren't going nowhere. I unloaded my mule and found not only the dynamite I'd bought but a miner's light and some carbide that I hadn't bought. It was Nora thinking I'd have to go through the crack in the rock to get to 'em. She knew the place well enough to know a small army couldn't get in there. "Let me see that there dynamite." Ransom was up and getting excited.

"Ya never said nothing about no dynamite."

"Because I didn't see no way of using it."

"We'll swing it down onto their roof from up above."

"How can ya do that when the rock overhangs the house?"

"We'll swing it back and forth till we got a big enough swing to hit the roof. Hey, Captain," he yelled. "Over here. Josh has got a load of dynamite over here."

Well, that drew a crowd. "What are ya doing with the miner's light, Josh?"

"Same thing as the dynamite. I might do a little prospecting while I'm out here."

"Well, I hate to spoil your prospecting, Josh, but I think Ransom has got the right idea." The captain turned to Ransom. "Ya get up there at daylight, and the rest of us will get ready to rush 'em."

Have ya ever put a round rock between your thumb and your finger and pressed it tight? The rock will spurt out a long ways if'n ya squeeze tight enough. Well, that's the way that log house did. I'd never seen a log house unroll before, but that one did. I mean the logs just kinda squirted out the side and down the hill. The Pinkertons were on 'em from their side and we had 'em from ours. To tell the truth, they was so dazed from the explosion they couldn't fight anyway.

CHAPTER 15

We had 'em from our side and the Pinkertons were on 'em from the other side. They wasn't in good shape. Most of 'em couldn't hear a thing we said and were too dazed to understand what was said if'n they had been able to hear.

It suddenly come to me that I was here to get the kid and Ann, if they'd pulled through, and I didn't see them anywhere.

I was busy moving logs and looking through the rubble when Ransom stopped me. "That feller over there, the only one that can talk, says they never had that girl and your friend. He says some woman named Nora heads up this gang and they was supposed to meet her here to divvy up the proceeds from their holdups. He says they weren't holding nobody for ransom, and weren't planning on it, that they was rich from all the robbing and stealing and was just waiting on this woman Nora to get here."

"That can't be right. I have it purty straight that they have the kid and Ann. Maybe he just wasn't in on it." So we talked to those we could as they recovered a bit from the shock of the explosion. There weren't none of them that even knew that Nora had took the money and ran. Not any of 'em knew where the money and gold was stored. I scouted around the woods in a circle around the place, but there weren't no sign I could pick up of any other folks, other than the ones we knew about.

I dug the logs back to find the cave Nora had said was there. There weren't no cave. There was a crevice in the cliff all right, but nothing a full-grown man could get through.

"I think you've got the wrong information, Josh," Ransom told me. "You best go back and see where your friends were last seen."

I nodded my head, but inside I knew that I'd been the fool for

Nora again. My guess was Ann and the kid were safe and free. Nora had got what she wanted. Her bunch was took care of and out of her way. She hadn't got to me one way, so she used another—her body. Whilst Ransom and the rest of them questioned Nora's bunch, I loaded up my pack mule and set out for Dodge, but I already knew she weren't gonna be there.

I made a pass through the rocks where Nora had said there was another way to the house through the rock. There weren't nothing there. I sat there and let my anger build. It would help nothing, but I couldn't stop it anyway. Then I had a thought. Nora was good at half-truths. Suppose she really did have a secret place up here and needed those varmints cleared out before she could get to her hiding place and get clear again.

Or maybe she just needed for them to be kept busy for awhile whilst she did what she had to. If that was it, she was up here somewhere, maybe watching me right now. What I needed to do was put on like I was pulling out and double back and beat the bushes till I found her. I left like I was really leaving, moving slow so I wouldn't be too far away at dark.

Moving slow was a good idea. It kept me from running right up on 'em. They was below me in a small valley, I could see Nora and the kid and Ann in a wagon. There was six mounted men riding alongside them. I got out of their sight as quick as I could. I followed along from above. They weren't going fast and it weren't no chore at all to keep up. When they stopped to make a camp, I angled that direction. I made my camp in a small cave that was just a dent in a cliff and hid from the front by rock boulders. I come on it whilst trying to get up close to Nora and her bunch.

They had a good fire going and when dark come, it made a good guide straight to 'em. They was all set around the fire, watching the flames. It takes awhile to get used to the dark after staring in a fire like that, so I was able to walk right up to them without being afraid of being found out, because I knew they weren't gonna be able to see me.

The first thing I noticed was that them six fellers with them was the only ones with guns, and the next thing I could see was that Ann and the kid were prisoners. I couldn't tell about Nora. She didn't act like she was afraid or being watched, but I didn't see no weapon on her. Maybe I had it wrong again. Could be this time she'd been straight with me.

Ann was closest to me. She had her back to me, and the gully I was moving around in ran right up behind her. I crawled up to her on my elbows and with one quick motion, I cupped my hand over her mouth and picked her up at the same time. Before they had time to notice, I had her and was gone.

Ann didn't know who had her, and I didn't have time to explain everything, so I kept my hand over her mouth and carried her in my arms like a small child, her head held in one hand and her legs hanging over the other arm. We was outta their range of sight and I was most of the way back to my camp before they saw she was gone. I could hear the shouting; they was hollering for her to come back in to the fire. They still hadn't put it together that she'd run off when they finally decided that she weren't coming back.

My fire was small and well hid from sight. You'd have to walk right up on it to see it. When I set Ann down, she didn't make no noise. She just looked all around and finally she looked at me. "I thought it must be you, Mr. Bonner. Obediah said you'd not be far away, that we needn't worry because he was sure you were watching."

"Why don't you try calling me, Josh. Most of my friends and even some of my enemies do."

She nodded her head like she would do that, but she didn't say anything else. I didn't know if'n she was shy or if she was scared of me. I tried to put her at ease. "Ann, I don't know what's going on, but you can be sure there ain't nothing gonna happen to you. I will make sure of that."

"I'm not afraid for me, Josh. They have my mother and they want her to give them all the money she has put away, or they are going to harm her, and they were going to kill Obediah and me if she don't give in."

With that, all the tears started to flow, and dirty streaks covered her cheeks. I picked her up and set her in my lap. She squirmed around and tried to get down, but I just held on to her tighter. "Please, Josh, this is unseemly, and I'm not a child."

I cupped her head with my hand and pulled her agin my shoulder. She pulled back for a while, but when she saw I was gonna hold her if'n she wanted to or not, she gave way to sobs and all the strain that'd been on her melted away, and she put her arms around my neck and cried into my shoulder. I just held her and rocked a little, and let her get it all out.

After awhile, she set up. "Are we going to be able to get Mother and Obediah back?"

"We'll see in the morning. Right now they got half of 'em out hunting for you, and we don't want to stir up anything tonight."

She looked concerned when I said they'd be out looking for her.

"They ain't going to find us, don't you worry none. We're hid real good here and even if they stumbled on us, they'd be the ones that was sorry."

She got down and covered up in my bedroll by the fire. "I'm not worried, Josh. I trust that you'll be able to take care of this whole situation."

And with that, she went to sleep. I've never in my life ever been able to sleep sound like that, and I've never seen anyone go to sleep just by closing their eyes before. I've always had to lay still a hour or so and listen to ever sound around me before going off to a light sleep, and every sound out of the ordinary wakes me. Except that time in the barn when Nora's men caught me, and that time I was not only wore out, but I was running a high fever.

Ever since I first saw her, I thought Ann was head high above any other girl. I don't know quite what I expected, but now that she is here, she's not as high up on the shelf as I had always placed her in my mind. She was just a purty little girl who was sure I'd be able to walk in and take her mother and the kid away from six tough gunmen who were on guard and waiting to kill me. I smiled to myself. This hero stuff could sure get you in a lot of trouble.

I dozed, but never slept, and she slept knowing I was gonna straighten this mess out come daylight. Daylight come, and I never felt better.

I took her back to a stream I'd passed coming this way and stood guard while she washed up. Then I made a good breakfast. I'd kept a eye on their camp. I figured they thought she had took off on her own. They wasn't acting concerned or beating the brush for her. They hitched up the team and they was moving out again. I packed up the mule and put Ann on Horse and led them along the high slope keeping pace with the wagon. We made slow time, and it come on me we was bearing back toward the cliff Nora's house had been built under. I wondered if'n any of the rangers were still around, but figured the chances weren't good.

Traveling with a girl can be bothersome. She was embarrassed the first time or two she had to stop to do the necessary things, but before the day went on long, she quit being formal with me, and it seemed she was always either stopping or needing a drink or needing to rest. It was good the wagon was going slow, too. I tried not to show any irritation and to be patient with her. There was more little girl in her than I would have thought for a young lady that was seventeen. At home, she'd have two kids by now and a house to run.

We had two more traveling days, and at least sixteen more necessary stops, maybe forty drink stops, and I was tired of being nursemaid.

Nora was taking them in a wide circle toward the cliff. We could have been there in one day, and I figured she was giving me time to make a move. Only what kind of move do you make agin' six experienced gunfighters?

The night of the third day, I could see Ann was wore out with this traveling across mountain ridges, up and down canyons and across cliffs where we had to lead the animals and climb at the same time. We was hot and sweaty when we come back across that same stream, only further up the mountain.

"Josh, can I take a bath? I'm so hot and I'm tired of smelling like this."

I looked at her. She looked tired and dirty. There was dirt streaks over her clothes and sweat stains. Her face was streaked with days of dust and sweat. Her eyes were showing tiredness.

"Ya set right there in that shade." I pointed to a shady place under a tree. I unloaded my mule and pulled the saddle off the horse. Whilst they took a rest, I found a small rope, and going from limb to limb, I strung a small square at the base of that tree. Then I took my bedroll and hung blankets on the rope, making a private, shut-in blanket room. I dug in my pack and come up with a clean shirt and a comb.

"You go in there and change into that shirt. Take everything off you want to wash, and I'll carry you and your stuff out there to that rock in the middle of the creek. I've got soap here and you can bathe and wash your clothes and hang 'em here on the rope till they dry."

She got everything ready just like I told her, and come out to be carried. I set her down on a rock and undid her hair. She had long, thick black hair that hung past her waist when it was let loose. I took the comb and combed the dust and tangles out. When I was done, it hung loose over her shoulders in thick waves to her hips.

She watched me in some surprise when I started. She never complained if'n I snagged a little tangle, and she smiled and stretched like a well-fed cat when I was done. I held out my arms to carry her, and she tucked my shirt in around her and put her arms around my neck and let me carry her out to the rock in the creek. Whilst she washed , I took off my sweaty shirt and waded out and did some cleaning up myself. I heard her giggle and looked up to see her watching me. "You look like a big black bear," and she laughed her little girl laugh.

I was covered with black hair and probably did look like a bear to her. I did my best bear imitation, and she squealed and fended me off like she was scared. We played like kids for a hour, and both of us was the better for it when we got out of the water. I'd felt like a kid again for a while, and it had took some of the tiredness away.

It didn't take long for things to dry. When she come out of the blanket screen I'd put up, she was fresh and clean, with her hair put up and in long curls coming from under her bonnet and curling around her face. She could tell from my face how good she looked, but I told her anyway, "You look just like I've always said you look. You're the girl all other girls should be measured by."

Her eyes sparkled just like the first time I met her, and she was fourteen and I'd never seen anything like her.

"Josh, you can be so sweet. I'm glad I've got to know you. Now you're not just someone I've seen on the street or heard those awful stories about, but I know the real Josh Bonner."

"I wished you'd taken the time to know me before ya settled on the kid to marry." My tone was blunt and a little bitter.

"You are mistaken, Josh. Obediah and I are not engaged. I reconsidered him and told him long ago that I did not love him and never would."

"I'm sorry, Ann. That weren't none of my business, and I had no business saying that." I was jolted clear down to my boots. I had figured her to be spoken for by a friend, and now to find out that weren't so, and to be told out here in the wilds by ourselves. My face, as always, told her what I was thinking.

"Josh?" Her voice was troubled. "Does that change things between us?"

"I figured to be taking care of a friend's intended. Now to find out you're not bound to him doesn't change things between us, but it sure come as a surprise."

"It's kind of like you were here with a woman that was spoke for and you weren't thinking that what you said or did mattered much, to find out that suddenly if you said or did the right things, she might like you better?"

She had said it just right, and she was looking at me with her head cocked a little and her eyes had a question in them. I didn't know how to answer her. "I didn't know if what I said or didn't say might ever matter between us. This ain't the time or place to have to worry about things like that. I come to get you and Nora and the kid free. I don't want to think abut anything else right now."

"I'm sorry. I don't want to be a bother, Josh, or to hinder you in what you have to do. I just wanted you to know I was glad I had a chance to get to know you."

I nodded a stiff nod and started picking up our stuff.

"We'd best get moving, or we might lose them."

She scurried about, helping me pack. I felt a little distant now. I don't reckon things will ever be as free and easy as they had been. I gathered from what she said that she thought that knowing she was free, I might be trying to win her and if'n she was judging by what I wanted in the past she'd of been right.

But now that I've met Peggy, I haven't been thinking on Ann anymore. There weren't no reason to tell her different but right now if'n I could have either one I wanted, I don't know who I'd pick. With Ann, I'd be wore out every day, just running around taking care of her. I weren't sure of Peggy. In private she'd be all a man wanted, but in town she might not know how to act around fine people. And I intended to be somebody important some day. I set up camp and got some biscuits and beans together, and went to check on Nora's bunch. They was about the same place, I didn't see how she was going to be able to stall much longer.

I thought about trying to do like the injuns do, and take out one or two of 'em from ambush every night, but that would work only one time, then they'd know I was there, and Nora and the kid would be in real bad trouble. The best I could do was let her light somewhere and make a plan then.

When I got back, Ann hadn't stayed put. She'd tried to follow me and her foot had slipped on a rock, and she'd fell a-rolling. When I got back to camp, she was bawling and dirt-streaked again, and there was blood showing through her skirt where her leg was. I tried to get her to stand, but she must of twisted her leg or her foot.

When I wanted to look at how bad she'd skint herself, she wouldn't let me raise her skirt to look at her leg to see if she needed a splint or a bandage. She was afraid the sight of her ankle might "enflame my passions." I really wanted to jerk her over my knee and blister her bottom, but I decided to leave her set till she hurt enough or bled enough to ask for help. So I just smiled and let her be whilst I cleaned up the pans and set the fire. I rolled up by the fire and left her settin', tears rolling down her cheeks and blood running down her leg. Any other woman would've fixed a bandage her ownself, but she set there like a baby and let the blood run, not knowing how to do or what to do, and I was so out of sorts I weren't gentle enough to tell her what she needed to know.

"Josh."

I didn't answer.

"Josh," a little louder.

I rolled over the other way and still pretended to sleep.

"Josh!"

She hollered loud, and I raised up, rubbing my eyes. I was almost enjoying myself.

"What?"

"Josh, you better come and see what you can do. I'm afraid I'm hurt worse than we thought."

"You sure? I don't know how I might act, seeing your foot that-a-way."

"Josh, are you making fun of me? Would you do that to me?"

Well, the tears started again, and I felt ashamed of myself again, so I got up and carried her over to the bedroll and gently laid her on it. Then I raised her dress up to see the leg, and I really was ashamed. She'd skinned it bad, and blood covered her leg past her bloomers, and they was all bloody, along with her petticoats and her dress, clear up to her hip. Blood was running from up on her leg or maybe on her hip.

I turned her over to her side and looked at her side. There was blood on her shoulder so thick it was sticking to her dress. I fixed a pan of water to heat and got some rags to soak the dress loose from her shoulder. She tried to stop me from undoing her dress, but I just set her hands aside and unbuttoned it all the way. Then I got a blanket, and as I lifted her dress to her waist and pulled her bloomers off, I spread the blanket over the part of her that weren't hurt. She was still exposed like no other time in her life and she had her face covered with her hands, sobbing her heart out.

I carried some more water and heated it whilst I tore up a good shirt for bandages. I had some laudanum I been carrying ever since I'd used some of the kid's when I had the arrow in me. I gave her a mouthful of that, and she closed her eyes and settled down enough to let the pain go away. She was groggy now, and I finished taking off all her clothes. I took care to keep her covered as best as could be done, whilst I was setting on a rock with her on a blanket on the ground. It weren't like having a bed and things to work with.

By the time I washed the blood off, I knew a lot more about her than anybody else, even her, cause she couldn't see her backside. The blood was all over her and places I'd just as soon I didn't see had to be cleaned. My folks at home had been a lot like Ann. The women were particular about keeping covered up, and I respected her for being like that.

I had some sulphur salve I kept in case Horse got hurt, and I got it now and covered her with it. She was going to be sore and smell like sulphur. We had to keep moving if'n Nora and the kid was to have a chance, and sore or not, she'd have to be able to travel come morning.

I took her clothes down to the creek and spent half the night getting the blood off and getting them hung up to dry. I was wore to the bone time I hit my own bedroll.

"Josh?"

I thought she was asleep and wished she was. "I'm here."

"Josh, am I going to die?"

"Not unless you don't let me sleep."

I heard her snuffles. "Josh, you can be so mean."

"I know, but I'm tired. You're all right, and I've got a lot to do tomorrow."

"I hurt."

So I got up and found the laudanum and gave her another

mouthful. This time she drifted off and I could hear her snoring. I went to sleep laughing.

Come morning, I fixed biscuits and bacon and had the coffee made afore she opened her eyes. I carried her a tin plate full of food and a cup of tea I'm made just to help her injured feeling.

"Oh! I didn't know you had tea. Josh, why haven't you been making me tea before?"

"Because you're spoiled enough already."

"Josh, you can be so mean."

I just grinned at her. "Ya said that last night."

"Well, it's true!"

"Whatever happened to that nice girl that told me, 'Josh, you can be so sweet'?"

"She didn't know you well enough."

I picked up the salve and the bandages. "Well, I know you well enough, and right now we are going to get reacquainted."

"Josh, this is hard enough without you being vulgar about it."

I peeled back the blanket and exposed the leg and side. "You're going to have to marry me now, you know."

She gasped in a whole lot of air. "Why?"

"Because when we get back, no nice boy will have you now that you have been bathed and diapered by me and lived with me up here for all this time."

I was just teasing, talking to take her mind off the washing I was having to do, because it was personal and I figured she was ashamed and embarrassed.

She put her hand to her mouth and looked at me wide-eyed in surprise, but it was about that time I had to roll her over and wash her bottom and apply more salve and wrap it. I took two wraps around her sore bottom and had to bring the end of the bandage through her legs like a diaper and tie it up along her side. I didn't leave her much privacy doing it.

"Josh?" Her voice was low and kinda pleading.

"I'm just about done, babe."

"I'm not a baby, Josh. I'm a full grown woman."

"Little girl, you're my babe right now."

"Josh, are you really going to marry me?"

Well, I'd said it, even though I was just teasing. No wonder she'd gasped and looked so surprised. She'd took me serious. Well, I hadn't thought on it till she asked it like that, and then I knew that, in spite of all the little girl in her, whatever it took, she weren't leaving these mountains till she was mine. Peggy was just a memory and didn't even know me very well. Ann was real and close by me.

"You are mine already, babe, you just didn't know it yet."

"Mr. Bonner, you'll still have to speak to my father. And I'm not jumping over a broom with you. I intend to have the biggest and best wedding Kansas City has ever seen."

I didn't know what to say or how to act just then. She'd gave me something I never thought would ever happen between us, and I couldn't get my thoughts together, so I went to get her clothes, but when I got back, there was Ann naked and spread out on the blankets.

I saw her there with her eyes twinkling at me. She was a little girl playing at being a temptress. I couldn't believe she was acting like this. Awhile ago, she'd of cried if'n I'd a uncovered her. What was the difference now? She must have a reason, but dogged if'n I could figure out the difference. My first thought was to cover her back up. But my heart was pounding so loud I couldn't hear my thoughts. "How do I look on a blanket, all scratched up and bandaged?"

She was beautiful. She was girlish pink all over, the pink of large round young breasts with nipples the color of pink rosebuds. The pink of a tiny waist and rounded hips. One look at her with all of her completely uncovered on the blanket took all my air out of me, and I couldn't seem to get breathing again.

"I don't think you know how you look to me when you're laying there like that. Even bandaged all over. There's something presses the air outta me, and I go weak all over and my heart swells up till it's fit to break clear out of my chest."

She held her arms out towards me. "That's how you look to me, silly. That's just how I feel."

I knelt by her and kissed her, and that's how we settled on marrying.

CHAPTER 16

No matter how good she looked, she was still all scratched up and sore, and we didn't have time for lovemaking, so no matter how much of a temptress she was, she weren't in the shape for it, and we didn't have the time for it. I handed her her clothes. "We got to get moving; we got to get you dressed."

"Oh, Josh." She dug her heels in the folds of the blanket and arched her back. "You could take time to be a little romantic."

"We don't have time for romance. That'll have to wait." I got her dressed and the camp broke, but we was late. The other bunch had been on the move a couple hours ahead of us. It was good they was going in a half-circle and had to deal with getting that wagon over all those humps and hills, because we'd have never caught up. I had Ann on Horse and had put extra blankets under her, but she was in misery the whole way. I kept a little laudanum in her, but not enough to put her sleeping again. She started bleeding again and I had to stop and wrap her leg with tighter wraps. And that left her with a wet, bloody dress rubbing agin her leg. I felt bad for her, but I didn't dare stop. I had to be there when they settled. That might be the only chance I had to get them away from them varmints.

Right after the sun passed its high point and after we'd stopped to eat, I changed Ann's bandages again and gave her a short time to rest. It started clouding up and turning cold. The wind picked up and Horse and the mule were twisting their heads around at me, as if to say we better find shelter. We got lucky for a change and come on a purty good-sized stand of trees. I took my ax and chopped some cross limbs for the walls. I tied them around the tree trunks with rope, and it weren't long till I had us a good-sized shelter, big enough for us and the animals. I cut small poles to lay between the limbs of the trees and used large ferns to weave a rainproof roof. I worked fast and got some dead stuff up for the fire. The sky was getting darker and I was worried that there might be a twister coming. This was the country for it and the right time of the year.

It rained first, great sheets of hard, wind-driven rain, the kind that stings when it hits you. Then it hailed, big stones that'd knock a man down if'n he was out in it. The trees broke the force of them big hailstones and still they hit our little shelter hard enough to keep it shaking.

Ann was on the blanket by the fire and she was tired and sick. But I'd fixed her some tea, and there was still a small smile in her.

"Josh, are we in danger here? This shelter seems like it's going to give way any moment."

"Not unless this turns into a twister, or a lightning storm."

"I'm glad we're in here, even if it does shake, and not out in the hail."

"I was just thinking this might be the time to get your ma and the kid outta there."

She squirmed a little and hugged her chest with her arms. "I wish you didn't have to leave me here all alone."

"I know this is scary, and I'm sorry. But if'n I'm going to get them free, I've got to take a edge when I can find it."

She held up her arms and I gave her my best bear hug. "Josh, those hailstones are really big, and they could hurt you. What if something should happen to you?"

I knew she was scared, not just for herself but for me too.

"I'll be back, Ann. You don't worry, I can take care of this."

She smiled at me and there was a knowing, proud look. "I know you can. You can do anything."

I was plumb happy to know that, I thought, as I ran from tree to tree doing my best to keep under the shelter of the leaves. It was better that she didn't know how scared I could get facing six gun-slingers. But her little-girl faith in my know-how and her trust that I had the knack and the might to get the job done, kinda built a little extra stock in my own self.

Them hailstones were big and hurt like thunder when they hit. Tree to tree I run, and still it was a good hour before I got clost to 'em. I'd been beat to pieces by the hail. I hurt all over my head and shoulders, but I was under a tree and looking right into their camp. The kid was under the wagon. They'd unwrapped a tarp from the side of the wagon and stood poles up under the loose end. All them gunslicks were bunched up there. Which meant Nora was in the wagon.

There just weren't no place for them to run to in time to be hid from me. And getting under the wagon wouldn't be no help to 'em, because I could cover it all from tongue to tailgate from where I was. All in all, I'd come on 'em just right. They sure weren't expecting trouble from outside in this kind of weather. After all, what kind of fool would be out here in this like I was, lettin' hisself get beat to pieces in a hailstorm. I guess the answer to that question would be a man who needed all the surprise on his side he could muster.

I lay flat on my belly under the tree and had a clear view of all of 'em. With any luck, I could hit all of 'em before they knew I was on 'em. I pulled down on 'em and took a deep breath. Who knows, this might be clost to the last breath I'd ever take. It was going to be clost to the last breath some of them were going to take, that much was certain.

I shot the one on the left in the head and quick as I could, I levered another shell in the chamber. I know it took just about the time it takes to blink, but right then it seemed to take way too long, and I was breathing hard and hurryin'.

The feller next to'm turned to see why his partner was falling and I got him in the neck as he turned, and that was two of'm, but before I could get the rest, they split both ways around the wagon running hard. I hit another one, but it was in the calf of his leg, because by then that was all I could see to shoot, and he went hopping off with the wagon wheel cuttin' off my line of sight. The rest got away. It hadn't been the turkey shoot I'd hoped for.

There was still four left and I was in trouble. I run forward and flung myself down by the closest wagon wheel, hoping it would keep me covered from their fire if'n they stopped runnin' and started to fight. I was laying even with the kid, he was just inside the wheel under the wagon. It took just two strokes with my knife to free him. He'd been tied so tight his hands were corded with red rings where the ropes had been. It was going to be a while till he was able to use his hands.

"How about it, Kid? You all right?"

"I'm glad ya finally got here."

"I was here. I just had to wait till I had some kind of chance."

"Them fellers won't run far. As soon as they figure out it was just one man, they'll be back."

"I know. Let's get Nora and get out of here."

"Nora? Them gunslicks are her hired hands that have turned on her. But she's never been tied up. She's in the wagon."

I saw feet and ankles at the end of the wagon. "I reckon she's out now. Let's get outta here whilst we can."

We didn't waste time on howdies, we just ran for the shelter I'd been shooting from. We made the trees and got down out of sight where we could see the wagon like I was before. Only they didn't come back to the wagon, and I had to figure they was working in a circle towards us. We weren't doing any talkin' at all. I motioned with a short hand sweep for them to follow me and I ran for the trees behind me. We kept that up for awhile, scooting from tree to tree till we was a good ways back from the wagon.

"We got to make sure they're dead or they'll hound us till they get us." Nora was pulling at her boot like it were giving her trouble.

"What's the matter with that boot?" I leaned over to help her.

"There's nothing wrong with my boot. It's just that I was slipping my knife out when I almost got caught and let go of it and it dropped down where I couldn't reach it."

I pulled her boot off to see that she was walking in blood from a knife cut deep enough to have almost cut her foot off. She had to have real guts, man-sized guts, to let her foot be cut like that and not let on. There's not a woman in ten thousand that could do that. My respect for Nora grew a little if'n my opinion on what kind of lady she was didn't.

I purt near said one of them words Pa used to get in trouble for. "Nora, how do you plan on walkin' on that foot?"

"Just shut up and fix it. I'm in some pain here." I could purty well guess she was in a lot of pain, so I shut up and went to work on her foot.

I didn't have no bandages except if I used my shirt, so I took my knife and cut the tail of my shirt off and wrapped her cut foot as tight as I could. "I don't think you'd better put your foot back in that boot, or we'll have to cut the boot off next time we fix the bandage."

She used the kid for a chair. She made him set on the ground, and then set on his knee. "Where's your camp? Is Ann with you?"

"Ann's with me, but she took a fall and she's cut and scratched up some." I took a stick and drew them a map where my camp was. I watched them hobble off, the kid half-carryin' Nora and her holding on to my six gun I gave them to take. It was gonna be a long time before his hands would be any use to him. He'd be lucky if'n he ever was able to hold a gun again. I wondered if'n I should have said something about me and Ann to them. It was going to be awkward with the kid being her ex-intended and Nora having spent time in my bedroll with me. The thought come to me that it would be nice if'n Nora didn't mention that we'd been in the sack together.

What if, by the time I got this thing done, Nora had let something slip about the night we spent together. I might not have Ann for my wife after all, and I would have something else to put to Nora's account.

"Lord, please don't let her shoot off her mouth to Ann about what we done. I ain't asked for much, but I need some help here. I don't reckon I could take losing Ann now on top of all the other things Nora took away from me." I ain't been one to ask for much, I purty much take what comes as best I can, but I was sure wishin'

I'd a-thought to speak to Nora private-like before she left. But then again, Nora might just spoil it for me just because that's her nature or because she might not think I'd be a fit husband for Ann.

By now I'm more worried about what was going to happen back at my camp than I was about them fellers with guns a-lookin' for me. I'd wished a thousand times I'd never got in the sack with Nora. It ruint things with Peggy and now might ruin things between me'n Ann.

Then I heard a shot. It was back toward where Nora and the kid were headed. It'd quit hailing but was raining steady, and the ground was muddy. I took off on the run, trying to stay sheltered and low to the ground and still run. I was leaving tracks all over the place, but it couldn't be helped. Besides, if'n I was leaving tracks, so was they.

I didn't need to run far. I come on Nora settin' on the ground and the kid stretched out with both hands reaching forward, like he was reaching for something. He'd been shot in the chest and he weren't breathing.

"Where are they?" I purt near hollered at Nora, because she was just settin' there as calm as could be, with the kid dead at her feet.

She kinda smiled at me, a sad little smile. "It was a accident. He left me standing here while he used the trees as a necessary. When he got back, I reached for him and got off balance and started to fall. That's when it happened. I must of touched the trigger while I was reaching for him."

It was more than I could take. I damned the trigger pull that Ransom had set for me, so light it only took a twitch. The same gun that I'd used over and over to save my own life had just took the kid's.

"What a way to die. After all we'd been through, for him to die like this." I was so beside myself, I cried in front of Nora.

She patted my shoulder, and I saw her watching me. She even had a curious look. There weren't no sympathy, not even a word of being sorry or being at fault. It was just a fact—she'd reached for him and when she done it, she started to fall and that made her clutch for his arm and the gun went off. She didn't feel responsible, or if'n she did, she didn't mention it.

I took my gun outta her hand. "Here, let me have that before you accidentally shoot me." I was mad through and through. I hurt from the kid's senseless death, but I was mad at her not caring.

Reaching for the gun caused me to lean forward, and little things like that mean a lot sometimes. It sure meant a lot today, cause there was a piece of lead whizzed by my ear before I heard the gun that had fired it. Nora was already on the ground and I never saw a person wiggle like a snake and move so fast before. She reached the shelter of the trees before I did. I'd threw myself forward and to the ground and hit rolling, a trick I'd used lots, and one that had saved my life time and again.

I hit the tree line running towards where the bushwhacker had shot at us. Usually a man will think on what's just happened for a while before he moves, but I'd decided long ago it were best to go with my gut feelings than to try to stop and think after the fight was already on. I guess "Sudden" was a good handle for me.

I come purt near to where I thought he was and dropped to the ground and started crawlin' injun fashion from bush to tree to bush, creeping up on him.

One of his partners had heard the shot and had run up to him. "Hey, was that you?"

"Almost got 'em. He got lucky and moved just as I lined up on him."

"Did ya see who it was?"

"It was that big feller that's been chasing Nora all over the territory."

"Ya mean Bonner?"

"That's the one!"

"That don't make sense. Ya mean he's the one rescued Nora?"

"Maybe it was that young feller with her he come for. I heard they was purty tight."

I crawled up close enough to hear real good, and so's I could get the drop on'm.

"If we'd a-knowed that, he could have had him. I'd a-rather let him have his partner than to have lost two of ours."

"I'd a-rather not had this hole in my leg either."

"Did ya shoot the kid that was with Nora? He's still laying out there."

"Naw, Nora was in the open, and that young feller was walking towards her, and she said something to'm and he started for her, trying to reach her before she done him in, but she shot him and him coming for her."

"She's a cold one. I wonder what that was all about."

"Ain't no telling. She holds grudges forever, it could have been anything."

Well, that was a whole different story than Nora had told me, and I didn't have no good reason to doubt him. He didn't know I was there and didn't even know I'd have cause to want to know. All the good feelings I was trying to have about Nora left right then. I didn't have no cause to believe she was trying to change, and truth was, she'd most likely kill me some day, because of the grudges she had agin me. I couldn't help remembering the night with her, the thrill of all she taught me, but balanced agin what that night had already cost me, I'd really paid for it. What was worse, she most likely intended for me to die when this was all over. Maybe in her own bed. She'd most likely think that was a fitting end for a fool. I weren't gonna let her get back to Ann. She's saw Ann for the last time in this life!

The one who had the hole in his leg was setting on a stump holding his leg with both hands. The other'n was facing him and tying a bandanna around the leg, trying to put pressure on the bandage they had on it, to keep the thing from starting to bleed again. I stepped out to where the one on the stump could see me. The other'n had his back to me. I can't tell you what the man said.

I ain't never used that style of talk, but he were surprised and scared and desperate all at the same time.

I shot him, but he was so fast, even setting down, that he got a shot off even though I'd been standing there with my gun out. The bullet hit the ground in front of my feet, but I was jolted and startled by his speed. The other'n drew and turned in one swift motion. The only thing that saved me was my habit of moving when I'm shooting, never standing in one spot.

He beat me to the first shot, and he'd had his back to me and hadn't even known I was there. That's what years of being on guard for your life does—it keeps your nerves so tight that you move and shoot without having time to think. You just do it.

I don't know why it popped into my head like that, but my first thought was he hadn't had a relaxed minute in years, and now he was going to have lots of time to be at ease. Both those rannys had been faster than me, and I was supposed to be a top hand with a gun. It was enough to unsettle me. Not only that, but there was two more of 'em out there just as good as these fellers were. I remembered my last promise to Ann and wondered if'n I was gonna be able to keep it.

I crept back to Nora, watching every shadow, every movement of a limb, or even a leaf. Nora was laying on the ground under a bush; she was well hid. I knew she was there and I still had to stand for a long while before I could pick her out. I come up on her from behind her and watched her for a spell.

This was the woman that had been my enemy all the time. Even when she'd been making love to me, she'd been planning my end. I'd half believed her, I'd wanted to believe her. I would have even helped her get her ill-gotten gains and helped her to get back east with them. Just because of that one night, and because she'd said she wanted a chance at a new life.

I reached down and touched her leg. I had to admire her, she didn't jump or scream. She just turned over and looked to see who was there. Not knowing if'n it was them or me, she still was under control. She didn't blink a eye, just asked, "Did you get him?"

I nodded that I had.

"How come it took two shots? You getting sloppy?"

"There was two of 'em."

She got excited. "Who were they? What'd they look like?"

"One wore two guns, come shoulder high on me, about twenty-five or six, seemed to be partners with the one I'd hit in the leg. He was older, maybe forty, skinny, wore a snake engraved on his boots."

"That's what they called him, 'The Snake.' He was supposed to be fast as one, and the other'n with two guns was from Texas. They called him 'Texas Joe.' And he's supposed to have killed twenty-six men already in stand-up gunfights."

She had a way of cocking her head and looking right through you. I remembered that Ann cocked her head that same way, which was strange, cause she hadn't been raised by Nora, or even spent that much time around her.

"You get 'em from where you was hid, Josh?"

I just stared at her. I was sure that was the way she thought. More and more what she said, when it was pieced together, gave a purty sorry picture of her. "I ain't never killed from ambush, and I gave these fellers more chance than they would a-gave me."

"You walked right out in front of two of the best gunmen I could find and killed them? You're some kind of man, Josh Bonner." She had that admiring look to her again, but this time I figured it out—she admired me for reasons other'n the ones I had wanted to be admired for. I had a anger in me that wanted revenge. I wanted to shout at her that I knew she'd murdered the kid. I wanted to hurt her.

"That Snake feller, he said you shot the kid on purpose when he was walking up to you."

"He'd lie, Josh, if he thought he could cause trouble between us, he'd lie. I told you how it was."

"He wasn't talking to me and didn't even know I was listening. He told that Texas Joe all about it, said you held grudges forever and always paid them back."

She had her eyes on my face, searching every thought that

showed there. "It might of looked that way to him from where he was, but the truth is it was a accident just like I told you. He reached for me to keep me from falling and I reached for him for help, and the gun went off."

She looked me straight in the eye. "I don't lie, Josh. If I'd killed him, I would have said so without apology. I wouldn't have waited till now, I'd have done it long ago. I'm sure it could have looked that way to someone that far away, but it was not my idea to kill him."

Well, I had to admit she could have done him in a long time back. She didn't need to wait till now. The kid and Ann had been took just like she said, and so far I ain't caught her in no lie. Maybe I had been thinking she had used me here lately when she hadn't.

"I had to ask. He was my friend."

"What about me, Josh? What am I to you?"

I stood up. "What about you? What am I to you? Lover? Just someone you need right now? What?"

"I don't see how you could ask that, Josh, when you know how I feel."

"That's the problem, Nora. I don't know how you feel. You make love to me and then you make this big decision that we are too far apart to get married. Did I have a say in it? Did you ask me what I wanted? You want me to come running when you need me, but what else am I to you?"

"I'm not used to talking things over, Josh. I've made all the decisions for the gang for years now. I was wrong." She had a soft look and I could feel more reasons coming than I wanted to hear.

"I've got to go. This ain't the time for this. You stay put and don't make a sound. I'll be back shortly." She nodded her head and crawled back into the brush she'd been hiding in.

I was confused. First, I'd thought she'd lied to me about Ann and the kid being held by her gang. Then come to find out it was true. Then I thought she'd lied to me about killing the kid, but the way it happened didn't make sense that she'd done it on purpose. Now she says she still wants me for her man, when I never was sure about her to start with. Not even counting I was supposed to marry Ann.

I got back to where the wagon was supposed to be, only they was moving it. They was headed to the cliff where the house had been under the overhang. I walked and run to keep up because they was headed in a straight line now. They'd be surprised to find there weren't no house there or men to help 'em. My guess was that the men to help 'em was what they was after. But if that was so, what did they take the wagon for?

They wasn't after either one, because they turned the wagon to come up on top of the cliff. They finally come to a stop about where Nora had said there was another way into the house. I knew that was a wild goose chase, because I'd already looked where she had said to look. I was wrong again; they found a boulder and used a iron rod out of the wagon to move it, and there was a hole in the cliff. I slipped up boulder by boulder and bush by bush till I was up close.

There was one stayed on guard whilst the other one let hisself down in the hole. How did they know where to look? Had Nora told them, and if she had, what had they been keeping her around for?

The one in the hole threw out a rope and the other'n pulled on it till he pulled some sacks out that he loaded in the wagon. I made it to the tailgate because his mind was on the money they was pulling out. I waited right there in a pouring down rain and waited till they had that wagon mostly loaded. Then I heard the one in the hole say, "Just one more trip and the rest will have to wait."

The next time he pulled on the rope, I reached out and hit him with my gun. He fell like a dead man. Then I moved over by the hole and waited for the other'n to come see why he weren't pulling on the rope. He stuck his head up and I hit him. Then I buried the two of them by piling rocks on top of them. It sure beat having to shoot it out with them and them being the kind of gunhands they was.

It was a long way back and it was daybreak by the time I got to Nora. I was worrying about Ann now, because I'd been gone so long and I hated to leave her alone all night like I'd done. I still had one more problem. I was determined not to let Nora get close to Ann. Except Nora was running a fever and thrashing around on the ground when I got there. I held her foot and took off the bandage. I'm no doctor, but I could see it was red and purple clear up her leg, and I knew I'd best get her back to camp. I didn't want to, but I had to if'n there was to be a chance to save her life.

It'd been so quick. When I left, she appeared to be fine, just a little sore where she'd cut her foot. Now she was in serious shape. I lifted her to carry and she was so hot she burnt me to hold her. I stopped at every stream and bathed her in cold water to kill the fever, but every time the fever come right back.

It seemed like hours, time I got to camp. Ann was asleep and the fire was still banked. Everything there was in good shape. But Nora was worse. Ann woke right up when I was heating water to wash the wound with.

"What happened?"

"She had a knife hid in her boot and purt near cut her foot off."

I put some whiskey on the cut and cleaned it as best I could, but her fever didn't go down. I poured some laudanum down her throat and she seemed to quiet down. I kept cold water on her by placing cold wet cloths all up and down her small body. Before they could dry, I'd have more wet cloths to replace them with. Ann held her hand and washed her face over and over with cold water. I kept pouring whiskey in the cut, but the red in her leg kept moving further up her leg. I knew we weren't gonna save her, but we didn't give up.

Suddenly Ann thought of the kid. "Where's Obadiah?"

I nodded at Nora. "She shot him!"

Her hands flew to her face and tears ran in a stream. "Why?"

"It was a accident. The kid was trying to get her back here and she was holding my gun. It went off whilst she was trying to grab his arm."

"Poor Mama."

I looked at her, wondering why she'd say that.

"She loved him, you know."

I reckon that was the last thing I expected to hear. She sure hadn't acted like they had any feelings between 'em.

"Are ya sure of that? They didn't act like they was in love."

"He come to me and confessed they'd been having a lurid affair. He stopped it because he felt so guilty, but she still wanted him."

"Is that why you broke off the engagement?"

"Yes. If he loved me, why would he be in bed with her?"

I couldn't answer that and I said so. I just hoped she'd never be asking me that question about me and Nora.

"Is that when you told her ya didn't want to stay with her anymore?" I asked her.

"How did you know about that?"

"She told me. But she let on like it was because once you'd satisfied your curiosity, you wanted your Pa again."

"No! It was because she stripped off her clothes and enticed my intended into her bed. She did it just to make sure she was still young enough and pretty enough to take him from me."

"How do you feel about her?"

"I hated her at first, that she would do that to her own daughter, but then I realized she had always did as she pleased, and that was her nature. It would be like hating a cat for being a cat."

I thought that was a purty fair likeness for comparison.

"The kid say why he did it?"

"She undressed in front of him, and he said he couldn't help himself."

Well, that purty much answered why Ann had pulled that little come-and-get-me-now stunt back when we had decided on marrying. She'd been scared Nora would decide to jump in my bed and figured she'd do it first to protect me from Nora.

Ann took a water bag and limped out to go to the creek for more water. Just as she left, Nora stirred and opened her eyes. She saw me standing there holding her hand and smiled. I couldn't hear what she said, it was so low, but I could read her lips. She said, "I love you."

I didn't know what to say, so I leaned down and kissed her. I think I done the right thing. She smiled at me and closed her eyes, then she just passed on. I shouldn't have been happy at her passing, but I was. Our secret was safe now, except for all them Lazy Rocking B hands and Tom and Cam. How could I have been so dumb as to do that right in front of the whole bunch? Was I cravin' to be the big man that bad? Maybe I'd just go to California.

Nora the Queen of the Golden Belle, Nora the outlaw, Nora the mother, and Nora the lover. How many other Noras there were, I didn't know, probably many more. I wondered for a bit if the kid had regretted being her lover as much as I had. Then, when I thought of what it had cost him, I was sure he had. What a life she'd led, and she almost made it out of here with all her loot intact. She's almost made that fancy new life for herself that she'd wanted. After all the danger she'd faced, and then to die from a cut foot. It weren't seemly.

I thought, I never got to ask her how them fellers knew where to go. Why did they take all that time and let her lead them around in a half circle if'n they knew where to go? I guess I'd never know the answer now. I set down and waited for Ann to come back. This would have been a problem for Pa to figure out. He had always been ready to tackle whatever come his way. . . . It come to me that I am a lot like my Pa. I've tackled everything that has come my way. Maybe I ain't always handled everything the way he would of, but except for the gold, I'd purty much done things the way he might've. I thought about that for a bit. I liked the knowing of that. I really am a lot like my Pa!

"Time and events, time and events," Pa would have said. I could almost see him standing there shaking his huge black-haired head when untoward things happened. And a lot of things had happened. I weren't the same mountain boy I'd been a few years back. I'd made good friends and lost a good friend. . . . I had Ann to marry and Nora's money to spend. I could hear Ann's footsteps as she was coming back. I reached over and closed Nora's eyes and said, "Time and events, Nora, time and events."

CPSIA information can be obtained
at www.ICGtesting.com
Printed in the USA
FSHW011529120421
80392FS

9 780738 809397